PAINLESS

S. A. HARAZIN

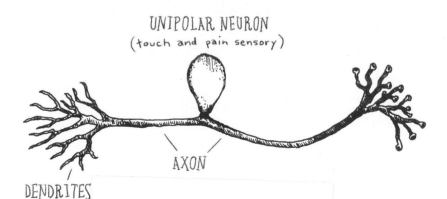

UNIPOLAR NEURON
(touch and pain sensory)

AXON

DENDRITES

ALBERT WHITMAN & COMPANY
CHICAGO, ILLINOIS

Library of Congress Cataloging-in-Publication Data

Harazin, S. A.
Painless / S. A. Harazin.
pages cm
Summary: After eighteen years of dealing with CIPA,
a condition in which he cannot feel pain,
David Hart sets out with new friend Luna to complete his "bucket list,"
starting with finding the parents who abandoned him.
[1. Coming of age—Fiction. 2. Congenital insensitivity to pain—Fiction.
3. Sick—Fiction. 4. Interpersonal relations—Fiction. 5. Self-reliance—Fiction.
6. Grandmothers—Fiction.]
I. Title. PZ7.H2114Pai 2015
[Fic]—dc23 2014027713

Text copyright © 2015 by S. A. Harazin
Published in 2015 by Albert Whitman & Company
ISBN 978-0-8075-6288-8

Printed in China.
10 9 8 7 6 5 4 3 2 1 NP 18 17 16 15 14

Cover design by Jordan Kost
Cover image © Shutterstock.com

For more information about Albert Whitman & Company,
visit our web site at www.albertwhitman.com.

In memory of Holly Ann Moore

PART 1

CHAPTER 1

Dr. Goodman brings a bucket of ice water into the exam room and sets it next to me. I'm sitting on a gurney naked except for a sheet. He's already checked my heart and lungs and felt my belly.

He's old-fashioned. He thinks of simple tests.

"You know what to do," he says.

I stick my hand into the water. His nurse checks my heart rate and blood pressure. After about thirty seconds he tells me to take out my hand.

"Did I pass?" I say with a grin. This is one thing I can do better than anybody.

The nurse checks my temperature with an ear thermometer. "Ninety-eight point one," she says.

"Your vital signs remained normal," Dr. Goodman says.

I already know that most people can't stand more than ten seconds in the ice water. One time he tested my heat tolerance by putting me in a hot room and keeping track of my temperature. I lasted about two hours, and then all of a sudden I had a temperature over a hundred and three—and I didn't even know it. The good news is that I didn't have a seizure.

"Feel anything?" he asks.

"My nose itched."

Dr. Goodman frowns. "I'd like to talk to you in my office," he says.

I stare at his stethoscope hanging around his neck. What's he going to tell me this time that I don't want to hear? I think I passed his made-up test, but I don't know what I'm supposed to feel when my hand's in the ice water. I know ice is cold, but what's cold? I don't know what that means.

The nurse hands me my glasses and then leaves the room. I wear glasses because I scratched my eyes when I was so young I don't remember. I heard Nana say my mom went into my room one morning, saw blood on my face and in my eyes, and started screaming.

Maybe that's why my mother ran away never to be heard from again. Google cannot even locate her.

I dress in jeans and a T-shirt. I get my jacket and walking cane. Years ago, I walked around with a broken leg. I was kind of unsteady. My leg didn't heal properly so I ended up with a limp and using a cane.

I go to Dr. Goodman's office, and I wait trembling. I'm scared he's going to tell me something's seriously wrong that I don't want to hear.

The thing is, most people don't know how long they have to live, and that's probably a good thing. I think knowing when you're going to die stinks. I know I'm living on borrowed time.

✦ ✦ ✦

Rod, Dr. Goodman's physician's assistant, walks into the office. "Hey, David," he says. "I heard you've graduated from high school." He places a stack of folders on Dr. Goodman's desk.

"Yes," I say. That was last month, and I didn't have a ceremony or anything.

"Waterly High?" he asks. "That's where my brother goes."

"No. I was homeschooled."

I remember when I went to kindergarten. I wore a helmet, gloves, and goggles so I couldn't hurt myself by accident. Sometimes I would chew my tongue and my hands. My baby teeth were pulled to keep me from mutilating myself more than I already had. By the time my permanent teeth came in, I had learned not to do that.

When I went to school wearing gloves, goggles, and a helmet, some kids would call me a monster and run away screaming. Some of the braver kids would pain-test me by punching me. They'd knock me down, and I'd get up again because I didn't feel anything. A couple of kids believed I was Superman, and I did too back then.

I was born not feeling pain or hot or cold, and unable to sweat.

"Congratulations," Rod says. "You are amazing."

Rod means I'm amazing because I survived for so long. I have congenital insensitivity to pain with anhidrosis, or CIPA for short. Maybe a hundred people in the world have CIPA, and the average life span is about the same as a hamster, but I've survived for more than seventeen years.

According to my grandmother, I'm one of the unique people in the world. *Unique* is the word some people use for *defective*. Other people use words like *monster* or *superman*.

"Dr. Goodman will be with you shortly," Rod says as he leaves the room.

Nana calls me a daredevil. She says I don't know fear because I don't feel pain. You know those guys who swallow fire or walk on hot coals? I could do it if I wanted to, but I'm not nuts. My skin would fry, and I wouldn't even know it until I smelled something cooking. I could have appendicitis or a heart attack and not know it.

The truth is, even wearing a thick sweater on a hot day could kill me.

My wristwatch alarm sounds. I stand, go to the door, and look out. I don't see Dr. Goodman or anybody so I head down the hall to the bathroom.

My watch monitors my body temperature. It also beeps to tell me when to eat, sleep, and go to the bathroom. I don't like that a piece of metal knows what I can't. Why stick a microchip in a watch when it could go into my brain?

One day in kindergarten, my watch beeped. We were sitting in a circle listening to the teacher, who was reading a book and showing us the pictures. Tyler said, "You better tell the teacher you have to go to the bathroom." Tyler was my imaginary friend.

I told the teacher.

But she went back to reading and showing us the pictures. It was a story with frogs flying on magic carpets at night. When daylight came, they returned to their boring routine.

I wet my pants. Kids laughed.

That day made me remember to always follow my routine and pay attention to my watch beeping, but mostly I remember the frogs and Tyler not laughing. He could've been my best friend if he were real. In another reality, maybe he is.

The teacher called my house sometimes, and then my father or mother would ask me if I hit the other kids. Didn't I know I hurt them? Didn't I know I caused trouble?

I became a kindergarten dropout.

After I use the bathroom, I wash my hands and glance in the mirror to make sure I haven't been chewing on my lip. I always try to remember not to bite myself because I can't feel it when I do.

I look okay.

When I was fifteen I had several operations on my face and hands to fix scarring left from me biting and scratching. My jaw and nose were fixed too. After the last surgery was over, Nana cried because of some swelling and bruising, but I didn't suffer at all. I probably would've suffered if I looked into a mirror, but I was surprised how much my operation hurt Nana.

A couple of months later, Spencer saw me for the first time since my surgery and did not recognize me. He said I looked great. He made me look in the mirror. I didn't look bad anymore. I looked like me but different without the messed-up face.

Spencer's my personal assistant and best friend. It's not like I'm his boss. He'd work for free, but I think it's hard to turn down easy money when you don't have any. We're both almost eighteen, but sometimes I feel more like he's twenty or thirty and I'm ten.

I still have a few scars.

One thick, ugly scar runs across my forehead. A dog bit me when I was a little kid before I went to live with Nana. I had stitches. They itched all the time so I picked at my face and pulled the stitches out. I kept scratching the spot. I didn't feel anything except the itching that wouldn't go away.

The next thing I remember is going to visit my grandparents. My dad left me there and didn't come back. That was eleven years ago. One of these days I'll find him and my mom. I'll ask them why.

✦ ✦ ✦

Dr. Goodman walks into his office, pulls over a chair, and sits facing me. "You need to become more independent."

"Are you serious?" I wrinkle my forehead.

Dr. Goodman has said his educated guess is that my pain tolerance is about thirty times that of a normal person. My best guess is that I don't know. I don't know what normal is. "You need to get outside," he says. "You don't need to be afraid of the hot or cold if you use caution. There's more to surviving than staying inside most of the time."

I want to shake my head. Dr. Goodman's wrong. Everything's dangerous. I look away from him. "Have you had any other patients with CIPA?"

"No," he says. "But Dr. DeLorenzo has."

My point exactly. Dr. Goodman doesn't understand.

Dr. DeLorenzo is a researcher at a university. I knew him back before he became an expert. Dr. Goodman sometimes consults with him about me.

"One of his patients lived until she was twenty-five. But you know what? She was okay with it. She went to her junior prom. She volunteered at an animal shelter. She had her driver's license. She got engaged."

I shift in the chair. "Why'd she die?"

"Complications from CIPA."

He's proving my point. "Was she in a wheelchair?"

"That's irrelevant. She had a rewarding life."

Dr. Goodman doesn't know anything.

"David, you have done better than anyone ever imagined. You're a good kid. You deserve a life. Get a driver's license, fall in love, do something nice for your grandmother. Make a list of things you want to do."

"A bucket list?" I say.

"Call it whatever you want to."

I'm not about to make a list of stuff to do before I die. I don't need to be reminded that I won't live long.

My grandmother says that when somebody dies, they've bought the farm, and their soul is free to wander through fields and grassy meadows with streams so clear you can see fish waggling back and forth.

✚ ✚ ✚

I ride the elevator down to the lobby where Spencer is sitting in a chair and texting. He stands when he sees me. "Do you want to have lunch?" he asks.

"Sure," I say. I can't feel hunger, but I have great senses of smell and taste. One time when Spencer and I were eating pizza, he asked if I could eat too much and explode. He was grinning so I knew he was joking around. I told him to sit back and watch.

Another time he asked me if I'd ever had sex.

"Only by myself," I told Spencer. "What about you?"

"Same here," he said. "But that doesn't count."

When he said that, I felt almost normal.

But I've never kissed a girl.

Everything I know about sex I learned from my grandfather's *Playboy* magazines stored out of sight in the basement. I make frequent trips to the basement in the middle of the night.

We walk out the automatic doors. Spencer clears his throat. "It's below freezing," he says.

I slip on my jacket. "I know," I say as my freakin' watch starts beeping.

When the weather's warm, I go outside once a day to swim. It's the only real exercise I can do. It's therapy. I do what I have to do to stay alive because I don't want to die. The thing is, I want to have some excitement in my life and to have more than a paper girlfriend.

Spencer watches me to make sure I don't drown or get overheated or hypothermic. Since I can't feel hot or cold, my body temperature can soar in a short time, and I can't sweat to bring it down. Then I'll have a seizure and maybe wet my pants. When my body temperature drops too much, it's like a tidal wave has hit me until I become unconscious.

The body temperature problem is mostly why I need a personal assistant.

We go to a pizza place and order a vegetarian pizza with extra cheese. Spencer gobbles down his slice while he watches me eat slowly and carefully. He really does a good job of making sure I don't hurt myself. Once, years ago, he saw me after I'd bitten my fingers, and they were bleeding. Unlike my mom, he didn't run away screaming. Instead he cried and ran to Nana for help.

I learned that I was hurting myself, and I hardly ever bit my tongue or lips or fingers after that. I didn't like seeing Spencer cry.

I can't make tears, and I've never cried in my entire life. I guess that makes me lucky. Otherwise, I'd probably be crying a lot.

"I got into Vanderbilt," Spencer says. He stretches a smile across his freckled face, and his oversized ears wiggle. His coppery hair shimmers like wet pine straw. I'm lucky I don't have big ears.

I blink at him. "That's terrific," I say. "Really terrific."

"I'm going to be busier than ever the last semester of school," Spencer says.

He means he won't be hanging around as much. His words kind of shake something up inside me. Spencer's my only friend, I guess, and he'll be moving on in a few months.

CHAPTER 2

After dinner on Christmas Eve, Nana and I go into the living room. The stockings are hung over the fireplace and the tree's lit up. Spencer and Veronica, the housekeeper, left earlier.

Nana sits in the recliner, and I move her walker to the side of the chair. Cataracts fog her eyeballs, and dementia has rewired her brain. Sometimes her mind's okay, and sometimes she stares like she can't see what's in front of her face.

Nana turns on the TV and clicks to a station that shows a fireplace and plays Christmas music. "Isn't this nice?" she says.

"Yes," I say. I get a hollow feeling inside watching the logs burn on TV.

I open gifts. A sweater. Shirt. Tie. Jacket. Underwear. There should be a rule against giving underwear. Next gift is a Bible. I flip through the yellowed pages. It was printed in 1850. Nana has written on a front page: *David, don't ever forget me. I love you.*

Then I open a package containing a VHS tape. The label's yellow and the writing faded. I turn around and hold it up. "Thanks. What's on it?"

"A surprise."

I can't wait. It's probably a movie she taped twenty or thirty years ago. She's got a whole shelf of them in the study.

I give her a framed collage of pictures taken of Nana and her family before I came along and got dumped here. I found the photos in a box in the attic.

I look over her shoulder at the pictures.

Nana and Grandpa getting married.

Nana and Grandpa playing tennis.

Nana and Grandpa at the Olympics thirty years ago.

Nana swimming in the pool.

Nana and Grandpa's rafting trip.

Nana holding my dad on the day he was born.

My dad's high-school graduation picture.

My dad waving good-bye.

Grandpa smiling and holding a plaque at a banquet.

My grandfather was a smart man who made a lot of money selling antiques at auctions. He sold one book for a couple of million dollars.

It's a good thing he left Nana money when he died or else she couldn't have afforded me.

There are no other family members except for Nana's cousin, Ruby, and Ruby's grandson, Allen. Once Ruby brought Allen over to play with me, and we pretended to be ninjas. He kicked me in the belly, and I socked him in the face. He cried. I had broken his front tooth and his nose. Ruby said I was dangerous. They never came back.

Nana smiles and says the perfect spot for the collage is on the fireplace mantel, so that's where I place it. "Check—check—your stocking," she says.

My heart's in my throat when I pull out two things. A wallet from Veronica. A gift card from Joe.

He's my grandmother's attorney and my guardian if something happens. He's the guy in charge of running my life. He's got me on speed dial on his phone. I'm number two. It's hard for me to talk to him, and it's usually when something's gone wrong.

"We need to have a party soon," Nana says out of the blue. "I haven't been to a party in years. We used to have parties. We'd dance and sing karaoke as if tomorrow would never come." She suddenly changes the subject again and talks about the rafting trip she went on with Grandpa and their friends. I've heard that story before.

It makes me feel empty—like the world is moving on, and we're moving backward in time.

I can remember when it wasn't so lonely around here. I guess loneliness makes you remember the good times, and then you go looking for something like love or excitement or maybe drugs. I chose excitement.

One time when I was sick of my room, I sneaked out to the railroad tracks and waited for the ten p.m. train. When the whistle blew and the lights were so close that I was breathing terror, I jumped out of the way. A wild sensation came over me. My heart was beating fast, and I was shaking.

I loved the adrenaline rush, but I'd rather find other ways to get it.

"We should've rode around and looked at Christmas lights," Nana says.

That would be some adrenaline rush with Nana driving on ice and not seeing where she's going.

"It's too late," I say. It was too late six months ago when she started showing signs of dementia. She left the house one day and got lost on the nature trail behind our house. Spencer and I found her a few hours later. I had to call Joe because we sent her to the hospital. He didn't yell at me or anything, but I thought he would. He was taking his yearly vacation. He never talks about his yearly vacation. It's a big secret.

"Why don't we watch the tape?" Nana asks.

"We don't have a VCR."

"We had a VCR," Nana says.

"Maybe twenty years ago. I've never seen it."

She says I need to get into the spirit of Christmas.

I'm trying. "I'll look for the VCR," I say. I hurry to my room.

I usually hang out in my room where it's safe. I have twin beds, a desk with a laptop computer, an entertainment center spanning one wall, and bookshelves lining another. Nana wants me to read three a week. Sometimes I do, but I'm better at other stuff like playing the guitar and piano. I also have CDs and DVDs, thick black carpet, and snow-colored walls with a world map tacked to one.

I can play video games for hours, and my friends mostly live inside the games. They don't laugh at me or turn away or treat me as if I'm a freak. Sometimes I just sit looking out my window.

I check my email, but all five messages are spam. I read them anyway just to be sure. Then I check Facebook and read "Merry Christmas" a dozen times from people I don't know. Anybody on Facebook this time of night isn't having a great Christmas Eve. Next I look out the window and see only one star.

I look in Nana's room and the study for the VCR so that I haven't told her a lie. We don't have a VCR. We've never had a VCR.

I go back into the living room, and the saddest Christmas song ever is playing.

When you're almost alone on Christmas Eve, hear sad songs on TV, and watch logs burning, you start wanting to jump off a cliff. I'd start a real fire, but Nana would start screaming, "You're going to catch yourself on fire!"

"I could play something on the piano," I say, turning down the volume on the TV.

I go over and sit on the piano bench. Nana sits next to me. I play "Jingle Bells," and Nana sings along in a raspy voice.

She can't sing, and she runs out of breath quickly, but I can feel her hand keeping time to the song on my back.

I've always been able to feel touch unless it's a slap. I can't feel a slap.

I play "Rudolph the Red-Nosed Reindeer" and sing for her. Next is "Frosty the Snowman."

Then I decide to surprise her. I play the theme from *Superman*. I like that it's fast and energizing. It's a great song to rev you up.

I think I'm getting the Christmas spirit.

I turn my head to ask if she wants to watch TV. Her eyes are closed, and I don't know if her mind has gone somewhere else or not.

"You okay?" I ask.

Nana opens her eyes. "I'm thinking." She moves back to her recliner, says she's tired, and asks me to keep playing.

I play "The Entertainer" from *The Sting* and then the theme from *Batman*. When I'm finished, I glance at Nana. She's asleep. I cover her with an afghan and watch TV for a while. It isn't like Nana's missing anything by falling asleep on Christmas Eve.

I text Spencer and ask if he has a VCR. He doesn't reply. I almost text him again to say "Merry Christmas," but I'd sound like I don't have anything better to do.

In the middle of *A Christmas Carol*, Spencer sends me a text.

Open the door.

I go to the door and open it slowly.

Spencer's there. "I don't have a VCR but thank you for the tickets to Aspen. Best Christmas ever!" Spencer hands me a gift wrapped in gold paper.

We go into the living room. Nana's still sleeping.

I unwrap the gift.

It's a scrapbook.

"We had to make a scrapbook of our life for our senior project. It's mostly about me and you, but Nana's in there too."

I open it and see pictures and sketches.

Under one picture of me standing on a bridge he wrote, *You know how your mother always says, "If your friends told you to jump off a bridge, would you do it?" This is the guy who would do it, my best friend David.*

I kind of laugh. I was only pretending I'd jump, but I lost my balance and fell twenty feet into deep water. I think if I had a bucket list, jumping off a bridge would not be on it.

But still, it's a pretty nice Christmas.

CHAPTER 3

My grandmother taught me to follow a schedule so I can stay alive. Half my life is devoted to checking my body and looking at details. I do the morning body check in the bathroom, and I'm always scared I'll see a burn, a cut, or a bone. Actually, I think I'd notice a bone right away. Then I shower and apply special lotion because my skin dries out from not ever sweating.

I dress and go back into my room.

"Happy New Year," Nana says. "Are you doing okay today?"

This is why I always dress in the bathroom. I never know when Nana will be waiting for me in my room.

"I'm fine," I say with a smile. "Happy New Year."

Last night we watched the ball drop.

"Did you do your body check?" she asks.

I sit on the bed. "Yes. You know you don't have to ask me that all the time."

She ignores my whining. "What's your temperature?"

"Ninety-seven." I could make up anything.

"Did you go to the bathroom?"

I cringe. "Don't ever ask me that again," I say.

It isn't the first time I've told her that.

With shaky hands, Nana checks my blood pressure and my pulse. She peers down my throat using a penlight. Then she looks into my eyes and ears. I don't know what I have inside me that's so interesting. Last of all, I pull up my shirt, and she takes a look at my back.

Spencer does this when he's around, but nobody sees me naked. I have my pride.

I smooth out my shirt, look at her, and see how pale and out of breath she is. "You okay?" I ask.

"I'm all right for now," she says. "But I can't even find my shoes. I'm old and tired and dying, and you need to be prepared."

I just sit staring. I can't move. Can't breathe. It's like the world is really flat, and I've sailed over the end.

Once in the hospital I had a pneumothorax—a collapsed lung—and I was fighting to breathe, and there was no way I could keep breathing without help. All I could do was gasp hungrily for air, and then I stopped gasping. I think I died for a moment. Everything turned black.

Later when I awoke, I had a big, fat tube in my chest, and I was breathing.

Nana's probably just saying stuff because of the dementia. Sure, she's old, but she doesn't drink, smoke, or eat unhealthy food.

In the kitchen, my vitamins and minerals are lined up on the counter. They're to make me smarter and stronger. They do not work, and I don't like them. I usually throw them away when Nana isn't looking.

She's sitting at the table. "What's the date?" I ask.

She looks up from her coffee. "January first." She smiles at me, shaking her head.

I didn't think she'd know. I take the vitamins. She's fine.

✦ ✦ ✦

"Happy New Year," Spencer says. He's carrying an old TV. "The VCR is built into the TV. Sorry I couldn't bring it over sooner. I got home yesterday. Aspen was great. You should've come with me."

"I wish."

"No, you don't," he says.

I can see it now. I'm sitting in the ski lodge in front of the fireplace reading a book. People laugh and head out to go skiing. I stay where I am.

Here's what I know about skiing. It's fun to watch on TV, but when you have a messed-up leg, it's not a good idea to go skiing unless you like hanging out alone in a lodge with only your brain to talk to you.

"I'd probably hit a tree," I tell Spencer.

"Look on the positive side," he says. "You wouldn't feel a thing."

"You wouldn't either," I say. "Because you'd be dead."

Spencer laughs and connects the TV. "What's on the tape?"

"Nana said it was a surprise."

He rolls his eyes and slides the tape into the TV.

The picture's fuzzy, but I can see a man sitting in a room and the white wall behind him. "We're Off to See the Wizard" plays.

Spencer adjusts the controls, and the picture clears. He increases the volume and sits on the bed.

I sit in front of the TV. Nana would say I'd go blind sitting too close. She's also said I'd go deaf from loud music. Wonder what I did to destroy my nerve endings.

I see a man and he starts talking.

Dear David, I've collected pictures from some of your birthday parties and made this video for you so you don't forget.

I think he's somebody I'm supposed to know.

Dear David, you turned two today. I am sorry I don't have a recording of your very first birthday, but you had two parties for your second birthday.

I see me. I'm wearing gloves, long sleeves, a mouth guard, and a pinkish helmet. I look like I'm from outer space.

Hi, son. Today you are three. We had your party in the hospital, and all the nurses sang happy birthday to you. I hung a stuffed elephant from your IV pole.

"HE'S MY DAD!" I turn my head toward Spencer. "MY DAD. DID YOU HEAR ME?"

"Yeah," he says in a depressing voice.

I look like I'm sleeping. I'm getting oxygen through a mask.

"I wonder what happened to the elephant," I say to Spencer.

"He probably dumped him somewhere," Spencer says.

I almost wish I was watching this alone. Spencer doesn't understand. The video continues.

21

Dear David, here we are, celebrating your fourth birthday. I can't believe how fast time flies. You are amazing. Don't ever forget that.

He quits talking. I'm sitting in front of a piano, banging on the keys, and singing "Happy Birthday to Me."

There aren't any kids in the picture, and I have a toothless smile on my face. If I was so amazing, why did he dump me at Nana's and never come back?

"If I Only Had a Brain" starts playing, and my dad speaks.

I thought if you could make it until you were a teenager, you wouldn't have as much to deal with because you would have learned so much about your condition. But things happened. Do you remember when we watched The Wizard of Oz? *The Lion wanted courage, the Scarecrow wanted a brain, and the Tin Man wanted a heart. But it didn't matter because they already had what they sought, only they didn't know it.*

There's a collage of everything with "Over the Rainbow" playing. Suddenly my dad starts talking and crying.

Dear David, well, it isn't your birthday, but today is a big day for you. I'm taking you to Nana's house for a while. You'll be safe and happy with her.

I can't believe this. He leaves me a lousy tape when he could've visited me. It's been eleven years, and he's never sent me a card or anything. He's pathetic.

Spencer turns off the TV and ejects the tape. When he hands it to me, he doesn't look at me.

It's the look-away that happens when somebody feels embarrassed for the other person.

"Anybody ever say you look like your father?" he asks.

I smile. "Only Nana. Nobody else knew him."

"If you don't mind me asking, what happened to your mother? She isn't in any of the pictures."

Maybe she didn't like me. Maybe she went shopping. Maybe she was taking a nap. Maybe she was filming the video. There are too many maybes. "I don't know," I finally say.

"They don't call or come to see you?"

I shake my head.

"It doesn't matter," Spencer says. "You know what your grandmother said about you? She said the Creator sent you to your grandfather and her. She said you saved them."

I probably did save them. I kept them from doing much of anything.

Spencer unplugs the TV.

I ask him if he wants to hang out a while.

"I can't," he says. "We have company, and Cassandra is coming over. My mom's fixing a huge dinner."

Cassandra plays the keyboard in Spencer's band. I don't know her very well, but she has an argument with Spencer about once a week. I overheard her talking to Spencer about me. "Aren't you embarrassed?" she asked. "Poor little rich kid has you to make up his bed for him."

She doesn't know about me. It's not like I advertise I can't feel pain.

He sits back down on the bed. "Remember a few weeks ago when I told you I made it into Vanderbilt and how I'm going to be really busy this semester?"

"Yes."

"I'm quitting, but I've found somebody to replace me. I'll be here early tomorrow morning to show Ms. Smith what to do," Spencer says. "You wouldn't believe how many people I talked to before I found the right person. You need somebody new anyway. We're around each other all the time."

I'm getting a sick feeling, kind of like I ate too much pizza and exploded.

"Not as much lately," I say.

"We do the same thing day in and day out. Trust me. It's time for both of us to move on. This way I can come over whenever I want to and not feel like I have to."

"Is it because Cassandra says it's demeaning for you to work for me?"

"No."

"I understand," I say. I really do. He knows it's his time to move on.

✦ ✦ ✦

"James gave me the tape the day he left you here," Nana says from her recliner. "I watched it back when we had a VCR and then forgot about it."

"But I don't understand why he didn't come back."

"I don't think we'll ever understand. Your parents divorced, and James brought you here. Then they disappeared," Nana says. "I've told you before. We searched. We filed missing persons' reports. We hired detectives."

"How can anybody disappear like that?"

"When they don't want to be found," she says, trying to catch her breath. "You were constantly covered with bruises. You'd jump out of a tree. You'd bang your head. You'd chew your mouth or your hands. They were accused of child abuse every time you were taken to the emergency room."

She's paler than I've ever seen. "It was like that for us when you first came to live here. Your grandfather was arrested once, but then Dr. Goodman explained to the authorities about CIPA. Even then, they did not believe him at first. Joe managed to make the authorities understand your condition."

"It's all right," I say. I can't ask her any more questions. Not now. Maybe not ever.

"Joe's trying to locate James," she says.

"He'll find him," I say, but Joe needs to hurry. Time's running out.

✚ ✚ ✚

My body-check routine is repeated in the evenings. Sometimes I turn on the song "Stayin' Alive" and listen to the music for inspiration. I'm so good at being careful that I hardly ever see blood anymore.

CHAPTER 4

I'm in the kitchen eating cereal when the doorbell rings. "That must be Spencer," I tell Nana. "He's bringing somebody with him to train her."

Nana doesn't answer. She's too busy staring into the kitchen cabinet to answer. I don't understand what's going on in her brain. Yesterday I thought she'd disappeared until I found her sitting in her car in the driveway. Luckily she couldn't get the key into the ignition. That was freakin' scary.

I don't need a personal assistant. Nana's the one who needs help. Veronica's taking her to the doctor this morning for a checkup. I think he can adjust her medicine and she'll improve.

I look up from my cereal when Spencer walks in. He pulls out a chair and sits at the table. "Ms. Smith will be here in a few minutes," he says. "She was a nurse's aide and has good observation skills."

"How'd you meet her?"

"Craigslist."

I roll my eyes. "And you think that was a good idea?"

"I talked to her. Joe ran a background check."

"So who's going to keep her from stealing something?"

"You can watch each other," Spencer says.

Then Veronica walks into the kitchen with a girl around my age. She's short and skinny. She's wearing blue scrubs, but the top has little white ducks on it. Her hair is short, sort of curly, and dark brown.

"This is Ms. Smith," Veronica says and rolls her eyes.

I almost start laughing and glance over at Spencer. He's grinning. Now I know why he talked to several people before hiring somebody. It's like he's hired me a girlfriend.

I like it when he accidentally makes me want to laugh.

"Hello," she says and sets a black bag on the table. "You can call me Luna."

"Luna?" I say. I don't know what else to say. "Like the moon?"

"Luna like lunatic," she says, tilting her head.

"I'm David."

"Oh my god. You're my patient?"

I nod.

She looks from me to Spencer. "You can't be serious," she says. "Is this a joke? You think it's funny? Oh my god. This is what I get for placing an ad on Craigslist. You guys are freakin' perverts."

"'It's not a joke," Veronica says. "David needs a personal assistant. Do you know anything about CIPA?"

"Not much."

"That's okay," Spencer says. "Nobody else does either. I'm Spencer."

I look down at my Cheerios floating in milk. I'd take a bite, but I'm scared milk will roll down my chin. I hate awkward moments when someone keeps looking at me like I'm an ugly painting. What am I supposed to say? It's time to check my blood pressure?

I don't want a girl checking me out and watching me.

And I really hate that Nana's still staring into the cabinet.

"Mrs. Hart, this is Luna," Spencer says to Nana. "Remember we talked about David getting another personal assistant?"

Nana gives him her I-don't-know-who-you-are look. Then she comes over and plays with my hair.

It's embarrassing.

"Nana's my grandmother," I tell Luna. "She's not herself this morning." I don't know who she is.

Veronica takes Nana by the arm. "There's coffee and cereal and juice on the counter. We have business downtown this morning."

"The car keys are in the spider plant," I tell Veronica.

"Will you be okay?"

I nod. I have to be okay or else Veronica wouldn't leave.

"Leave the bedroom door open," she says, and I give Luna a sideways glance.

Luna rolls her eyes.

"Does that hurt?" I ask.

"What?"

"Rolling your eyes like that."

"He's not a child," Luna says to Spencer. "I thought I was hired to help a disabled kid."

"He can be very childish," Spencer says.

Luna lowers her voice and speaks to Spencer. "Retarded?"

"No," I say. "There are five categories of CIPA. With type V there isn't mental retardation. That's what I have. But each case is unique, I think. I don't feel pain, but I get by okay. I've been taught to recognize what can harm me."

I can tell we're off to a great start.

"I don't really need a personal assistant," I say.

"That's some bruise on your arm," Spencer says.

I cover it with my hand. "I ran into the edge of an open door," I say. "That could happen to anybody."

"It doesn't hurt?" Luna asks.

"Is it supposed to?" I say.

"David once walked around with a nail in his foot," Spencer says. "But his grandmother thought he had swallowed it. He was x-rayed and everything, but the whole time the nail was in his foot."

Luna snorts. I bet she's thinking, *This place is a loony bin.*

"Give me some credit," I say. "That was years ago. I would know if I swallowed a nail. I can taste metal."

"Sherwood Anderson swallowed a toothpick and didn't know it," Spencer says. "He died."

"I'll be sure to check David's feet and mouth," Luna says.

You know what's so bad about what she says? She is serious. I don't want her or anybody looking into my mouth. What if I have bad breath?

"I usually start by checking his blood pressure, temperature, and pulse," Spencer says.

"I think we're going overboard with this," I say.

She opens the bag. She checks my blood pressure, temperature, and pulse, and writes down the numbers.

"The room temperature is kept at sixty-eight. Outside, if the temperature's over eighty, he can't take more than two hours. Do you have any questions?" Spencer asks Luna.

"I have no idea what to ask," she says.

"Just remember to check his body," Spencer says. "He doesn't need to be naked. I mean, just look at his arms and legs and back to make sure nothing's wrong and observe him."

I'm feeling like a monkey inside a glass enclosure at the zoo.

"For what?" Luna asks.

"Broken bones, seizures, hallucinations, confusion, coma, cardiac arrest from a high fever, or low body temperature or hemorrhage."

"Oh my god," I say. "Spencer's exaggerating. He spends most of his time here playing video games or texting."

"David would not know if something was wrong. Something minor like appendicitis could be fatal for him," Spencer says and stands. "I have to head to class. There's a list of emergency numbers on the refrigerator. You do know basic first aid and CPR, right?"

"Yes," Luna says.

Spencer says he'll see me later and leaves Luna and me at the kitchen table.

I should feel good that I have a cute nerd sitting at the kitchen table, but I don't. Not when I'm on exhibit. I place my cereal bowl in the sink. It's still full of last night's dishes. "You can do the dishes," I say to Luna.

"Are you helpless too?" Luna asks.

"No."

"Then go ahead."

I've never loaded the dishwasher before. It's because of the glass incident. I broke a glass, picked up the pieces, and threw them away. My hands were cut, but it's not like I didn't notice the blood. I said "ouch" like I was taught to do.

The weird thing is that Luna is observing me intently as I load the dishwasher. After I'm finished, she gets up from her chair. "Here you go, Helpless. You don't know what you're doing." She starts rearranging the dishes.

"Don't call me Helpless."

"Okay, Painless. Pay attention."

"My name's David."

I hate people who call me names. I hate people who treat me like I'm less than a person.

"Always place the sharp objects downward so you don't stab yourself."

"I'm careful."

"You're bleeding onto the table," she says like she's won a prize.

I look down and see drops of blood, but I'm not about to say "ouch." My right hand has a puncture wound. I get a napkin, wrap it around my hand, and head upstairs to my bathroom. Luna follows me.

I wash my hands, open the medicine cabinet, take out rubbing alcohol, and pour it over my hand.

"Doesn't that sting?" Luna asks.

I turn around. "No."

"It's supposed to sting and feel cold."

Whatever that means. I get a Band-Aid. Luna snatches it away, opens it, and sticks it onto my hand.

"There you go, Helpless," she says, still holding my hand. "Next time don't use alcohol. Soap and water are enough. Don't forget to clean up the blood on the table."

"Screw you," I say. I can't believe I said that.

She releases my hand. "Don't get your hopes up, Hopeless."

We walk back to the kitchen. She goes online. I wipe up the blood. It's only four drops. I've seen more. Then I say I'm going to my room.

She shuts her laptop and trails behind me like she thinks I might stumble.

It's embarrassing and demeaning. I'm going to ignore her.

I sit on the floor and pick up the game controller.

I've been playing a video game, trying to make it out of the World of Darkness into the World of Light, but I'm lost. In the game, my character's named Davy. He's kind of my alter ego. Davy can use magic to cure himself whenever he's injured, poisoned, or paralyzed.

Crap. I forgot that Tyler's dead. He's the other character and Davy's sidekick. The one with the answers. I revive him with a potion, but now Davy's slumped over from a hit, and the enemy casts Devastation.

Then both Tyler and Davy are dead.

"Get the girl wizard to cast Revive," Luna says. She's lying on my bed with a book in her hands.

She's obviously played role-playing games before. I didn't know she was watching.

I scroll to Revive. I've never had to use it before and that's why I forgot. The wizard casts Revive and saves Tyler and Davy.

"I have other games," I say. "I mostly play the classics."

"Why?"

"I have trouble with sensory perception. I can't keep up."

"I don't know what that means."

"It sucks. When that's messed up, one of your senses misinterprets the environment. I don't know all the science behind it."

I'd look it up, but I don't like reading about the bad stuff and what's going to happen to me sooner or later. Probably sooner.

"But the video games help me with hand-eye coordination."

"You're pretty good."

"Thanks. The other games are on the shelf. I have a couple of game systems in the closet if you want to play."

She opens the closet and sits on the floor. "You have six game systems," she says at last. "That's absurd."

She's probably the most absurd person I've ever met, wearing scrubs with ducks on the shirt. I wonder what she thought she'd be doing today. I get back to playing the game.

"You can wear regular clothes," I say.

She's looking around my room. "You play the guitar?"

"Yeah, and the piano."

I keep playing the game and she watches me, but we don't talk. She reminds me of someone watching a goldfish in a bowl. Then she sits on the floor next to me. I'm trembling, and I never tremble or shiver. The hair on the back of my neck never stands up like the hair on people in books I've read. I wonder what happens to real people when they're nervous.

I don't even realize Nana and Veronica are home until I hear the vacuum cleaner. I stand and say I have to find out what the doctor said about my grandmother.

We head to the kitchen. Veronica has placed sandwiches and fruit on a serving platter. "Where's Nana?" I ask.

"Sleeping."

Then Luna touches my arm and says, "Why don't you set the table?"

I give her a long, hard stare and then get plates.

"Thank you for staying," Veronica says, which surprises me. I figured she'd make a fuss about Luna. The whole thing is weird.

Luna sits and picks up a sandwich. "I forgot to ask. Exactly what hours do you need me?"

"Anytime," Veronica says.

"Spencer would always come over whenever he could," I say.

"Perfect. Do I call first?"

"If you want to," I say. "I'm always home."

"We'll start doing things," Luna says. "I'll make a schedule."

After Luna goes, I hang out in the kitchen with Veronica. She's unloading the dishwasher.

"How come you changed your mind about Luna?" I ask.

"I'd like to have somebody around to make sure you're okay," Veronica says. "I've had my hands full making sure your grandmother doesn't set the house on fire."

"When'd she do that?" I ask.

"She left water boiling on the stove."

"The doctor can't do anything?"

Veronica shakes her head. "The dementia is progressing, and she is in congestive heart failure."

I know about congestive heart failure. It makes her short of breath from the fluid in her lungs and her feet swell. I haven't noticed her feet swelling, but I usually don't look.

Veronica continues. "The doctor gave her something to get rid of the fluid in her lungs, and adjusted her heart and blood pressure medication. He suggested sitters, a hospital bed, and oxygen. I've left a message with Joe."

"But she's okay now?"

"She may need to be placed in a nursing home," Veronica says. A rooster crows, and she answers her cell phone. "Hey, Joe," she says. "I'm afraid I have some worrisome news."

I sit listening to Veronica repeat what she told me, and then she hands me her phone. I'm already not feeling too good, and now I'm feeling like the time I did when a hot dog got stuck in my throat.

"Hey, Joe," I say in a squeaky voice.

"We need to talk about you," he says.

No, we don't.

"There's an upscale community not far from you called Twin Falls. It has walking trails, a swimming pool, a clubhouse, horseshoes, and shuffleboard."

"I know about Twin Falls. I overheard the conversation you had with her about what to do about me if something happens to her."

"That conversation was at least a year ago," Joe says. "And you should not be listening in on private conversations."

"*So what?* I should be included in important conversations." I say. "Twin Falls is an assisted living community. Nana does not want me there, and I'm not going. Dr. Goodman said I could be independent."

"I've talked to him. He said you had some growing up to do. You're immature."

"He said I should get out more," I say. "That's all."

"Exactly. That's why Twin Falls would be a great match for you. Listen, I'll be over in a couple of hours, and we'll discuss this further." He disconnects.

My stomach knots up. If he hardly ever went outside or spent months of his life in the hospital, he'd be immature too.

✦ ✦ ✦

I'm playing the theme song from *Jaws* on the piano when Joe arrives.

He sits on the sofa, and when the song's over, he asks me if I know any nice songs.

I turn and look at him. "I'm in a bad mood."

"I noticed. Listen, I don't have all day. You need to be somewhere where you're safe. You're different."

Joe's right about that, but it isn't like that's big news. My mind works strangely. Nana said it's because of my condition and what I've experienced. That's the problem. I haven't actually experienced much of the outside world.

"Some people will take advantage of you," Joe says. "That could happen at Twin Falls."

Nana already gave me this talk. A couple of years ago, we went to the bank and opened an account for me. Nana said, "After I buy the farm, don't discuss money with anybody or else you'll have a lot of fake friends and long-lost relatives showing up."

The only long-lost relatives I have are my parents. My dad didn't leave me any family photos when he dropped me off here, but I've looked at Nana's album. Dad's my age in the pictures, and my mom isn't in any. Sometimes I see a certain margarine commercial on TV, and the man and woman eating breakfast remind me of my parents. I change the channel.

"Don't make this any harder than it already is," Joe says. "I've researched your condition, and I've read your medical record. In order to survive, you will always require some supervision."

I could've told him that. *Some* supervision is what I need. Not being sent away where I don't know anybody.

"Give me a chance to show you I don't need to be sent away," I say.

"Then you better grow up fast. You cannot get hurt or cause trouble. Can you make sure your grandmother eats? Can you watch TV with her and read to her? Can you make sure she is comfortable and safe?"

"Sure." Joe doesn't know anything about my life. I do some of those things already.

"And you'll fix your own meals and do your own laundry."

I shrug. "I'm not allowed to touch the stove or the washer and dryer."

"Why?"

"They're hot?" I guess.

"The washer and dryer aren't hot," he says. "Every evening, I'd like for you to send me a report. Then we'll talk about what's best for you, okay?"

"Okay." Some of what he wants is what I do anyway, but this feels too much like a threat. He already has everything figured out.

"How do you like Luna?" he asks.

"Fine."

"I think she'll be able to teach you some social skills," he says.

Then the doorbell rings, and Joe stands. "That's probably the medical equipment arriving."

I wait for him to go, and then I go to my room, stare out the window, and see a truck from a medical supply company. Suddenly I'm more scared than I've ever been. I shut the blinds.

CHAPTER 5

On Saturday I walk down the basement stairs and stop at the bottom. Spencer's band, Geo, is here to practice. I head over to the bar and sit on the stool. I should feel good that they come over here to practice, but I know it's not to hang out with me.

Marcello, Spencer, and Cassandra say hello to me.

"Where's Seth?" I ask.

"Late as usual," Cassandra says.

"I've been trying to call him," Spencer says. "All I get is voice mail."

"We don't need him. Let's get started or else we'll be here all day, and I have things to do," Cassandra says.

"You have a gig?" I ask.

"Fiftieth wedding anniversary next Saturday night," Spencer says. "The songs we need to learn are old."

Geo mostly plays at weddings and funerals. I wouldn't want to play at a funeral. It would be too hard. Too real.

First Cassandra and Spencer practice "Something Stupid." The way they look at each other is like there's nobody around but them. I'm close enough to Spencer to see him gaze into Cassandra's eyes. I wonder what he sees that makes him smile like somebody in a toothpaste commercial. One of these days somebody's going to gaze into my eyes. I hope they don't say, "Your eyes are bloodshot."

They mess up a couple of times, but I don't think it matters. There is passion in their voices.

"I guess Seth isn't coming," Spencer says after the song ends. His forehead wrinkles.

"It doesn't matter," Cassandra says. "We can do this without him."

Then they play "Earth Angel," and Marcello sings. Marcello hardly ever talks because he stutters when he's nervous. When he sings, I stop what I'm doing and listen to him. I bet everybody does, but I've never heard him sing any place but my basement. It's hard to believe such a smooth, clear voice is coming out of his mouth.

When it's over, Spencer says he's calling Seth.

"Oh my god," Cassandra says. "We're never going to finish rehearsing."

Spencer takes his phone from his pocket, walks over to the TV area, and sits on the couch.

Cassandra goes to the refrigerator and gets some water for herself and Marcello. "Have you noticed how Seth sweats after we play a couple of songs? It's gross."

Marcello shrugs. "Only when a room is hot," he says.

I wish I could sweat.

"How do you like your new personal assistant Spencer hired?" Marcello asks. "He said she was cute."

"She's okay."

"Is she here today?"

I shake my head.

"Spencer did good," Marcello says.

Cassandra's eyes widen. "Wait a minute. He hired a playmate for you?"

Marcello laughs. I shake my head. "She's not a playmate. He found his replacement."

"So what do the two of you do all day in your room?" Cassandra asks.

"Read. Watch TV. Play video games."

"Right," Cassandra says. "My parents would never allow me to have a guy in my room." She takes a drink of water.

"My grandmother knows I can be trusted," I say.

"Is Luna coming over today?" Marcello asks.

"No," I say. I wish she was here. I'm not sure why, but I miss her. I like her. She fills up the emptiness—everything I do, she does with me.

I usually wait for Luna to arrive. I sit at the window wearing shorts and a T-shirt. That way she can quickly look me over and then take a glance at my back. It's like she really cares. Then she writes everything down. I had a red spot on my arm that she measured to see if it was growing.

We hardly talk. I mean, what do you say to a girl who's mainly interested in your wounds and body temperature? It's a weird relationship.

Cassandra takes another sip of water. "Spencer finally told me that you don't feel pain. I understand why you need a personal assistant, but I don't get why it's a secret. Imagine how badass it would be if the doctors could develop a medicine to switch pain on and off in a normal person. I'd love to not feel pain."

"I wish I could feel pain," I say.

She snickers. "It's not like you have cancer."

It's not worth the effort to explain anything to her.

Marcello raises his eyebrows. "Uh...actually CIPA is fatal. Most kids die before they turn three. David's already beaten the odds." He throws his empty water bottle into the bag for recycling. "Maybe David can fill in for Seth. I don't think he's coming."

I'd do that, but I'd turn into a rock onstage and not be able to move.

Cassandra shakes her head right away, and I'm sort of relieved. A long time ago Spencer asked me if I wanted to be in the band he was starting. Nana said no. Crowded rooms get hot.

"*Oh no. Oh no,*" I hear Spencer say. I glance his way. He's talking on the phone and running his hand through his hair.

Cassandra walks over to Spencer with her bottle of water. She holds it out to him, but he shakes his head.

I get a funny feeling something bad has happened, but I'm not going to think about the possibilities. When you imagine something bad, you never know if you're making it come true. Still, I can't stop thinking about where Seth could be. Maybe he got a speeding ticket, and he was arrested. Or maybe Seth's been grounded. No, that can't be it. He'd call. He couldn't call if he's in jail. For some reason I'm hoping he's in jail.

Spencer slides his phone in his pocket and whispers to Cassandra. She covers her mouth with her hand. Then they walk over to us.

"Has the gig been canceled?" Marcello asks.

"Spencer called Seth's phone but his mother answered," Cassandra says.

"Why?" Marcello asks.

"He was in an accident last night."

My legs get weak. I lean against the bar and stare at Spencer's worn-out sneakers.

"Last night during the storm, a tree fell on his car while he was driving," Spencer says.

I look up and see Cassandra hugging Spencer.

"What are you trying to say?" Marcello asks.

"Seth is dead."

I close my eyes. The minutes or seconds before dying must've been awful for Seth.

For a few minutes we stand around in shock and don't know what to say. Then Marcello and I make eye contact. "You okay?" he asks, and I nod. I ask him if he's okay, and he says yes.

"Seth's mom wants you to sing," Spencer tells Marcello in a shaky voice. "And she wants you to play the piano," he says to me, sniffing. "It's a short service."

At Thanksgiving Seth brought over a pumpkin pie his mother made. Seth, Nana, and I ate it and drank glasses of milk. Then he and I played "The Entertainer" on the piano together. We were almost friends.

Spencer tells Nana what's going on. We choose "Hero" to play at Seth's funeral, and then we play music in the basement, but nobody goes home until it's totally dark outside.

Seth wasn't a hero, but I bet he could've become one if he had a chance.

✚ ✚ ✚

When I was younger, I'd imagine I could be some sort of hero because I don't feel pain. One time Spencer and I were with Nana shopping for clothes. We stepped into the parking lot and saw what I thought was a guy pulling a woman into a van. I was only a few feet behind him so I grabbed the man from behind. Luckily, my arms have always been strong from swimming. Unluckily, the woman pointed a gun at me, and I almost peed in my pants. I heard people screaming. She took my wallet, jumped into the van, and squealed away.

"Congratulations," the guy said. "You have saved the universe. You're a real superhero, helping that woman steal my van."

"Think of it this way," Spencer later said. "He freaked out when all she wanted was his keys and wallet. You kept her from shooting the guy or herself. Know what I mean?"

My fear of getting shot almost did me in. But then again, I wouldn't have felt a thing if the woman had gone ahead and fired the gun.

I sit at my desk and email Joe. I've been emailing him every day just like he asked me to do. I usually copy and paste the same email, and he hasn't noticed. See, he doesn't really care. But today is different. I tell him about Seth.

Today I played the piano for Nana and watched *Jeopardy* and *Wheel of Fortune*. I also read to her. Also, a friend died last night in an accident. His name was Seth.

To my surprise, Joe replies right away. *I'm sorry about your friend.*

CHAPTER 6

I feel like it's some sort of omen when the first thing Luna and I do outside of the house is go to a funeral. Spencer, Marcello, Cassandra, Luna, and I sit together.

When it's time, Spencer, Marcello, and I walk up to the front of the church. Seth is in the coffin looking better than ever.

So far all the music has been religious, and people have been sobbing. My fingers are trembling and I'm shaking when I start playing "Hero." I'm afraid people will be thinking, *What the heck is that*?

I block everything out except the reason I'm here. It's to play a song for a guy named Seth who liked pumpkin pie, milk, and playing "The Entertainer" on the piano so passionately that you'd think there would be no tomorrow. But there really was no tomorrow for Seth.

After the song ends, I go back to my seat next to Luna. She rests her face against my shoulder.

✚ ✚ ✚

I go online to find new information about how long a person with CIPA could live.

Age twenty-five.

Dr. Goodman was telling the truth.

I've got eight years maybe. That's almost a lifetime if I stop wasting time.

✚ ✚ ✚

I lie in my bed, arms and legs stretched out, and I stare at the ceiling.

Spencer and I once watched this movie called *Rudy*. It's about this kid who dreams about playing football at Notre Dame. He's poverty stricken and dyslexic, and after a lot of rejection, he gets to play for a few minutes at the end of the last game of the season. It's an awesome movie.

I think about how I want to live the next few years. I have the money, but I don't have the know-how. I don't even know how to go shopping, but shopping won't be on my bucket list. That's what the Internet is for.

The clock's ticking.

The first thing on my list will be *learn to drive*.

After I learn to drive and get my license, I'll go anywhere I want to go. I'll drive to the beach or just down a scenic road. I will email Joe and tell him. He'll be surprised and relieved that he doesn't need to worry about what's going to happen to me, and I'll be free.

CHAPTER 7

My grandpa once let me drive his John Deere tractor. I was going as fast as I could across the yard, the wind blowing my hair, my grandpa laughing, my hands controlling the big red monster.

"Look at me! I'm a superhero!" I yelled to Grandpa.

When he was alive, I wasn't scared of anything.

Suddenly I heard Nana. "Oh my god. Oh my god. He's going to run over something or kill himself."

I looked her way.

"I'm Superman!"

"Watch out!" she yelled.

I hit a tree. My head hit the steering wheel, and I saw stars. I threw up. I got a concussion, but I don't think it was my first.

I learned that when your head hits in just the right spot, you get two black eyes. Driving the tractor was worth the concussion and the black eyes. The stars were beautiful.

+++

I go online and search for how to drive. I read the instructions and then download the driving test handbook to my reader.

I'm reading in my bed when Luna arrives.

"Are you sick?"

"No, and I've done everything I'm supposed to do."

"I didn't know you knew how to read books without pictures," Luna says.

"I read three books a week."

"What are you reading?"

"Driver's handbook."

"I haven't heard of that one," she says. "What's it about?"

I kind of laugh. "It's about using your blinker when you make a turn."

"Oh." She pulls a book from her backpack and lies on the other bed.

"What are you reading?" I ask.

"*Siddhartha*. He goes on a spiritual journey to find the meaning of life."

My ears perk up. "Where did he find it?"

Luna smiles. "The journey led to the discovery. It took until he was old and near death."

I don't have years and years to make discoveries.

And I don't read books I have a hard time understanding.

"Have you read 'Allegory of the Cave'?" I ask.

"No. What's it about?"

My mouth gets stuck in the open position. Embarrassment is what I get for trying to act smart. There's no way out. I can't run and hide. Luna's waiting for me to answer.

"Well, uh, people who have been prisoners since birth are bound so they can only face a wall in a cave. Statues stand on top of the wall and a fire behind the prisoners makes shadows appear on the wall." I shrug. "The prisoners believe that the shadows are reality. A prisoner is freed, and when he turns around and sees the fire, he experiences pain from the light. He has to be dragged out of the cave, and the sunlight blinds him even more than the fire did. After a while he finally sees the trees and flowers and everything that's real."

"Enlightenment," she says. "He sees reality and truth."

"Yeah. I have a Kindle you can have," I say. "It's old, but you wouldn't have to carry all those books around with you."

"No, thanks." She turns a page and another one falls out.

I lean down, pick up the yellowed page, and hand it to her.

She gets back to reading, her face serious as if she's lost somewhere in the story. I'd be lost too, but it'd be because my brain would be saying, "Ugh. What's happening?"

I kind of lied about reading "Allegory of the Cave." Nana read it to me. She read hundreds of books to me before her eyes went bad. Nana said I needed to exercise my brain. I'm afraid if I don't, my brain will deteriorate like Charlie's brain did in *Flowers for Algernon*. He couldn't do anything about it, but if he had somebody like Nana, he would've been better off.

I hope I don't lose my brain, and I want to be smarter.

Even the driver's handbook is confusing, filled with ads for driving schools and messages from the governor and other people.

I take a deep breath and smell Luna's perfume. I glance at her. Her body's stretched out, and she's lying on her stomach.

"Stop watching me," she says.

I was only looking at her for a few seconds.

She shuts her book. "If you're going to stare at me, we should go downstairs," she says, looking away from me. "This feels too weird."

"I'm sorry," I say. "It feels weird to me too. I'm used to Spencer being here. This was like his second home, but it was time for him to move on. Most everybody does when they finish high school or college."

"What about you?"

I shrug.

"Listen," she says. "I can teach you to drive. I like doing things I've never done before. I like challenges."

I'm not a challenge. I'm a person. "I have to get a learner's permit first, and you're not twenty-one," I say.

"You can practice in the driveway," she says. "Or on the road out front."

Our driveway branches off a two-lane country road that dead-ends in front of my house. There aren't many other houses along the way.

"I don't know," I say. "I need forty hours of practice."

"You know what your problem is? You need confidence. If you don't do it now, you'll never do it." She shrugs. "I hate to say this, but one of these days you'll be stuck here alone, doing nothing but breathing. All the effort your grandmother made to make sure you survive will be wasted. It's time for you to move to the next level. She wouldn't want you to end up alone or with somebody you pay to keep you company."

She's saying I'm a loser and a failure. I'm not. Just to prove her wrong I say, "Let's go."

✚ ✚ ✚

In the garage I slide into the driver's seat of the Lexis. Luna sits in the passenger seat. Nana has a Mercedes too, but I'm more familiar with the Lexis.

Luna points out the controls, but I already know where everything is. Back before Nana was diagnosed with dementia, she'd drive me to doctors' appointments, and she'd forget where the windshield wipers or headlights were. Sometimes, we'd get lost. I should've known something was wrong a long time before she was diagnosed.

"I got it," I say at last. I turn on the motor, put the car in reverse, and open the garage door. I press the gas, and all of a sudden the car's moving! A few seconds later I hear the scraping of metal, and a sick feeling lands in my belly. I've hit the side of the garage door.

"Yes, you did," Luna says.

I turn off the motor, get out of the car, and check the bumper. There's barely a scratch. I run my hand over the bumper a couple of times and then get back in the car. Luna has a smirk on her face, and then she starts snorting.

"It's not funny," I say.

She covers her mouth.

For the next hour I drive around the circular driveway with Luna. I only need to do this for thirty-nine more hours to get my permanent license.

"I'll make a new schedule for you," Luna says as we get out of the car. "One that doesn't include me checking your temperature or blood pressure or whatever."

I roll my eyes.

"I hate it when you do that," she says.

✛ ✛ ✛

The next morning Luna prints out my new schedule. At nine o'clock I have driving lessons. Then at ten o'clock I have a life-skills class, followed by public service and art.

"I don't know how to draw," I say. "But anyway, today is Saturday. Spencer's band is practicing in the basement."

She spins around. "That's perfect. Why aren't you in his band?"

I tell her what Nana said about hot, crowded rooms and how I don't sweat. I don't remind her I could have a seizure.

"One step at a time. You won't know what will happen until you try. First ask him if you can join," she says. "I've heard you play the piano and guitar." She scribbles out "art" and adds "music."

Luna's the most enthusiastic personal assistant I've ever had.

✛ ✛ ✛

"You can try out for the band," Spencer says. "But the thing is, I don't know how much longer we'll keep doing this." He says they canceled the gig playing at the anniversary party because they weren't ready. They're all busy with summer coming, vacations, and preparing to go away to college. "We are planning on playing at the Spring Festival."

Nobody mentions Seth's absence. I feel sad not seeing him.

We play three Beatles songs, but in the middle of the third, Cassandra suddenly yells, "Stop! This isn't going to work. I'm sorry to say this, David, but you look weird when you move around."

"He can stand still," Spencer says.

"That would look weird too," Cassandra says.

Cassandra and Spencer start shouting at each other. She says she's saving me from embarrassing myself. Spencer says to give me a chance.

They seem to think I can't hear them.

Marcello keeps trying to say something, but Cassandra drowns him out.

Luna comes down the stairs. "Shut up!" she shouts, and the room suddenly becomes quiet. "What are you trying to do? Upset his grandmother? That's just what she needs." She asks what's going on, and Cassandra tells her.

Luna starts laughing. I missed the punch line of the joke.

"You are idiots," she says loudly. "David doesn't need you for anything."

Oh god. I don't want her saying stuff. I'd rather just walk away. Then she looks at me and smiles. I've never seen her smile like that before. It's like I'm special in a good way.

"What did you say?" Cassandra asks her.

"You are idiots," Luna says.

"You're a scammer," Cassandra says.

Luna heads toward Cassandra.

I'm freakin' irritated. I step between them. "I don't need your help," I tell Luna. I want to crawl into a deep hole.

Cassandra laughs. "You're just a research project for her."

"So what?" I ask.

Years ago, one of my tutors was a medical student who did his research project on me. Nana had him sign a contract that no identifying information could be used. She said he might be able to help other kids and families. He's the doctor at the university who Dr. Goodman consults.

"I'm out of here," Luna says.

"Me too," Marcello says, stuttering. "This is stupid."

I guess I should leave too. I'm just standing around with my mouth open, and nobody's saying anything. "You guys don't need another person anyway," I say. I look at Cassandra. "You shouldn't have called Luna a scammer and me a research project."

"She is not your friend," Cassandra says. "You pay her."

I shrug and head up the stairs. I don't think I was given a fair chance to be in the band, but I learned a long time ago that life's unfair.

Besides, I was only doing this for Luna. I kind of thought I was a research project for her because of all the notes she'd take.

Veronica tells me we caused too much of a commotion, and that confuses my grandmother. "She thought there were intruders in the basement, and it scared her," Veronica says. "I think Spencer and the others should find another place to practice."

Nana sits in her recliner staring at the turned-off TV.

"You okay?" I ask.

Nana's stare fills me with dread.

I escape to my room and watch a movie, but I don't pay attention. I'm not mad at Veronica. She's been like a family member and a second grandmother to me.

I fall asleep and awaken when the movie's over. I'm pretty depressed. I check Nana's room and see she's asleep. The sitter is too. I go downstairs. It's dark. Nana's asleep. Veronica's gone. I get a Coke out of the refrigerator and drink it. Loneliness is worse when most everybody you know is mad at you.

CHAPTER 8

The next morning I'm not in the mood to play a video game or read or look out the window, so I decide to drive the car around the circular driveway. It's pretty long.

I back out of the garage into the driveway, put the car into Drive, and go to the road. I turn around and go to the other end of the driveway. I do that over and over again, hoping Luna will show up today.

I haven't run over anything so I'm going to drive down the road. I'll turn around before I get to the stop sign. I'm cheating by counting my driving time without having somebody with me. I know that. But who's going to help me? I have to do it myself.

Spencer's probably with Cassandra today, and Luna's probably looking for another job.

I drive down the road and pass Cameron's house. He's sitting on his porch with a dog that never even gets to go for a walk. I wave to him. He's lived in the broken-down house ever since he came back from Afghanistan.

Right before the stop sign I pull into a dirt drive that leads to a fenced-in field to turn around. I make the turnaround without problems, but right before I pull back onto the road, a car runs the stop sign and another car collides with it. Metal flies into the air and drops to the ground. Other cars stop to help. I can see one of the victims leaning forward inside his car.

I get out of my car, go over, and tell the man that help's coming. He nods, and I can hear a gurgle when he breathes. I wonder if that hurts. It sounds like it would.

The paramedics arrive within minutes, and I get out of their way. I head home.

Luna's standing in the driveway holding her notebook. I don't know how I missed seeing her.

"Don't you know it's cold today?" she asks when I get out of the car.

I'm not wearing a jacket. "I was in the car most of the time," I say. "You see the accident?"

She nods. "I saw you turning around too. I am sorry about yesterday. I embarrassed you."

"I'm sorry too."

"I'm not a scammer."

"I don't know where Cassandra got that idea," I say.

"I spend hours a day alone with you in your room and get paid."

"My grandmother is thankful you come over. So is Veronica."

"They want you independent."

"I try to be. I can take care of myself."

"Maybe," she says.

I glance at the notebook. "Taking more notes?"

"Yes," she says. "If that's okay."

I tell her she cannot use my name or any identifying information.

We talk about her one day going to graduate school and hopefully getting her PhD.

We walk into the kitchen. Nana's sitting at the table working on a word-search puzzle. Some days she's fine. Some days I can't tell. Other days she's out of her mind. The sitter's across from her.

"Where's David?" Nana asks.

"I'm here, Nana."

"She asks about you dozens of times a day," the sitter says. "She thinks you're in the hospital, and she wants to go see you."

I don't know what I'll do if—when—Nana dies.

✦✦✦

"You have a bucket list," Luna says. She's at my desk revising my schedule. "You should have told me before."

"Lots of people have them," I say.

"Not like this." She reads it out loud.

1. *Graduate from high school.*
2. *Meet a girl I really like.*
3. *Live in my own apartment where somebody's not watching me all the time.*
4. *Find a job.*
5. *Get my driver's license.*

6. *Go to the beach and swim in the ocean at least one more time.*
7. *Perform random acts of kindness.*
8. *Find my parents and laugh in their faces.*
9. *Don't break any more bones.*
10. *Fix my temperature problem.*
11. *Feel pain.*
12. *Make tears.*
13. *Stay alive and die of old age.*
14. *See something spectacular.*

"See something spectacular? Like what?" Luna asks.

"I don't know yet."

"I've never heard of a bucket list like this," she says. "It's different. It's heartbreaking."

Great. I've broken a girl's heart, and I'm not even trying. "I'm a beginner," I say.

Our eyes meet. "All those times you were in the hospital, did you ever see the tunnel of light?" Luna asks.

"Just ducks. I heard quacking. I figure I made a wrong turn."

"Maybe you had a quack doctor," she says and starts quacking. I laugh with her.

"Once, a doctor got this idea that if I was tasered every day, it would stimulate the growth of nerve endings," I say. "Obviously, it didn't work, but I shook and laughed. It felt like tickling."

"So you can feel some things?"

"Yes. I feel touch, pressure, and itching," I say. "So what about you?"

"I'm boring."

"Probably not to a duck. You quack well."

She laughs. "I grew up competing in beauty pageants. I loved dressing up and pretending to be a princess. It was my mother's life. We competed nearly every weekend. She'd make me beautiful," Luna says. She smiles.

That's what makes her go from plain to beautiful.

"You are beautiful," I say.

Luna laughs. "I can merge some of the things from your bucket list to the schedule. That way, you'll have something to work toward."

I'm looking at my revised schedule, which includes a calendar. "Spring Festival?" I ask.

"It's part of life skills," she says. "I'll meet you there."

Under Spring Festival, I see "cab" circled.

"Maybe you'll meet a girl there you like," Luna says.

I stare at my bucket list. I already have met a girl, but I'm a research project to her.

CHAPTER 9

I blow-dry my hair and comb it carefully. Then I dress in black jeans and a button-down shirt. I splash on Terre d'Hermes. It's for the man who has his head in the stars and his feet planted on the ground or something like that. I want to be him.

I grab my jacket and cane. Stepping into the hallway, I shut my door, and then I walk down the hall to Nana's room. I glance in. She's lying on her bed talking on the phone. I wave bye to her.

"Wait, James!" she calls out. "Got to go," she says into the phone.

But I'm not James. You'd think after eleven years, she'd remember my name. "I'm David," I say with a squeak in my voice. I try hard not to make a big deal out of it.

Nana motions for me to come in. "You look so much like your father," she says, staring at me.

James hasn't been around for over a decade, but I figure

at seventy-eight years old she has a right to get mixed up once in a while and forget today and yesterday and years of her life. If I had all those memories floating around in my head, I'd get mixed up too.

"Who called?" I ask.

"Stanford asking for a donation."

I stay quiet. Nana graduated from Stanford in 1959. You'd think somebody as smart as her would never get mixed up.

I stand at the foot of her bed. She's dressed in pajamas. "Where's the sitter?"

"In the kitchen."

I'll have to check to be sure. I never know what to believe, but if the sitter's not here, I can't go anywhere.

"I'm going now," I say.

"Where?"

"The Spring Festival," I tell her for the second time today. "Remember? The band's playing in the *Waterly's Got Talent* show."

I'm not playing. I haven't talked to Spencer since the day I found out I looked weird onstage. They haven't practiced in my basement.

Nana starts to get up. "I forgot. I'll be ready in a minute."

I grab onto the bedpost. "I don't need you to drive me. I'll call a cab, and Luna's meeting me." From the look on Nana's face, I know she doesn't have a clue what I'm talking about.

I'm not calling a cab. I lied to Luna too. I don't need riding in a cab as a life experience. I got my learner's permit yesterday, and there's a hardly used car in the garage that's calling to me.

Nana lies back down. Her eyes droop, and her head falls forward.

"Be careful, David."

At least she got my name right. "I'm always careful," I say, kind of sad. She's always been afraid for me and sometimes terrified, but I've been doing better while she's been getting weaker.

Nana looks up and throws me a kiss.

I smile at her and throw a kiss back.

As I'm going downstairs, the sitter's headed up. She's carrying Nana's protein drink. Tonight it's strawberry.

I smile, breathe a sigh of relief, and tell her I'm going out.

I grab the keys from the spider plant, and then I check the thermostat. It's a perfect fifty-six degrees outside. Two hours ago, it was a perfect fifty-seven degrees.

I get into Nana's Lexis and take a deep breath. I can do this. I have to do this. I want to see Luna, and I don't want to arrive in a cab.

At the end of the road, I look left, right, left, and then slowly turn left. My heart pumps as hard as a fire hose when the hydrant's turned on. Driving is scaring the heck out of me. I thought I'd feel powerful. I thought I'd feel like I was in control of something. I wonder how Seth was feeling when he was driving before the tree fell onto his car.

When I finally arrive at the Spring Festival, I park where there aren't any cars for me to hit and walk across the road, the air tasting like smoke and new flowers. The sky's star-filled. I walk along a trail toward the bonfire in the middle of the field. About a hundred people I don't know are celebrating spring.

Along the sides are booths with vendors selling popcorn, pizza, hot dogs, and drinks. I smell cotton candy and see pink clouds in my head. Best of all, there's a lit-up Ferris wheel on the other side of the field. I've never ridden a Ferris wheel or been on a roller coaster. All I've ever ridden is a merry-go-round, and Nana was afraid I'd fall off the horse.

I look around for Luna, but I don't see her.

She said she'd be standing near Spencer's band. She said I should act like I didn't care that they didn't want me. "If they don't want you, then you don't want them," she said. "It's like falling in love. If somebody doesn't love you, then forget them."

There's Spencer next to the stage at the north corner of the field, and for some reason I think about the time I helped him with math. My answers were wrong because I did the wrong page. Spencer said it was all right. He said that he would've done the wrong page too.

Another band is playing right now, and people are dancing. I weave through the crowd. I say hi to Spencer as I pass him, walking like I'm on my way somewhere important.

"Hi," he says, but that's all. I find a place to stand near a soccer goal somebody forgot to move. There are not many people hanging out at the soccer goal, and it's easier for me to keep an eye out for Luna.

Then the MC says, "Now we have Geo." The audience applauds.

All at once I feel like my heart's fallen into the dirt. They go onto the stage, and the music erupts. *She was just seventeen…*

They're strong, loud, and playing better than ever. I feel only the music, barely aware of anything else around me. I imagine I'm up there with them.

Then it's over, and the audience applauds wildly. Cass takes a bow, throwing kisses, eating up the attention. I look away. Then I gasp in disbelief. I think I see my dad maybe thirty feet away. I head in that direction, weaving through the crowd, but then he's lost among all the bodies. Thing is, the guy's too young to be my dad. My dad would be middle-aged by now, and he wouldn't come back here for a million dollars. After all these years, he's probably dead. I blink him away.

Around three years ago, a car was found in Paper River, which is not too far from us. Skeletal remains were inside. For a few days we thought the person was my dad, but later we were told the body was Noel Peeples, who had gone missing forty-five years ago.

I buy a bottle of water and twist off the cap. Then I feel a touch on my arm.

"Hi," Luna says. She's wearing jeans and a sweater. She smiles. Her breath smells like apple mints. I love apple mints. "Want to dance?" she asks.

"Not really."

"You don't know how?"

"Actually Nana taught me to waltz."

"That would be cool," Luna says. "I've never waltzed before."

"Nobody's playing a waltz. I bet you added dancing to my life-skills list."

She doesn't answer.

We end up waltzing to a song. Luna, my cane, and me. I like the feel of her hands touching the back of my neck. I get butterflies in my stomach. It's how I imagine I'd feel on a roller coaster the moment right before the fall. I won't ever forget this. I count, "One, two, three," and I could do this forever just to be close to Luna.

Then the music stops. I hold Luna for a few seconds, even though we're a foot apart. Then she says we should go over to the bonfire. "See that girl?" she says. "You should say hello to her."

"And then tell her I don't know any pickup lines?" I say. "No thanks."

"You have to start somewhere," she says and hooks her arm around mine. We go over and stand near Spencer, Marcello, Cassandra, and the girl Luna wants me to meet. They're talking and laughing. Luna punches my arm. "Tell Spencer they did great," she says. "And then introduce yourself to the girl."

"She's with Marcello," I say as Marcello puts his arm across her shoulder. I turn my head and see a guy squirt lighter fluid onto the fire. Flames erupt. The guy drops the lighter fluid can at the edge of the fire, too close to the blaze. A can of lighter fluid exploding is like a bomb with shrapnel going everywhere. It could kill somebody, and I'm not in the mood to die. I go over, pull the can away from the fire with my cane, and pick it up.

Luna screams. I look down and see my jacket sleeve

burning. I drop the can, pull off my jacket, and stomp on the flame. I fake scream a little too, to sound like a normal person. At the same time, I hear Spencer yell, "David!" and then he's charging toward me, but everything's moving in slow motion. I keep hitting the fire until it's out. Smoke fills my lungs, and I smell burned hair. Coughing, I quickly touch my hair to make sure it isn't burning. It isn't, but the odor's probably caused by singed arm hair. I'd rather smell hair than flesh.

A crowd is gathered around me. Luna's crying. "It's all right," I tell her. "I'm not burned." I make that up. I don't know if I'm burned or not without looking.

Spencer walks up to me, his face sweaty. "Didn't anybody ever tell you that metal in a fire is hotter than hell?" he whispers.

I look at cotton candy somebody's holding. "Yep. It would've hurt anybody else. I figured I had to do something."

"But it hurts you too, only you don't know it. You're not a superhero," he says.

"I know." I stopped believing that a long time ago.

Spencer's shaking his head. "You're either the luckiest person I know or the unluckiest."

A security guard yells, "Move along. The excitement's over." He picks up the can.

I kind of laugh. The Spring Festival is supposed to be the excitement. I can smell smoke and lighter fluid on my clothes.

Spencer takes his keys out of his pocket. "I'll give you a ride to the hospital."

"No thanks. I know where it is."

The girl I was supposed to talk to touches my arm. "You're a hero."

"I'm only pretending," I say. I look away. I'm not a baby, but sometimes I think I'm waiting to be born. The first time, God forgot the neurons.

Now I'm embarrassed and feel like crawling into a hole. Luna's seen the stupid part of me too many times.

"I'll talk to you tomorrow," I tell Luna. I can't walk around smelling like a gas tank.

"Don't your hands hurt?" the girl asks.

"Nah. I'm an alien from outer space," I say and walk away.

✛ ✛ ✛

In the car I turn on the light and check my hands. They're red, but the light's bad. I don't trust it. A burn on my wrist looks like a tree turned red in the fall. Little blisters are forming. I'll be okay. I'll put some ointment on my hands later.

On the way home I'm thinking about what a loser I can appear to be. The Spring Festival will probably be going on for hours. I was only there for a short while, but I want to start over and not end up looking like an idiot.

I look for the stop sign at the dead end where I need to turn right. My fingers squeeze the steering wheel. Darkness engulfs the road, and I glance down at the switch to turn on the bright lights. When I look up, I see the stop sign ahead, and I brake, but the car keeps going. Gasping, I pump the pedal. *Please, please, don't let me hit anyone.* The car enters the intersection and refuses to slow down. I'm in the middle of the road. My grip tightens on the steering wheel. I'm crossing the road, hitting the grass on the other side, and bouncing down an incline into a ditch. The car stops. Ten more feet, and the car would've been sinking in a pond full of catfish.

My heart's pounding, but I'm not in shock. Well, maybe I am in shock. I can't move. Two times tonight I've come close to getting hurt. I've got the right to be in shock.

And there's only me to do something. Unwilling to move, I don't. I can't believe I'm having all this bad luck in one night.

"Do you need assistance?"

At the sound of the voice, I jump, and then I remember that the Lexus has an onboard emergency response system.

"I only need a tow truck," I finally tell the person, balling my hands into fists. "I don't need the police or an ambulance." I'll be in big trouble for driving without a license. *Do they put you in jail for that?* I wonder.

"Help is on the way."

I shove the airbag out of the way, put the car into Park, and turn on the inside light. I check myself. I don't see blood or bones sticking out. I must feel fine. Good thing there were no cars coming. Good thing I missed Mr. Henderson's pond.

The brakes went out. I don't know why. Brakes can fail suddenly. I've seen it happen on TV. Maybe I hit the gas instead of the brake, but the car never sped up. Suddenly, I know what happened. I panicked. My foot kept hitting the floorboard, and my brain was telling me it was the brake.

I get the flashlight from the glove compartment and then pick through the contents until I find the insurance card. Nana had a flat tire once, and I remember what she did. I could've changed the tire, but it was a hot, summer day, and Nana wouldn't let me.

I grab my cane, open the door, and tread through high grass and briars to the front of the car. Shinning the light across the fender and then the hood, I don't see any damage.

I climb up the slope behind the car to the side of the road and wait breathlessly for the wrecker. It's dark, and I can barely see anything. I look down the road and see a car coming. It can't be the tow truck.

I think about a commercial from TV where the first person to arrive at an accident scene was a lawyer in a hot-air balloon. Then I remember a movie I watched about a girl breaking down on a highway. A serial killer stopped to save her. But the car I'm watching speeds past me.

While I'm waiting for the tow truck, I think things out. I'm going to be in trouble for driving without a license, and I'm going to be in trouble for having an accident. I cannot hide that. But to avoid the most trouble, I have to get checked at the hospital or else I'll end up being taken by Joe, and I'd rather have him yell at me on the phone than in person.

The tow truck pulls up. Sticking my hands into my pockets and walking over to it, I breathe a mix of relief and fear. The truck has "Hills Towing" written on the side of the hood, and a hook and chain in the bed of the truck. You'd think he towed hills instead of cars.

I ask the driver if he'll drop me off at the hospital.

✚ ✚ ✚

I don't want to go to the hospital, but who would? Doctors never say anything I want to hear, and they always find something wrong I don't want to know about.

After I check in, I'm taken to one of the semi-private rooms where patients are examined.

The nurse pulls the curtain around the gurney and leaves so I can undress. When I have everything off but my underwear, I sit on the gurney with a sheet wrapped around me. A man's moaning on the other side of the curtain. I'm used to hearing all sorts of human sounds when I come here. Burps, cries, screams, grunts, wheezing. You wouldn't think a body could make so many different out-of-control noises. The worst is when somebody's gurgling, and then you know there's a good chance that soon you won't hear anything else.

Dr. Wilensky appears. I've met him before. One time I cut my foot and glued the skin together. It got infected, and I had to come here. Dr. Wilensky gave me an antibiotic in the vein and said I was lucky I didn't have to have my foot amputated.

"Let me guess," Dr. Wilensky says as he reads my chart. "You didn't know you were on fire until you smelled something cooking."

I stare at his stethoscope. "Not exactly," I say. It's embarrassing.

"And you were in a car accident?"

"It was a minor accident, and I don't have any injuries. I didn't hit my head or anything."

Dr. Wilensky checks me from head to toe, and I think about what Nana's going to do when she finds out I ran into a ditch. She'll probably kill me if she's herself.

✚ ✚ ✚

When I was about ten years old I found a razor blade in the bathroom medicine cabinet, and I decided to do a pain test. I cut my arm, but it only bled and didn't hurt. My grandfather opened the door and screamed.

"Please don't get rid of me," I said.

"You want to know how bad it's supposed to hurt?" my grandfather said. "Remember how your dad hasn't come back? That's how bad it hurts."

At the hospital a doctor asked if I was trying to kill myself. He didn't understand about a pain test.

Back at home Nana made me write "I will never do a pain test again" a hundred times. There are thousands of my "I will not" papers in the closet in her room.

✚ ✚ ✚

I don't have to worry about what Nana's going to do or say.

Not one bit.

When I exit the treatment area, Joe's standing in the waiting room. I'd forgotten that because I'm a minor, the emergency department would notify a parent or guardian.

"I never thought you'd take the car without permission. You could have killed yourself or someone else."

"I'm sorry." I stick my hands into my pockets. "I made a mistake, and then the brakes failed."

"You need to pay attention and stop walking around with your head in the clouds. What did the doctor do?"

I shrug. "He checked me. He didn't find anything wrong."

"What's wrong with your arms?"

I have marks from when Nana digs her fingernails into my arms. "Sometimes Nana won't use her walker," I say.

Joe doesn't say anything on the way to my house.

I unlock the door. He follows me inside. We go into the living room.

"I don't know what I'm going to do about you," he says and sits on the sofa. "Because the buck stops with me."

"Why?" I ask.

"I'm your legal guardian now."

I groan and plop down onto the sofa. I can hear the grandfather clock in the corner ticking. "It's time?" I say. "Things are getting worse?"

"I don't know, but your grandmother is in no shape to make decisions for you."

I stare at a stain on the sofa where I once dropped a burrito, wondering if I can actually take care of myself. I don't want to be left alone. I hear the hum of the heat or maybe the air conditioner, but how the heck am I supposed to know? I figure it has to be the heat because it's fifty-six degrees outside.

I pull my knees to my chest and hold on to my legs. The grandfather clock ticks so loudly that I want to break the glass over its scary face and stop time. Sometimes I've dreamed I'm walking through the house. It's empty, and I can't find a door or Nana to show me the way.

I'm thinking that if I was never born, my parents wouldn't have disappeared on purpose, and Nana wouldn't have gotten stuck with me. I remember overhearing Ruby tell her I should never have been born. That's the same as wishing I was dead.

I rest my head on the back of the sofa and stare at the crystal chandelier.

I figure my parents are as pain-free as me but in another way. All they cared about was dumping me so they could go on with their lives.

So I figure it's my fault nobody ever came to get me. I'm damaged.

What's sad is that whenever anybody would ask Nana, "How's James?" she'd say, "He's fine. He'll be coming home soon." Then she'd quickly change the subject. After a while, people stopped asking about my dad, and she didn't have to lie about him coming back.

"What's going on?" Nana asks from the doorway. She's stooped over and holding on to the walker.

"We're just talking," Joe says.

"Is it time for breakfast?"

I shut my eyes and take a deep breath. A stranger is living in my house.

"It's eleven o'clock," Joe says. "At night."

She's not confused. She's been sleeping for a while. So what if she woke up and thought it was morning? That's happened to me.

Joe stands. "I'll be back in the morning." He looks at me. "You be ready. We're taking a ride."

CHAPTER 10

When I was ten I was pretty stupid, but my grandparents wanted to adopt me anyway. They were in the study talking to Joe. My tutor was on the back deck either talking on his cell phone or texting, and I was hanging out behind the door to the study.

Joe said I would require care the rest of my life, and they were already at the age where they did not need a disabled kid. "What's going to happen to him if you die?" he asked.

"For god's sake, David is our grandson. He's our responsibility now," my grandfather said.

Joe asked if they would like him to check into experimental studies or interviews to help with my medical expenses. My grandparents said no. They didn't need money.

I remember thinking I'd like to have my picture on a magazine cover because of my condition. I'd make a lot of money and pay a doctor to fix me to be like everybody else. The sooner I got normal, the sooner I'd be loved.

How stupid is that? Not even all normal people are loved.

✦ ✦ ✦

Joe's car has been in the driveway for ten minutes, and I'm not going downstairs to hear him lecture me again. He's not my dad. He's not even related to me. Unfortunately, I hear a knock on my door. Nana doesn't knock. Luna will knock, but she'll say, "Hey, David. It's me." And Spencer would just walk in.

He knocks again. I better answer. Maybe it's not Joe. He never comes to my room. I open the door and see Joe.

"Look," he says. "I know you want to see me about as much as I want to see you." He looks me over. "Time to go."

"Luna's coming over," I say.

He doesn't say anything. I guess it won't matter.

I follow Joe down the steps, out the front door, and to his car. I get inside and hear my door lock. I don't ask where we're going. I don't want to know.

Joe's perfect as far as Nana is concerned. You'd think he was her son or grandson instead of her attorney and my guardian.

"We have an appointment," Joe says.

This is not going to turn out well. "Where?" I ask.

"Twin Falls," he says.

I knew I wouldn't be hearing good news. He doesn't think he can just drop me off there today, does he? He wouldn't try to get rid of me, would he? I hold my hands in my lap, folded together. "You can't do this to me," I say.

He turns onto a private road. "You did it to yourself."

Twin Falls has golf-course grass covering rolling hills

and a stream running along the side of the winding road. Joe stops at a gate, presses a button, and says his name. I hear a buzzer and the gate opens.

For a minute, I look for a way out. I see a redbrick wall along the perimeter, probably built to keep someone from leaving without permission. The driveway winds past redbrick buildings. Joe stops in front of the one that has *Office* written on double glass doors.

A lady shows us a studio apartment on the second floor, and it's pretty nice, but there wouldn't be enough room for my games and stuff. From the balcony I can see a pond with ducks.

"I'm allergic to ducks," I say.

"David," Joe warns.

I stare at him.

The lady says I'd have an aide to check in on me and help me shower and dress if needed. The aide will bring my lunch too, unless I want to eat in the restaurant.

We go into the hallway and ride an elevator to the fifth floor. The door opens and I see a circular restaurant. A few senior citizens sit at tables. I don't see anyone that's not a senior.

"Once a week, a shuttle takes our residents to a movie and shopping," the lady says.

"That would be too much fun for me," I say sarcastically. I get a sick feeling inside. Here I'd be going in reverse instead of moving forward.

"You'll feel at home here," Joe says.

Only if I keep my eyes shut.

Joe tells her he'll be in touch.

Looks like Joe's trying to scare me, and he's good at

that. But he'd never dump me here, would he? Then I think about how my grandparents never expected my dad to dump me and never return.

In the car, Joe starts lecturing me again. "You have bad judgment," he says. "You should not have taken the car last night."

"I won't do it anymore," I say.

All my life I've been trained to live by the rules or else I won't survive. Check your body. Take your temperature. Don't bang your head. Don't bite. Don't pick scabs. Don't scratch your eyes. The thing is, I'm grateful I was reminded. Now I'm feeling like "Don't breathe" has been added to the list, and I'm ungrateful.

"I don't suppose you can come up with a good reason why you were driving without a license and why the wreck wasn't your fault."

"I don't suppose you've checked with the mechanic," I say. "Maybe it wasn't totally my fault."

"I did. The brakes are worn out." Joe clears his throat. "I should have discussed a few things with you earlier, but to be honest, I don't know what to say to you."

"You're doing fine," I say.

"You go through life like a bull in a china shop," Joe says.

"That's a myth. A bull can actually be very coordinated, but I get what you mean. I know what's dangerous."

The world's a scary place for me, but I want a life even if it's short. If I mess up, I don't have anything to lose. The worst that can happen is I'll die from disease complications. Lately I have realized there's more to life than staying inside, afraid to go out.

Considering I've been in the hospital dozens of times, I'm doing all right. I've heard doctors say I wouldn't survive. My lips, hands, and legs are scarred, and I've had a hole in my throat, tubes in every opening in my body. Wouldn't the doctors who said I'd be retarded and die young be surprised to see me now?

"You could say you'll try to find my parents," I say. "Give me a chance to meet them."

"And you think they'd want you with them?"

"No."

"Even if I found them, I would not trust them with your future. You had two broken legs when your father left you here," Joe says. "Dog bites on your arms, bruises, and I don't even remember what else. You thought you were like Superman with super-genes."

I remember using crutches and going fast. "I'm not a little kid anymore," I say.

"You had been in the hospital ten times."

Nobody wanted me. Not my mother or father or my make-believe friend.

"I have hired a detective to find your father and let him know his mother's condition. I'm warning you, though. Only one of three things can possibly happen. We find him, and he wants to be left alone. We don't find him because he doesn't want to be found. Or he's dead. Somebody's going to get hurt, no matter what."

"He'll come if he's alive and knows Nana is sick," I say.

"We tried to find him when your grandfather died," Joe says. "And many times before."

CHAPTER 11

The morning sun hangs over the top of the mountains in a clear sky. The light makes the backyard look like a garden in a magazine.

Luna and I go down the steps of the deck to the swimming pool. When Nana was well, she'd sit on the deck and watch me. Sometimes she'd swim too. She swims better than she walks. A long time ago she competed in the Olympics.

Luna sits cross-legged on the side of the pool. She's wearing jeans and a heavy sweater, and I'm wearing a swimsuit.

I sit next to her and kick the water.

"Where'd you go yesterday?" she asks.

"Joe took me to an assisted living community. He's trying to force me to live there."

She shakes her head. "I think he was trying to scare you," she says. According to her, the management of a retirement community doesn't usually allow someone my age to live there. The residents who don't want to be around kids would move.

"Joe's serious. He doesn't kid around. He's perfectly content not to have to worry about me."

"Then don't annoy him," Luna says, shutting her eyes and looking upward. "The sun feels good."

"Like what?" I ask.

"Warm," she says. "Like when somebody says, 'I think I love you.'"

A girl's never told me that. Nana frequently says, "I love you," and it feels good unless she adds the "cutie patootie" part and somebody's listening.

"You should go swimming," I say.

"The water's too cold for me. You have no idea what it's like to freeze."

"It's bad."

"How bad?"

"You can become dehydrated, numb, and get frostbite, and the entire body is affected," I say. "When I was eight, I sneaked outside to play in the snow. I tried to make a snowman, but he turned out to be creepy. My grandmother caught me before I could give him arms or legs or a smiling face. She wrapped a blanket around me." I shrug.

"I was dressed in pajamas and wasn't wearing shoes. Back then, I didn't understand that I could've gotten frostbite and end up losing fingers or toes. I'd like to know the feel of snow on my skin or in my mouth, but she scared me when she said I could lose a limb, so I never did that again."

"Cold is like somebody you care about telling you they don't care any longer," Luna says.

I nod. I like how she simplifies things. Sometimes I wish I could switch the inside and outside of me, but then I'd have guts hanging all over the place.

There are things I can try to fix, but I can't fix me. Not feeling pain or temperature are my weaknesses. It's the way I am. It's like kryptonite and Superman.

I swim for about fifteen minutes, and then I go underwater to practice holding my breath. It will make my lungs stronger, and it's fun to do something that most people can't do.

The next thing I know, Luna's in the water grabbing me under the arms. She pulls me to the shallow part and holds on to me.

I don't see the point in letting her go. I look into her green eyes. I smile at her. At the same time she's panting and shivering and asking me if I'm okay. "You were under for four minutes," she says.

It didn't seem like four minutes. For the moment it's just the two of us looking at each other, and I'm not about to make her mad or embarrass her by saying I wasn't drowning. "I'm okay now. Thank you," I say. I think I'm feeling warm. "You better change clothes before you freeze to death."

We climb out of the pool. She takes a couple of steps toward me. "I work for you," she says and pushes me into the pool.

✛ ✛ ✛

Luna leaves early, and I think it's because she's mad at me. I don't understand her, and she doesn't understand me. I wish she did. I wish I hadn't crossed an invisible line.

I'm in my room when I hear Nana arguing with the sitter.

"I'm going, and nobody's going to stop me," Nana says.

That sounds like something she'd normally say.

"Calm down," the sitter says.

I go to Nana's door. It's open. She has her shoes on, heading toward me, pushing the walker. The sitter's holding on to her arm.

"She only wants to walk around," I say. And that's good. That will help her get stronger.

"Call Spencer," Nana says.

"Why?"

"It's your grandfather's birthday. We're going to the cemetery, and you're getting your driver's license."

"It's okay," I tell the sitter. "She always goes to the cemetery this time of year."

I'm a little worried about the driver's license part.

"This is an emergency," Nana says to the sitter. "David wants a driver's license, and I'm going to be the one to take him. It's a life event."

That makes sense to me. I probably have forty hours of practice by my way of counting.

But I should ask Spencer in person so that he doesn't feel like he has to do us a favor. We haven't talked to each other in a while, and he seems to be avoiding me. He's been busy with Cassandra and getting ready to graduate. He doesn't have time to hang out.

"I'll be right back," I say.

I cross the road in front of my house and then head down a path to his house. His house is kinda small, so we've never hung out there. I can hear kids yelling as they play in his backyard. Last year, Spencer's dad lost his job, and now his parents run a day care.

On his porch is a box. I pick it up and knock. His mom answers, smiles, and invites me inside. She takes the box and says she's glad the graduation invitations have finally arrived. She wants me to come to Spencer's graduation, but it's going to be on the football field, and it'll be hot. The ceremony will take a couple of hours. "Maybe you can come for part of it?"

"I'll try," I say. I could've been graduating with Spencer. If I could go back in time, I'd go to school and not have tutors.

Spencer comes into the room.

"Nana would like for you to drive us to the cemetery and to get my license," I say. "If you're not too busy."

"No problem," Spencer says. "I have to find my wallet."

We go to his room, and he searches through the clothes on his floor. I take a look at a college brochure on his desk. I imagine myself going to college, but only for a couple of seconds. I need a driver's license to get anywhere.

On the way out, Spencer's mom tells me that if I need help during the day, I'm welcome at their day care. It's awkward. It's embarrassing. Why does everybody think I'm helpless?

The sitter's car isn't in the driveway, and Nana's not in her room.

We hurry through the house, calling her. We find her alone in the study.

"Where's the sitter?" I ask.

"She scratched me, and I fired her."

Nana has a small scratch on her forearm, probably from when the sitter was trying to keep her in her room. She tells me to open the fireproof safe. She can't remember the combination.

Spencer's shaking his head in an I-can't-believe-this kind of way.

I've come this far. I'm getting my license today.

I thumb through the important papers: my passport and social security card, a copy of her will, an advance directive with my name on it, stocks, and my birth certificate. I take it and start trembling. It feels like the beginning of the end. I feel like a monster for being more afraid of what's going to happen to me.

✦ ✦ ✦

"I love this car," Spencer says about the BMW. Actually, it belonged to Grandpa.

"Then it's yours," Nana says.

I glance back at Nana. She's holding a sheet of paper with about ten things on it. She likes to make lists of things to do or else she forgets. I drum my fingers on the console. I wonder if she ever had a bucket list.

"I can't take it," Spencer says.

"I have already arranged for you to have it," she says.

"Thank you." Spencer smiles and looks over at me. "Relax. The test is easy."

"You don't have to act like we're friends just because Nana gave you a car we don't want," I say.

Spencer stares straight ahead. "We are friends, and I'm allowed to be annoyed with you. I get annoyed with my brothers and sisters all the time."

When we pass the elementary school, I turn my head and glance at it. It's changed over the years. There's a new playground now and about twice as many buildings. Nana let me restart school for a while so I'd be around other kids. I only made it to second grade. I always had trouble paying attention. One day my class went to the auditorium to hear an author speak. I sat next to the teacher's aide who was assigned to supervise me. She was wearing a fuzzy sweater. My arm brushed up against it. Fascinated, I touched the sweater with my hand, rubbing it over and over. My brain was thinking, *This is what a cute lamb feels like*, and I was seeing one in my head.

Finally, the aide went over to the teacher and whispered to her. She took me to the principal's office, and Nana was called. Nana later said I shouldn't do stuff like that. It's inappropriate. I didn't mean anything by it. I only liked the feel of a lamb against my skin. School was awful after that. The kids—and my friends—somehow found out what happened and called me "freak" and "pervert." I got into a lot of fights. I bled a lot.

Nana and Grandpa fought for me. They tried to explain why touch was so important for me. But the thing is, what's best for me didn't fit the school policies. The school wanted me in special ed. Grandpa decided to hire tutors. He said it was cheaper paying for the best teachers than risking my future.

At the DMV, I flunk my road exam. I bet I'm the only person in the world who failed the test. I was nervous. I only shake my head when I walk out of the DMV.

"Sorry," Spencer says.

I smile at him, and he places his arm across my shoulder.

I don't look his way again as we head slowly to the car with Nana pushing her walker next to me. What if I fail at everything else on my bucket list? Walking between the two of them, I'm feeling like I'm smothering in a box and can't get out. I shove Spencer's arm off my shoulders and walk ahead of them.

"It's not the end of the world," Spencer calls to me.

He's right. I'll be seeing the world from the balcony at Twin Falls.

On the way to the cemetery, I'm thinking nothing can turn me into a normal person: not a license or a car, or even a mom or a dad or a girlfriend or a million dollars.

✦ ✦ ✦

Spencer turns into the gravel parking lot between the two-hundred-year-old church—no longer used except for a few community events—and the small cemetery, the final resting place for Grandpa's family, which includes a few soldiers, farmers, a teacher, a doctor, and four children. Before Grandpa died, we'd come here for picnics.

Oak trees shade the cemetery. There aren't any other cars or people around. It's so quiet I can hear the grass growing.

Spencer stays in the car texting Cass. They text each other all the time. I don't know how Spencer gets anything done.

"Need help?" I ask Nana as she gets out of the car. She shakes her head and says she doesn't need help to go to the bathroom. I watch her as she pushes her walker to the church door.

"I'll keep an eye on her," Spencer says.

I walk over to Grandpa's grave and say hello to him. His headstone reads *Return to sender.* That was his idea.

"What's new? How are things on the farm?" I ask.

I give him time to send me some sort of sign. I don't see anything different except a squirrel in the oak tree.

"I flunked my driving test today," I say. "I couldn't parallel park. I kept backing over the orange cone, and the examiner laughed at me. If you get bored, feel free to haunt him. Nana is okay, and she's planning to head to the farm soon. I'm going to be fine." I see her coming my way. Spencer's helping her walk with the walker.

Next I walk over to Noel Peeples' grave. She never has flowers or visitors.

Then I go see Seth and say hello. Somebody's left him a teddy bear.

Leaning against a tree trunk, I watch Nana bend over Grandpa's grave, her long, white hair falling in front of her face. She talks for longer than usual. I watch a squirrel watching me. I'm glad it isn't a zombie. You can imagine anything in a cemetery, especially when you want to forget failing.

Nana's grave site is next to Grandpa's. My grave site is next to hers. I don't like to look at mine.

✦✦✦

Grandpa had a heart problem, and whenever he had chest pain, he'd take a nitroglycerin pill under his tongue. Afterward he'd get a headache from the medicine. I was amazed that one tiny white pill could cause so much pain.

One afternoon I was sitting on his bed. I tried one of

the pills to make myself get a headache. It didn't work, so I tried another one. It didn't do anything.

I stood to put the pills away, and that's all I remember. The next thing I knew, paramedics were putting me onto a stretcher and elevating my legs. I was practically standing on my head.

That ambulance ride was great.

I didn't have to stay in the hospital. My blood pressure had dropped dangerously low from the nitroglycerin, and I fainted. No big deal, but Grandpa started keeping his bottle of nitroglycerin inside his shirt pocket where he could get to it quickly, and it was safe from me.

One day Grandpa said, "You're changing. You're becoming a man."

To me that meant I was closer to dying, and I was only ten years old. The next morning when I got up, I said hello to myself in the mirror and listened to my voice. I didn't sound like a man, and I smiled at myself.

Not long after, Grandpa went to the hospital and never came back except in my thoughts and sometimes in my dreams. He has his arms folded across his chest and he's saying to me, "Where's my nitroglycerin?"

✚ ✚ ✚

It's evening, and I get my laptop. I go into Nana's room and sit in the recliner.

Nana reaches for her bottle of pain pills.

"You took a pill after dinner," I say. I pick up the bottle and read the label. "You are supposed to take one every four hours."

"I'm hurting," she says. She looks so small when she

leans forward in her bed and slumps her shoulders. "I'm worn out."

I don't know what to do. "I think a pain pill takes a while to work." I don't know. I have never taken a pain pill in my whole life. I take off the cap and then twist it back on so it's child-proof. "I'll tell you when it's time." I set the bottle on the table.

"I'm losing my mind," she says. "If something happens to me...don't let the paramedics...doctors do anything," she says, out of breath. "Understand?"

I look away. "I know." I can't take this. I email Joe.

Need a new sitter immediately. Maybe a nurse.

Joe calls and I tell him what happened with the sitter. Then I tell him we went to the DMV and cemetery.

"You've been sending me the same email every evening," he says.

"It has the important parts," I say. "Me flunking a driver's test isn't important to anybody but me."

"You're wrong, David," he says.

CHAPTER 12

It's Sunday afternoon, and I didn't go swimming because it's raining. I'm in the kitchen with Luna. She's wearing casual pants and a shirt because she went to church.

Nana and I don't go to church. You never know what Nana might say or do.

Last time we went, Nana said loudly that the sermon was making her sleepy, and her butt was numb. The people in front of us turned, looked at her, and shushed her. Some kids laughed. I felt sad and remembered how I was laughed at when I was a little boy dressed in goggles and a helmet.

I hear a crash. Luna and I jump up from the table and rush upstairs to Nana's room. She's pulling out a dresser drawer. It hits the floor with a bang. Three other dresser drawers are turned upside down, and the contents are piled up like garbage. The sitter's in the chair by the bed. A family album is lying open on the floor to the pictures of my dad's high-school graduation. He gave a speech that night, and Nana probably cried with happiness.

"What's going on?" I ask.

"I'm cleaning out the drawers."

"You don't have to do that," I say.

"She wants to do it by herself," the sitter says. "She doesn't want help."

I wouldn't want anybody going through my stuff either.

Now Nana's crawling around on the floor. This could get embarrassing.

"What are you doing?" I ask Nana.

"I lost my glasses."

I look around, see them on the floor, and give them to her. Luna and I help her up and back to her bed.

She puts on the glasses. "These are not my glasses."

I take the glasses, walk around the room, and then give them back to her. Nana's having one of her bad days. She has a lot of them. They're going to get worse.

Nana blinks. "I told you these are not my glasses," she says in a mean voice.

I want to scream. I say, "Yes, they are," and she says, "No, they aren't," and then I say, "I'll look for them." Things have been getting lost after being put somewhere and then forgotten. Car keys, house keys, a car title, a sticker for a new car tag, Nana's wallet, her mind.

Nana points at Luna. "That woman is a thief and a whore. All she wants is your money."

Luna heads out of the room.

There's no point in arguing with Nana. She'll only get sweaty and short of breath, and she doesn't know what she's saying. I pick up a garbage bag of stuff and get out of there. I'm pretty sure her glasses are in the bag.

In the kitchen, I open the bag of garbage and dump everything onto the floor. Luna and I sort through it. It's weird. It's like Luna knew exactly what I intended to do with the bag.

"Nana didn't mean what she said," I say.

"I know. I was agitating her. That's why I left."

The bag contains mostly underwear and pajamas.

Then I pull out a graduation cap and a gown. Both are dark blue. "Look," I say to Luna. "I think this was my dad's." I'm not throwing away his cap and gown. It's bad luck.

"Uh-huh," she says and holds up the glasses.

I take the rest of the throwaway clothes to the garage. I'm thinking that when people start getting rid of stuff, they're getting ready to die.

I walk back into the kitchen. "You need to get out of here for a while," Luna says. "You're losing it. Want to go for ice cream?"

I know I'm losing my mind.

"It gets to me too," Luna says.

"She's better when her medicine kicks in," I say. "But it doesn't last."

Luna's driving her old Toyota, even though the Lexis has been repaired. The rain's stopped, and I'm keeping time to a song on the radio.

She drives around the square in Waterly.

"Know a good place?"

"No," I say.

"Look," Luna says. "The rainbow ends at Burger Barn. We have to go there. It's spectacular, right?"

"Yes." If I'm looking for rainbows, I could find one in my yard after it rains.

She gets a banana split, so I do the same. I've only had regular ice cream in flavors and not with bananas or chocolate or nuts.

While we're eating, I'm thinking this would be a good time for a conversation, but I don't know what to say.

I love your eyes and your hair and the way you smell? I know this from some TV movies I've seen.

Luna takes a bite of her banana split and then wipes her chin. "I understand why Joe wants you somewhere else," she says. "It's not about you being helpless. It's about you getting a break from your grandmother."

"It's about him getting me out of the way," I say.

"I have another job," Luna says.

"You're quitting?"

She nods. "It's full time."

"Where?"

"The information desk at the Holly Building."

That's where Dr. Goodman has his office and the tallest structure in town. At night when I've gone there, the lights from the building shine over the entire town.

"It's a great job with benefits." Luna takes a bite of ice cream. "You'll be fine, and I'm still going to come over. It's just that I need more money, and I don't like it when people assume I'm using you."

"I know you're not," I say, mixing up the chocolate with the ice cream. "You're not happy being my personal assistant?"

"Not anymore, but I'm going to miss you."

A while later we get back into the car, and she looks around, maybe for the rainbow. I'm not seeing one.

CHAPTER 13

The housekeeper cooks and cleans, the sitter sits, and I bring Nana's meals and snacks to her. I don't tell anybody that Luna's quit, and nobody notices. Nana's been dwindling. She's lost weight. She barely eats. Sometimes in the middle of the night, I'll go to her room to watch and make sure she's breathing.

I've been working on proving I can be independent, not getting into trouble and staying alive, which is pretty easy when you don't do anything.

Saturday morning I'm awakened by the sitter. She's sorry to bother me, but my grandmother has been calling me for hours, and she's worked herself into a sweat.

I step into the dark room. It smells like medicine. "I want you to get me a bottle of wine, a strawberry cheesecake, and cigarettes."

"You don't smoke," I remind her. None of that stuff will help her.

"Please, James." She grimaces.

I think she hurts. I think she feels all the pain I missed out on. I hate what's coming. I ask the sitter to go get cigarettes and a strawberry cheesecake. We already have wine, left over from New Year's Eve.

"I can't do that," the sitter says.

"She's dying," I say. I go to the study, find the checkbook, and write out a check. On the way back to Nana's room I grab a bottle of wine and two Waterford crystal glasses.

I give the check to the aide. "It's yours if you get the cigarettes and the strawberry cheesecake," I say.

"I'm on my way," the aide says.

✦ ✦ ✦

Joe's at the front door, and I'm feeling pretty good, but it's probably from the wine I drank with Nana. The only time she's ever let me have wine is New Year's Eve when the ball drops.

He comes into the living room like a strong wind blowing through a forest of pine trees, bending and breaking limbs and trunks. I let out a heavy sigh and recover from the almost happy feeling right away. He's carrying a legal-looking folder. He probably has papers for Nana to sign. Sometimes I wonder if she knows what she's signing. I know she signed something to give him power of attorney for both of us. She said everyone needs somebody who can legally make decisions when they can't.

"Have you been smoking?" he asks.

I shake my head and take two steps back.

Joe heads to Nana's room, but I try to stop him before he smells all the smoke in her room. I tell him she's sleeping, and he shouldn't bother her. He looks at me and then talks on his cell phone. He cancels all his appointments for today.

I might be in trouble for giving Nana wine and cigarettes.

I play "The Entertainer" on the piano to get myself revved up before Joe kills me.

Then Joe returns and stands next to the piano, but I keep playing. I'm not ready to die. But when the song ends, I stop and stare at the keys.

"You gave Nana alcohol and cigarettes. Really, David, why can't you use common sense?"

"I'm going to give her anything she wants."

He sits on the sofa and starts reading the newspaper. "A nurse is coming to evaluate Nana for services. Why don't you go to your room and think of ten reasons you should not have given Nana alcohol and cigarettes and email them to me?"

"If I knew ten reasons, I wouldn't have done it," I say. "I figure last wishes trump everything."

Joe's either grinning or smirking. It's hard to tell.

"May I be excused?" I say, and he nods.

In my room, I reset the game I was playing and start from my last save point. This time I'm going to build up my characters and make them stronger before they go anywhere. For the next three hours, they fight monsters right outside of the town and gain awesome strength and mental abilities.

At seven p.m., I go to Nana's room to watch TV with her. She likes game shows like *Wheel of Fortune* and *Jeopardy*. She says watching them keeps her mind sharp.

"James?"

"I'm David," I say.

She twirls a ring on her finger. "Where's James?"

"I don't know." Probably he's somewhere having more fun than I am. In my head, I picture him at the front door with my mother. They come inside and tell me everything's going to be okay. That's as far as I can imagine. It sucks when you can't imagine good stuff in your life because you know it won't ever happen.

I see her wallet open and her credit cards by the phone on the bedside table.

"You haven't been giving out your credit card numbers over the phone, have you?"

"I don't think so," she says, sounding like a kid.

I take her credit cards and stick them into my wallet. I won't use them. I don't want her giving out credit card numbers to strangers over the phone.

I think one of the saddest things in the world is losing your mind. I don't want that to happen to me. I'd rather be dead. My memories suck, but they belong to me.

When we watch *Jeopardy*, I know most of the answers in the human body category. After it's over, I ask if there's anything she wants to do. It doesn't matter what, and it can be now or tomorrow or the next day.

"Read?" she says.

So I read *Pride and Prejudice* to her. It's her favorite book. It's not my favorite book, but I'm almost at the end, and reading's easy compared to the other stuff.

CHAPTER 14

I'm in the living room, looking online for apartments, and Nana's upstairs screaming. The doorbell rings, and when I answer, I see Luna smiling. I'm so relieved I would cry if it were possible. She hugs me and asks if I mind if she hangs out and does homework.

"Sure," I say. "You don't know how happy I am to see you."

She laughs. "Yes, I do." She sits on the sofa, and I tell her what's been going on. Then she glances at my laptop. "Are you moving?"

"One of these days, I'm going to live somewhere that has a mild temperature all year long. I want to be near theaters, restaurants, stores, and parks."

Then I can go outside without always checking the thermostat.

"You should," she says, and that makes my heart sink. I wouldn't ever see Luna if I moved to another city.

"Whatever you do, don't get a roommate," she says.

"You'll end up hating them."

"You don't like your roommate?"

"She's a slob, and she's always late paying rent. Plus, she has a different guy over every few nights, and sometimes he doesn't go home."

"Do you think you'd end up hating me if we were together all the time?"

"Honestly, I don't know. I like being with you, but it's hard when your grandmother is so sick."

"You should be the one to move," I say.

"I am as soon as the lease is up."

Luna pulls out paper and pen. "I have to get this done by tomorrow," she says.

"Where do you go to college?"

"I'm taking online courses right now."

I could do that. I imagine sipping coffee outside a café. My college textbooks are on the table, and there's a dog at my feet. Luna's across from me and asks, "Are you ready for the anatomy exam?" I'll nod and smile. I'd do great in anatomy. I think I already know the bones in the body. I've broken some of them.

I shift in the chair. "How's your new job?"

"What?" she says. "I'm sorry, but I have to concentrate."

✚ ✚ ✚

The phone rings. The nurse scheduled from seven p.m. to seven a.m. injured her back last night while helping Nana, and she would've called sooner, but she thought she'd feel better by now. I believe her because I've seen how Nana hangs on to a person and how she doesn't cooperate. I tell the nurse not to worry and to rest. I go into Nana's room and ask the day nurse how she's doing. We walk into the hallway, and she tells me Nana's blood pressure is lower, her heart rate is fast, and her breathing is shallow.

Then I think about how quiet it's been in Nana's room. She hasn't screamed.

I ask the nurse if she can work all night. She shakes her head and says she'd call the agency for me, but the other nurse has probably let them know.

"I took the phone away from her," the nurse says. "I stepped out for a moment earlier today, and when I returned, she ordered me to find her credit card so she could donate to some cause. I took the phone and told them not to call here anymore." She takes a deep breath. "Your grandmother got snippy with me. She'll probably complain."

"Don't worry about it," I say. "She never used to be this way."

After the nurse leaves, I check on Nana. She's sleeping soundly. I hope she doesn't wake right away. At least she won't need to get up to go to the bathroom. She has a tube in. I turn on the TV and sit in the recliner.

I've watched the sitters and nurses so I have an idea of what to do.

Watch TV. Talk on the phone. Eat. Sleep. I have all those categories covered.

I'm half asleep when I hear Nana mumbling "James." Turning on my side, I ignore her. Nana keeps talking. I turn toward her. She's lying on her side with her hands under her face. "I knew you would come," she mumbles. Her eyes are watering.

I get up and stand next to the bedside. "I was asleep."

"Like Rip Van Winkle." Her speech is slurred.

I don't know what she means. Rip Van Winkle is a make-believe character. He left his home, got drugged, and fell asleep under a tree. When he awoke, everything had changed because years had passed.

Trembling, she stretches out her arms. "Aren't you going to hug your mother?"

I get it now. Nana thinks I'm my dad. It's because she's confused and the room's dark. I hug her. She smells like baby powder.

This is my chance to make her happy. "I'm sorry it took me so long to get here. I'm sorry for what I missed all these years." That's what I'd want my dad to tell me.

She wrinkles her nose. "Where's David?"

"He's around." I'll keep pretending I'm her son and say what he should be saying. "Thank you for taking care of David, and thank you for always loving me even when you should have hated me. Thank you for giving up your life for David and me. I love you."

"Love you too. Are you taking him with you?"

"Do you want me to?"

She moans. "If he wants to go. I need water. They don't give me water here."

I grab the plastic pitcher on the bedside table. "Nana, you have plenty of water." I start to pour some.

"I need clean water. They're trying to poison me."

"I'll be right back," I say.

"Don't forget the ice," she says with a groan. "One cube of ice."

In the kitchen, I fill the pitcher with water and add one cube of ice. I go back to her room and pour her some water. She's clenching a bottle of pills in her hand. The top's off. I open her hand and take the bottle. It's empty. I read the label. It's the Percocet she takes for her arthritis, leg pain, and headaches. I roll the bottle around in my hand. "How many pills did you take?"

"One," she cries. "I'm hurting."

I groan. *Please don't be lying to me. Please.* Am I supposed to call somebody and ask? What would they do? Pump her stomach? That would make her suffer even more. She has an advance directive. Even if I called an ambulance and sent her to the hospital, nothing is supposed to be done to prolong her life. She made sure I knew what she wanted. I promised.

"I would like to sit in the recliner," she says.

She must be all right. She wants to get up. I pull the recliner close to the bed and help her into it as she's screaming. I cover her with a blanket and sit on the foot of her bed. I watch tears roll out of her eyes as she groans and grimaces.

"What hurts?" I ask.

"Everything. I have to go to bed," she says.

So I help her back into bed, but she only moans this time.

The ceramic clock on the shelf ticks away the time. I made it and gave it to her one Christmas. I think about a message I'd written on the back. *To Nana. Love, David.*

I sing "Kumbaya."

Finally, I see Nana's eyes close, and she's breathing slow and easy. After a few minutes I think she's asleep. There are eleven hours until the sun comes up. Things will look better then.

"David?" she says.

"I'm here." I swallow. It was easy for me to speak for my dad. It's hard for me to speak for myself. "I don't want you to worry about what's going to happen to me. You taught me well." I'm flunking breathing. It's too hard. I take in a ragged breath and let it out. "I've made mistakes, and I've learned from them, but you always loved me anyway. I'm going to be fine. I love you, and I always will."

Nana touches my face. "You have tears."

I've never been able to make tears before, and it's a miracle. I lick the side of my face, and for the first time ever, I taste tears. They're salt water like the ocean. I picture the time Nana, Grandpa, and I went to the beach. Early one morning before the sun was up, we walked in the sand, and I felt it between my toes. I tasted seawater and watched waves tumbling to shore. We sat on the beach and watched the sun rise. The sky was red and gold. Grandpa and Nana took me out into the water. We jumped waves, and then they pulled me out farther and let go of me.

Grandpa said, "Swim, David. Swim as hard as you can." And I did. I made it to where I could stand, and the waves pushed me forward, and then the undercurrent pulled me back, but not too much. I made it to shore.

Now I pull up my shirt and wipe my face. Nana looks comfortable and content. She's smiling at me, and the sparkle from the bedside light shines in her eyes. I don't remember ever seeing her eyes this clear. It's like she's telling me something without words. It's like another way of saying, "I love you."

I fall asleep with her holding my hand tightly. When I awaken, she's let go of me, her hand curled next to mine. I nudge her shoulder. "Nana? Nana?" She isn't breathing. For a couple of minutes, I rest my head on her chest. I say good-bye.

✜ ✜ ✜

I call Joe. Trembling, I finally get the words out. "Nana's bought the farm."

He says he will take care of everything.

Then I go outside, wait under a dogwood tree at the side of the house, and let the wind dry my tears. The flowers are blooming, and lilies are poking through the ground.

Luna's calling my name. I look up and she's hurrying toward me. For a second I think I'm dreaming, but then she's next to me, hugging me, saying Joe called. "I came as fast as I could. I'm sorry."

I feel her wet face against mine, and I touch her hair. It's wet too.

I move a strand out of her face. "You should have waited until your hair was dry."

"No, I couldn't. She would have wanted someone with you."

"I was with her when she died," I say. "I let her take pain medicine. I let her die."

"You did the right thing. You didn't want her to be in pain."

"I don't know anything about pain," I say.

Luna strokes my face. "You know more than you think you do. Pain is when somebody you love dies."

PART TWO

CHAPTER 15

Today I'm eighteen, and I'm watching Luna pull into the driveway, which is a surprise. I didn't know she was coming over, and it's early evening. Joe's not here, and Veronica left early.

The last few weeks I've planted my body in front of the piano and hit the keys, or I've driven the car around and around the driveway. I haven't played video games. I'm not in the mood to see my make-believe friends lost in a cave or mountain or die over and over again, even if I can revive them.

My head's been stuck in a black cloud.

Joe has practically moved in. The study is his office. "Stay out of the study," he said to Veronica and me. "I have everything arranged so I can find what I need."

I'm super-kid. I'm super-polite. I'm not going to annoy anybody.

I meet Luna at the front door, and she wraps her arms around me. It feels good to be squashed against her, and

I wonder if she can tell how fast my heart's beating. "I'm sorry I haven't been around," she says into my ear. Then she steps back. "I have two jobs now, and I'm working all of the time."

"I understand," I say, smiling. I haven't seen Luna since we went to the lake a few days after the funeral. We rented paddle boats, but I could only be outside for a half hour. Then we came back to my house, and Spencer arrived. We played our guitars for a while.

"Want to go to dinner?" she asks.

I get it now. Joe's probably giving me a party somewhere.

And I'm hoping my father or mother will be there. The last time I asked him about them, he said, "I'm working on something."

He's always said no before and nothing else.

"Sure," I say to Luna.

✛ ✛ ✛

She pulls in front of an Italian restaurant, and we go inside. She speaks to the hostess who leads us to another room where people shout, "Happy Birthday, David!"

Happy Birthday, David is written on a streamer on the back wall.

I don't really know any of these people.

Joe walks over to me, and I smile. "This is great," I say, not sounding like I mean it. We head toward a long table. On the way, Joe says, "Nice to see you," to everybody we pass. I've never heard him talking so friendly before.

I glance around the crowd, and I don't see anybody who could be my father or who might be my mother. I mean, if they were here, they would've said hello by now. Something inside of my mis-wired brain had hoped Joe would've found them. That would be the ultimate surprise for me.

But this is enough for now. "This is fabulous," I say to Joe. I have a little more pep in my voice.

Luna and I sit at a round table with names on cards. Pretty soon Spencer, Cass, Cameron, and Marcello take their places at my table.

They're the only people my age at the party. The other people are Nana's age.

I lean over and whisper to Luna. "Do you know these people?" I ask.

We make eye contact. "Probably people who came to the funeral," Luna says. "Your grandmother's friends."

"It's cool," I say. In a way. I'm with Luna.

Then I see Veronica and her husband, and Spencer's parents. I wave to them.

A waiter brings plates of spaghetti.

"You were in the army, right?" I ask Cameron, my down-the-road neighbor who sits on his porch in a wheelchair most of the time. I cut my spaghetti with my knife. Luna keeps glancing at my hands, probably to make sure I still have my fingers.

"Yes." Cameron says he'd been stationed in Afghanistan and came home after he was wounded in an explosion.

I take a sip of water and swallow.

"It must be really difficult for you," Cassandra says to Cameron.

"It's hard for all of us," he says.

Cass rolls her eyes.

The time's coming when I'll have to be independent or

else. If Cameron can do it, I can do it.

Then Spencer moves over next to me. His eyes are red around the rims and bloodshot. I wonder what's happened.

"So did you break up with Cass?"

"How'd you know?" he asks.

I shrug. "You're not sitting next to her. You haven't spoken to her. She's flirting with Cameron."

"She said she didn't want to have a long-distance relationship." He says she was his soul mate, and he'd thought about transferring to her college to be with her.

I don't know how they ended up together. They've spent a lot of time together in the band and fell in love, just like in a romance novel with a bad ending. I don't know anything about girls, but I think there's more to it than not wanting a long-distance relationship.

"I can't believe you'd give up Vanderbilt." I shake my head. "You chose it because of the music program and the scholarship." I clear my throat. "It's a great scholarship."

"I know," he says. "I shouldn't be complaining. You have bigger stuff going on."

"Different," I say. I figure losing somebody is important, no matter what the cause.

"Did you get my graduation invitation?"

"Yes."

"I want you to come," he says. "It wouldn't be the same without you."

"I'll be there," I say. I don't know how I'll get to graduation, but I know what I'll wear.

After dinner, Geo plays "Happy Birthday" and everybody sings.

A waiter refills my water glass, and then I hear static. I watch Spencer step onto the stage. "Thank you for coming to David's celebration," he says. "I'd like to propose a toast. Would everyone please stand."

I don't stand. I can't move.

"David, happy birthday. May you have a hundred more."

Everybody repeats, "May you have a hundred more."

Then people raise their glasses and toast me. I hear sniffing, and I look over at Luna. She's trying not to cry.

✚ ✚ ✚

"Hey, Joe," I say the next morning from the doorway of the study.

"Hey, David. You can come in."

Piles of papers and folders litter the desk.

Nana told me once that Joe isn't as heartless as he acts. He was engaged years ago, but his fiancée died in a car accident. Joe doesn't have any other family but us. Now he only has me, and I bet he's depressed about that.

"Thanks for the party," I say, standing in front of the desk.

"You're welcome. I wasn't sure if you had a good time or not."

"It was great." I glance down at the desk and its scattered papers. "But I always hope my mom or dad will appear out of nowhere. Has the detective said anything?"

"No."

"He is still looking, right?"

"For now," Joe says.

I see a glossy Twin Falls brochure and pick it up. "I didn't think I would have to move to Twin Falls," I say, looking at a photo of the shuffleboard court.

He takes the brochure and sticks it on top of a stack of papers. "We'll see how you do living alone."

"I'd like to take the driver's test again," I say. "Would you take me?"

"Again?" Joe says.

"I failed the first time."

Two hours later, I walk out of the DMV. I wave to Joe, my driver's license in my hand, and I'm thinking about how free I feel. I can go anywhere.

CHAPTER 16

Spencer jumps into the pool. I have to get an early start these days because in a couple of hours, it'll be harder to maintain my body temperature even in water. I take a deep breath. Hold it. I keep expecting to see Nana on the deck watching me. When I'm in my room, I expect her to open my door and ask if I did the body check.

Other times I'll hear a car outside, and I'll look out the window, hoping Luna's stopped by. I don't call her.

The only time I'm actually unsupervised is in the evenings and when I'm sleeping. Sometimes during the night I awaken with feelings of dread, and I can't breathe.

Veronica's keeping an eye on me when nobody's around. She's almost as old as Nana. I remember that at the funeral she didn't walk to the front of the church to see Nana. She didn't place a rose on the casket at the cemetery. I bet she was thinking the same as me. *That will be me one day.*

"Coming tonight?" Spencer asks, drying off with a towel.

"I will."

"As you come onto the field, turn right and go to those bleachers," he says. "Hardly anybody sits there. The other side gets way too crowded." Then he says he has to go to graduation practice. I did not know anybody would need to practice for something they've waited twelve years for.

✚ ✚ ✚

"I'm going to Spencer's graduation," I tell Veronica.

She stops dusting the china cabinet. "You should've invited Luna to go with you."

I would've if she had answered my emails. "I'll be fine."

"She's a nice girl. You need a girlfriend."

"She's all right," I say and look away.

"She likes you."

She's stayed away.

It's eighty degrees when I get out of the car at the high school, but I have come prepared with a wet bandana around my neck and a cooling vest hidden under my clothes. I don't know if this actually will work to keep my body temperature down. My watch will tell me if my body temperature starts rising.

The parking lot is packed with cars and people headed to the graduation ceremony. I slip my dad's graduation gown over my head, put on the cap, and grab my cane. I head to the bleachers on the opposite side of the field where hardly anybody's sitting.

I know this seems crazy. I know. I don't need anybody telling me that, and I'm afraid I'll see somebody who knows me. I won't run and hide. I'm not going to be ashamed. I swallow. I've finished high school, only I never had a ceremony.

Until now.

The band's playing, and the graduates come onto the field dancing. Their gowns are blue, just like mine. Getting an adrenaline rush, I stand and kind of dance along. Then the kids line up on the field and "Pomp and Circumstance" plays. They walk around the field, and I see Spencer. My heart's running away. I think I almost know how he feels, but I want the real thing. I want to be walking on the field in a cap and gown, hearing the song, holding my head high.

I wave to Spencer, and then I see him running toward me like he knows how I'm feeling. He grabs my arm, and we hurry onto the field. We get into the line and walk toward the chairs. "Congratulations," I say and then keep going back to my seat on the bleachers.

Then I'm listening to the speeches, but not really listening.

You know what I mean? My mind's drifting. I'm on the stage in front of the microphone.

"Congratulations to all of us," I'll say and that'll be enough. Sometimes a single sentence or word is enough.

I watch Marcello get his diploma, and I applaud for him. I even applaud for Cassandra. Spencer's name is announced, and he walks across the stage. He turns and waves in my direction. It's like he's saying, *This is for you too*. I cheer loudly for us.

CHAPTER 17

I hear footsteps. I turn and see Joe. Something's up. He hardly ever comes out to the pool, especially when he's wearing an expensive suit.

"Let's sit on the deck," Joe says.

We go up the stairs to the table and chairs. I pull out a chair and sit. "What's wrong?"

"Ruby wants Nana's clothes."

"Ruby who?" I ask, pretending I don't know. She became nonexistent for me after I heard she'd said I was dangerous and said other mean stuff about me. Sure, I hit her grandson and broke his nose, but he kicked me in the belly first.

"Your grandmother's cousin," Joe says.

"Was she at the funeral?" I ask.

"Yes, and she sent flowers."

"She didn't speak to me."

"Get over it, David."

I frown a little. Nana's room has stayed shut up the past few weeks. "I thought Nana wanted Veronica to have her clothes and take what she didn't want to the women's shelter."

"I didn't know that. I'll talk to Veronica. Ruby is going to be here in the next half hour. I'll be in the study."

"So you already told her yes."

"You stay in your room," he says.

"I will," I say. "Whatever happened to her grandson?"

"I don't know," Joe says. "Why?"

"Because nobody's ever said," I say.

✚ ✚ ✚

First, I get the baby monitor out of my closet. Nana would keep it turned on when I was a little kid. I place the receiver on my dresser and go to Nana's room with the other part. Her room's dark, kind of like my brain right now. I turn on the light, and the room looks the same as it did the night I stayed with her and she died when I was sleeping.

"What are you doing?" Veronica asks.

I spin around. "Ruby's coming over for Nana's clothes. I thought you were going to take them to the homeless shelter."

"Joe said I could get a few things," Veronica says. She opens Nana's walk-in closet. It's filled. Veronica pulls out a blue silky dress. "Jan wore this when she left on her honeymoon with your grandfather."

I turn around and place the baby-monitor transmitter on the dresser and plug it in. A tiny green light blinks.

"You're going to listen in?" Veronica says. She has Nana's nice coat in her arms, a couple of silk blouses, the blue dress, and a red robe.

"I am."

"Better get the jewelry and lock it in the safe," Veronica says and gets shopping bags out of Nana's closet. She gives me one. I place the jewelry box in the bag. While I'm here, I may as well get the clock I made when I was a little kid and wore a helmet, and Nana's box of special stuff from Grandpa's closet. All of his clothes were given away years ago.

Nana's box is mostly filled with pictures I've drawn and cards I made, and I'm shocked to find the stuffed elephant that hung from my IV pole when I was a little kid. It's like going back in time. In my mind I can see my imaginary friend giving me a tiny fire truck, and my dad tying the elephant to the IV pole.

I smile when I see the *I will not* papers I wrote.

I thumb through them. *I will not kick. I will not touch the stove when it's turned on. I will not slide down the banister. I will not do a pain test. I will not take out my stitches. I will not injure myself to get attention. I will not glue a cut together.*

The *will not* papers stopped when I was eleven. I was a slow learner.

When we're done raiding Nana's room, we take everything to my room, and I stick the stuff into my closet. Veronica carries her things downstairs.

I sit on my bed and read. After a few minutes Veronica returns and sits in the chair. "I'd like to wait in here," she says.

"You want to hear what she has to say too?" I ask.

Veronica frowns. "Something's going on," she says.

"Like what?"

"I heard him tell her that the house and everything else

were yours. I think she was expecting something," Veronica says in a serious voice. "I don't understand her."

"Did you ever meet my mom or dad?" I ask.

"I was here the day he brought you," Veronica says. "When it was time for him to go, you begged him not to leave you, but I bribed you with cookies." She kind of smiles. "You had a speech impediment back then."

"I talk okay now?"

"Yes. You talk fine."

"Was Joe here?"

"I don't remember."

I look down at my book. "Do you trust him?"

"Yes," she says. "Do you?"

"I don't know."

Then the doorbell rings. Veronica and I look at each other. "That's probably her," I say. Then I stand.

"Don't answer the door," Veronica says. "Joe can."

"Did he tell you to make sure I stay in my room?"

"He mentioned it. Ruby says cruel things without even thinking."

I shrug. "I'm going to the top of the stairs."

"Wait for me."

Veronica hovers behind me. From where I am, I cannot see the door, but I can hear. "You've done this before," she says.

I nod. I hear Joe say, "Hello, Ruby."

"Good afternoon, Joe. Beautiful day, isn't it?"

"Yes, it is," he says. He asks how she is, and she says fine. He asks how her family is. Her daughter and son-in-law live in Alaska, and her grandson is attending Harvard.

"Terrific," Joe says.

Ruby asks if anyone has heard from James and says that she's shocked he wouldn't even show up for his mother's or father's funeral. But James was always a weird kid. He never had any friends. He'd rather watch butterflies than socialize. She hopes Nana left him out of the will because he'd spend it all in a week.

"She believed he was dead," Joe says. "If you'll come with me, I'll take you to Jan's room."

Nana never told me she believed my dad was dead.

"I'm sure you're busy," Ruby says.

"Not too busy to help you," he says.

Veronica and I hurry to my room and wait for the baby monitor to come alive with talk. A minute later I hear Ruby say she's flabbergasted at the mess in the room.

She should've seen it before we stole the important stuff.

"You should fire that lazy housekeeper," Ruby says. "I bet the rats have already moved in. I bet she allows that boy do whatever he wants to do. Have you considered my suggestion?"

I bite my lip and look at Veronica. She appears to be holding her breath.

"He's not going to Twin Falls," Joe says. "And the house is not for sale."

"He's a child with a serious disability. I'm not comfortable with him living here. His own mother was scared to death of him."

"You've heard from Carlee?"

"It has been a few years," Ruby says. "It was back when David beat up the mailbox across the road."

I was around nine years old then, but I never beat up a mailbox. The woman that lived across the road tried to blame me.

Several minutes later I hear: "Nana had her prescription filled the day before she died, and the bottle is empty."

"You need to finish up and go," Joe says.

Veronica turns off the baby monitor. "I should not have let you do this," she says to me.

Then I see Joe and Ruby standing at my door. Veronica pretends she's dusting my desk. Ruby's frowning. She eyes me. "What happened to your grandmother's pain medicine?"

I shrug.

"He doesn't show a grain of remorse," Ruby says.

"You don't live here," Veronica says. "You don't know David."

"I know what he did to my grandson."

Joe snorts the way a dog does when sniffing something gross on the ground.

I turn away.

"This is pointless," Ruby says to Joe. "I don't know how in the world you deal with a kid like him. I'll let myself out."

After she's gone, I turn around. "She's trying to get me into trouble," I say to Veronica. "She wants revenge."

CHAPTER 18

I'm in my room bashing monsters in the video game and trying to forget a dream I had last night that Luna was make-believe like Tyler was. Then Veronica knocks on my door and says a police officer wants to talk to me. He's waiting in the study with Joe.

"It's probably nothing," I say. Nana usually makes a contribution to a fund for wounded officers. I figure that's why somebody's here. Or maybe this could be about my dad. I bet it's about my dad or maybe my mom. Or somebody's been in an accident.

A sick feeling builds inside me. Veronica heads into Nana's room with a duster, and I have to go downstairs.

In the study I sit on the love seat. Joe's in the big chair. He introduces me to Officer Paige who is sitting in a wing chair.

"David," Joe says. "Officer Paige wants to know where you were on May first."

I look down. I have a cornflake stuck to my T-shirt. "Here. My grandmother died sometime during the night," I say and look at Joe. "You could've told him that."

"I did," he says. "The nurse was here too," he tells the officer.

Oh no. I better tell the truth or else. Once you lie, nothing else is believable. "The nurse didn't show up. She'd hurt her back, and the agency didn't send a replacement. I stayed with my grandmother." I glance at Joe. "I would've called you, but the day nurse was coming early the next morning."

"Did you give her pain medication?" Officer Paige asks.

"No. She took pain medicine."

"You saw her?"

"No. I went to get her some water."

"Was she confused?"

"Part of the time. I didn't know she could reach her medicine."

"Did you fill her prescription that day?"

"No. I don't do stuff like that. The medication is delivered."

"A person could make a lot of money selling drugs."

"I don't need money."

"Don't say anything else, David," Joe warns.

"I'm finished," Officer Paige says.

Wait a minute, I think. *What does he mean by that?*

Joe stands.

"It's routine. He is not under arrest." Paige looks at his watch. He explains that an unidentified caller said I gave my grandmother an overdose of painkillers. He had to follow up.

I try to stay calm. "What's next?" I ask.

"He'll turn in his report," Joe says. "Then we'll hear."

"And I may be in trouble for something I would never do in a million years? That sucks. That's not right to listen to somebody who's out to get me. Why would I do that when she was dying?"

Joe keeps standing, and the officer's sitting. It's his way of showing power. He does that to me.

"Euthanasia, perhaps," the officer says.

An unsmiling Joe looks down at him. "David has a rare condition where he doesn't feel pain. He doesn't understand physical suffering. It's documented on his medical record."

I could be in big trouble. I chew my lip. I don't want people thinking I'd do anything to Nana. Just about every night, I've gone to bed thinking, *Tomorrow when I wake, things will be better.*

Veronica walks into the room. "I have her pain medicine right here," she says. "The pills had fallen onto the floor. Count them if you want. There are twenty-eight of them. I can't believe you would harass a boy who is grieving without checking the details first. It makes me want to puke." She looks at Joe. "And you should be ashamed of yourself."

I lick my lip. It tastes like a penny.

The officer takes the bottle. He opens it and looks inside. He gives the bottle back to Veronica. "Ma'am," the officer says, "we want to be informed whenever there is a concern, especially when there has been a questionable death." He stands. "Thank you for your time."

Joe escorts him to the door.

"Can I have the pills?" I ask Veronica.

"Why?"

"To turn them in to the drugstore so they can be disposed of. Nana told me never to dump pills into the garbage or toilet."

She trusts me. She hands me the bottle.

But I have lied to her. The thing is, I don't know if Veronica would lie for me or not, and I'm feeling like she would. Nobody asked to see the pills she placed in the bottle. Nobody wanted to count them.

But I do. I want to know if Nana took the pills when I wasn't paying attention. I'm going to check them out.

I'm in a bad mood when I go to my room. I go online and look up Percocet. I find a picture. Then I open the bottle and dump out a couple of pills. I examine one.

This is Percocet.

I put the pills back into the bottle and set it on my desk.

How can somebody accuse me of murder? That's what Ruby was doing. I'm thinking I should tell Ruby she could've ruined my life.

I imagine what will happen.

Ruby will answer the door. I'll smile. First I'll say, "Veronica found all of the missing pills."

Ruby will smile. "I'm an idiot for thinking you'd ever harm your grandmother. Can you ever forgive me? Would you like to come in? I'll tell you about your parents."

I'll go in. She'll tell me about my dad. "He's living with an isolated tribe in Peru in the Andes. He's teaching the tribe to read. He is very dedicated and forgets everything else when he's working. And your mother never has seen you. She gave him complete custody before you were born and then went on her way. That's why nobody knows anything about her and why you have no memory of her. Have a cookie?"

Wrong. Ruby talked to her a few years ago.

It'll be more like this.

She'll open the door. I'll tell her Nana's medicine was found and wait for her to apologize.

She'll nod and look at me as if I'm a stranger. Then she'll say, "Get off my property or I'm calling the police." That's probably what she'll do, and I'll end up in big trouble.

I have to let this go.

I go into the kitchen thinking about how to show Ruby what an idiot she is. I say hey to Joe and Veronica. I open the cabinet to get a glass, feeling as if they're watching me and shaking a little as if I've done something I shouldn't have. A bowl slides out, hits the counter, and breaks on the floor. I turn around. I was right. Joe and Veronica are staring at me.

"I'll clean it up," I say.

"I'll do it," Veronica says. "You'll cut your hands to pieces, and then I'll have to mop up the blood. Go practice the piano. I haven't heard you play in a while."

I'm a total klutz. I can't do anything right. I feel depressed—like I want to go to sleep and wake up with everything almost the way it was and get asked questions by Nana. I never liked her asking before.

I head to the living room. I sit on the piano bench and start playing. That way I can't hear anything but the music, and it's the only beautiful thing around here.

"You're getting better and better," Joe says. He hovers tall over me.

I stop playing. "How come you're still hanging around?" I ask, looking at the keys.

"I have news about Carlee."

"Really? What?" My heart pounds in my ears.

"The detective found her. She sends her condolences about your grandmother. She doesn't think it's a good idea for the two of you to meet."

"Ever?"

He nods.

I'm shaking. "Why?"

"I don't know. Your grandmother had asked her to visit several times. One Christmas, Carlee was supposed to visit. She didn't show up."

"Nana never told me that."

"She felt it was better not to tell you," Joe says. "She didn't want you to be disappointed."

"It doesn't really matter to me," I say with a shrug. Talking about my mother makes her too real. I'm doing fine with a figment of my imagination. I turn around and look toward the window. "I don't need her. I never have." I don't understand why a mother would get rid of her kid. Maybe she's like a guppy. Sometimes guppies eat the babies.

"Did Carlee say where my dad is?" I ask Joe.

"She hasn't heard from him in years."

I don't need him either. I run my fingers across the piano keys.

"You're okay?"

"Yeah." I don't really want to talk anymore.

"That's not all," he says. "My trip to Belize is coming up. I've had this trip planned for a year, but I can cancel if I need to."

"You don't need to cancel," I say. I sound sad so I try to smile. "You need a vacation."

He rubs his forehead. "I'll probably have sporadic Internet or cell phone access."

"I could go with you," I say.

Joe frowns. "I have to go alone," he says. "You'll be better off here with Veronica."

It's not like I need him. Or anybody. It's actually all right that Joe would rather not take me to Belize with him. I don't want to get too attached to anybody.

"Tomorrow is your checkup with Dr. Goodman. I'm taking you so that I have a chance to consult with him. I want to make sure you're okay before I leave for Belize. Be ready at eleven."

"I will," I say.

It's crazy, but this is the best news I've heard all day. Luna works in the building where Dr. Goodman has his office. I might run into her. I might not. My best hope to see her is to ask her to lunch. We could eat in the snack bar, and I could take a cab home.

I like who I am when I'm with her.

Then Veronica brings a stack of cards and tells me I need to write thank-you notes for the flowers Nana received and mail them tomorrow or else. I don't know what "else" means.

I better get the thank-you notes written.

I better be ready to see Dr. Goodman.

Or else.

Anything can happen.

I text Luna.

I have a doctor's appointment. Want to meet at the snack bar at noon?

While I'm waiting for a reply, I look up Belize on the Internet. It has tropical forests, Mayan sites, caves to explore, the longest barrier reef in the Western Hemisphere, and snorkeling. The summer's a great time to go, even though hurricanes are a threat.

I check my cell phone. No reply from Luna.

All of a sudden I'm wishing I hadn't sent her a message.

CHAPTER 19

Dr. Goodman has a look of shock on his face after Joe asks him if I need to live someplace where I'd be checked on frequently. He tells Joe to go to Belize, have a good time, and don't worry about me. Then he turns to me and asks me if I made a list.

"Yes," I say. "I got my driver's license."

"Good for you," he says. "Keep going."

Joe and I get on the elevator. "What kind of list?" he asks.

"A bucket list," I say.

Joe presses the button to go to the lobby.

In the lobby I look over at the circular information desk. I don't see Luna, and she didn't answer my text last night. She's probably not going to show up, but there's no reason for me to go home. Having lunch here might be interesting. I can watch people, pretend I'm normal, and then go home.

"I have something to do," I tell Joe. "I'll get a ride home."

"What?" he asks.

"I'm meeting Luna," I say. I hope.

He nods, gives me a slow smile, and offers me money.

"I'm good," I say, shifting my feet. I brought some money, and I have a credit card and a debit card. It isn't like I didn't plan ahead.

Joe says he's glad I have friends. He reminds me to text or call when I get home. He's going to his office. The truth is, I could text or call from almost anywhere, and he wouldn't know the difference.

I head for the snack bar. Luna's not there either. I check for a new message on my cell phone. There's no way I'll text her again. Then I buy a hamburger and water and sit at a table. She could at least message me and say she can't make it.

I know what I'll do. I'll text her again in a half hour. I eat the hamburger slowly and watch people coming and going.

I think Luna lied to me about having a job, just like she made me believe we'd be seeing each other. I stand and take my burger wrapper and napkin to a trash can outside the entrance to the snack bar and then go over to the desk.

But I don't ask. It's obvious Luna doesn't work here, and I'm scared I'll never see her again. It kind of feels like that hamburger is stuck in my throat.

I'm not going to call or message her.

When I turn around, I see Luna getting off the elevator. She looks toward me, and I don't know if I should wave or not. I'm not sure she sees me. But tomorrow, the next day, or maybe next year I'll be wondering if she saw me, why she didn't answer my message, and why I didn't do something when I had the chance.

So I wave. She can pretend not to see me if she wants.

She waves back and walks my way, perhaps because she feels like she has to now that I've seen her getting off the elevator.

"Hi, David," she says. She's wearing scrubs like she did the first few times she came to my house.

"Hey!" I say, sounding too eager to talk to her. "How are you?" I should've said hi in a normal voice.

"I'm fine."

"That's good," I say. Pretty soon I'm going to ask her what's going on, if I get brave enough. I imagine she'll say we have nothing in common or that she has a boyfriend. She won't say she doesn't want to be around somebody like me.

"How are you?" she asks.

I shrug and look away. "Fine."

"You had a doctor's appointment?"

"Yeah. Joe dropped me off. He had to go to his office. He's way behind."

Blinking, she smiles slowly. "I can't believe he left you alone."

I'm not alone. "Did you get my message about meeting for lunch?"

"No. I dropped my cell phone into the toilet and haven't replaced it yet."

I have a funny feeling it was disconnected. "You never need to call before coming over," I say.

"You had all those people around, and I haven't had extra time working two jobs."

"I didn't see you working at the information desk." I say.

"I work at the main desk in x-ray," she says. "At night I'm a waitress. She looks at me. "Oh my god. You think I'm lying to you."

"I guess I did, but only because I never knew anyone who had two jobs."

Luna touches the back of my neck. "Wow. You've been living in the dark." She studies me for a moment. "Do you want a ride? I took the afternoon off to get my car fixed, but it's not an emergency."

I shift my feet. She looks pale, but the fluorescent light causes that.

"Yeah, but maybe you should get your car fixed too."

"It'll be okay," she says with a laugh.

CHAPTER 20

Duct tape holds Luna's back fender onto her old Toyota. I slide into the passenger seat, look down, and fasten my seat belt. "You had an accident?"

"Somebody rear-ended me." Luna cranks the motor. It sputters. "His insurance paid, but I've been waiting to get the damage fixed." She pulls through the gate of the parking deck, and a minute later drives onto the interstate. Within seconds, the speedometer reads seventy. We're in the far left lane, and she's going around every car in her way, but she's a confident driver even with the car shaking. I'd probably be driving about fifty in the right lane.

"What's the hurry?" I ask.

"I'm going the speed limit."

The backseat's loaded with boxes and junk. She says she's moving when she finds a better place with a thirty-day lease. Right now, she lives in a high-crime area so she keeps her important stuff with her.

I slump in the seat like a box overfilled with something heavy. I'm wondering how she survives with an old car that shakes and two jobs.

Suddenly, the engine sputters. The temperature light's turned red. "Oh no," Luna says. She pulls onto the side of the road, cuts off the motor, and leans her forehead against the steering wheel.

"The car just needs to let off a little steam," I say nervously. "Or it needed a smoke."

She starts crying.

"Don't cry," I say. "It isn't the end of the world. It's all right."

"But the heat—"

"No problem," I say. "We can call a tow truck." I shrug, take out my cell phone, and call Hills Towing. The night my brakes failed, I put Hills on speed dial.

The dispatcher says it will be a couple of hours before they can come.

"Why so long?" I ask.

"It isn't an emergency."

"What?" Luna says.

"This isn't an emergency," I tell her.

She takes my phone. "This is an emergency. My friend is gravely ill." Then her forehead wrinkles, and she gives me my phone. "She said I should call nine-one-one," Luna says.

"No way," I say. I call Joe and leave a message. It could be hours before he gets it. Then I call Spencer. He says he's at college orientation in Tennessee. I'd call Veronica, but she's scared to drive on the interstate.

It's ninety-eight degrees and humid. I bet the heat index is at least a hundred and ten. It's probably more.

"I just had the thermostat fixed," Luna says. She pulls a tissue from the console.

"It's probably the radiator or a fan belt causing the problem." I glance at Luna. She's pretty. She's really pretty even when she blows her nose. Cars are passing. "How far is the nearest place to get water?" I ask.

"Several miles."

"I'll check the radiator," I say.

"What are you going to do? Spit on it?"

I don't know what I'll do. Luna reaches down and pops the hood. We get out and go to the front of the car. I start to pull the hood open, but the engine's steaming. "Let's wait," I say.

We walk over and stand under a tree by a barbed-wire fence.

"I'll jog to a gas station," Luna says.

I shake my head. "It's too hot for anybody to jog that far. I'll call another towing company. We can't just stand around waiting for what's not going to happen."

"We're not. You start calling, and I'll see if I can flag somebody down."

"No," I say. "That's dangerous."

Luna doesn't listen. She goes to the side of the road and stands behind her car. She waves her arms.

I don't know who to call. I do a search for roadside towing and find Erwin's Auto Service. They have a twenty-four-hour towing service, so I make the call and talk to a woman. Somebody will be here in an hour. I walk to the road, shielding my eyes from the sun. "It'll be an hour," I say.

"Oh no," she says.

"Do you have any water?" I ask.

"No."

"Okay," I say. "An hour is okay." I go back to the shaded area and watch Luna waving. I make a couple more calls. The dispatcher at Ace Wrecker says a truck will be arriving within fifteen minutes. Fifteen minutes pass, and there's no truck. I call again. The tow truck is on the way.

An hour passes, and then a van stops in front of Luna's car. A big guy gets out. He has tattoos on his arms and neck.

Luna starts talking to him, and I walk over and ask him if he would drive me to get water. "I have water," he says.

I follow him over to Luna's car, and he looks at the radiator. Then he goes to his van and returns with a couple of gallons of water. He uses a rag to twist off the radiator cap, and then he pours in the water.

"Try it now," he says.

Luna cranks the motor.

I open my wallet and take out two twenties.

"No thanks," he says. Then he gets into his van and leaves.

Sweat's running down Luna's face. "That was lucky," she says, speeding toward my house. It's twenty minutes away. I'll be fine. My temperature is only a hundred and one.

I'm really happy the guy with the tattoos came along when he did. He doesn't know he probably kept me from having heat stroke. He probably saved my life and Luna's.

✦ ✦ ✦

We make it to my house, and I tell Luna we have some gallon jugs for recycling in the garage. She can use them for water until she gets her car fixed tomorrow. I hurry onto the deck and down the stairs, and jump into the pool. A few minutes later, Luna comes outside and sits on the pool steps.

I go over to her.

"This is embarrassing," she says. "What's your temperature?"

"Around a hundred," I say. I can think of ten more embarrassing things. Dying in a hot car with a hot girl is one of them.

"How long do you stay in the water?"

"Fifteen minutes," I say.

"Do you care if I take a shower?"

"No."

"I'll be back in a few minutes."

I go underwater, hold my breath for a couple of minutes, and then sit in the shallow part of the pool. Luna's right. This is embarrassing.

After a while Luna comes outside, and I ask if she's hungry. She says yes. I dry off, and we go inside.

I open the refrigerator and take out two bottles of water. I hand one to Luna and then quickly drink mine. "Want some leftover pizza? I haven't had anything to eat today except for a hamburger."

"Me either," she says and turns to look at me. "You okay now?"

"Yeah. Don't I look all right?" I wish she wouldn't ask me stuff like that. I wish she wouldn't see me as an invalid.

It was too risky to run the air conditioner on the way here, because the car could have overheated again. But I had the window down and the wind blowing in my face.

"You want your pizza warmed?" she asks.

"I like cold pizza."

Cold or hot doesn't make any difference to me if I'm eating.

"I'm going to change."

Back downstairs, we eat pizza and then we eat giant cinnamon rolls that Veronica made, and we talk. I've gotten over my embarrassment, and now it's like I've eaten too much happiness.

After we eat, we watch *Star Wars* on TV. "Feel, don't think. Use your instincts," Qui-Gon Jinn says to Anakin Skywalker.

Luna says she does not like this movie because she knows what's going to happen to Anakin. I ask her if she'd rather watch *Spider-Man*.

"No," she says. "I hate superhero movies. They're sad, really." She drinks water. "Superheroes tend to be stereotypical except they look different and have different powers. They're tortured, misunderstood souls, and they're lonely. If most everybody was a superhero, can you imagine how boring the world would be?"

"Chaotic," I say.

"I should go anyway," she says and finishes her water. "Work tomorrow."

"I have a crazy idea. Stay here tonight, and I'll take you to get your car fixed before work. I don't know everything that's going on with you, and you don't need to tell me, but I think taking a chance that the car won't overheat is a bad idea. We could walk around or watch TV, or you can fall asleep on the sofa. We're friends, right?"

"Friends," she says.

"We have a nature trail behind the house," I say. "With amazing weeds."

She blinks at me. "You want to show me weeds?"

"Nature," I say.

✚ ✚ ✚

I open the back door and take her hand. We step outside onto the deck and walk down the steps. A wondrous and scary full moon hangs low. I can smell the chlorine from the pool, and I don't know if it's my imagination or not, but I smell barbecue. We go through the back gate and step onto the nature trail.

Solar-powered lights shine along the path. We walk slowly. I haven't been here since winter, when the trees were leafless and I could see everything.

"How long is the nature trail?" she asks.

"About five miles, but it winds around. My grand-parents built it when I was a kid so I could ride my bike in a safe place. They talked about getting me a horse, but it would've been a big responsibility for them, and I was almost more than they could handle. I hoped I'd get a horse every birthday and Christmas for a couple of years."

"I've never ridden a horse," she says.

"It's great," I say. "How'd you end up in Waterly, of all places? I don't think it's on a map."

"I was living at home and unable to find a job. One day I told my parents that I was moving to Orlando on December first to work at Disney World."

"Why Orlando?"

"My best friend from high school was living there.

She said she'd get me on at Disney World, and we'd be roommates. When December first came, I put my stuff into the car, said good-bye, drove halfway across the country, and my car broke down here."

"This is not Disney World," I say with a grin. "This is not even on the route to Disney World."

"Yeah," she says. "I took a wrong turn and was heading north instead of south. Then my car broke down, and I was stuck here."

"You didn't call your parents?"

"They'd help me if I asked." Luna stops and touches a flower. "I've never seen a flower like this." She's looking at a bush with heart-shaped leaves and purple flowers.

"Morning glory," I say.

"So my car needed a new motor, and I knew I wasn't going anywhere for a while. I got a temporary job as a waitress, found a roommate, and moved in with her. We do not get along. I'm moving as soon as possible."

"Home or to Orlando?"

"One or the other. I won't be staying here."

My heart feels like it's breaking. "When?"

"Soon," she says.

I hear leaves crunching behind me. I twist around as my heart's jumping into my throat and see a raccoon. I hear chirping, hissing, howling, and there's a rhythm to it. It's like the forest has a beating heart that's about to explode.

"You should've told me before," I say. "I would've helped you."

"No thanks. I have a place to live and two jobs."

"Will you tell me before you go?"

"I will."

We walk back to the house. "You want something to drink?" I ask when we're on the deck.

"Do you have Coke?"

She follows me into the kitchen. "My dad warned me about moving a long way from home," she says. "He said there wouldn't be anyone to help me."

"But things are better now?"

She sighs. "Pretty much. I've lost my car keys and had to have new ones made. Then I had a flat tire and a wreck. I think I'm cursed."

I open the refrigerator. "Joe has said I was born under the accident-waiting-to-happen star." I hand her a Coke and lean against the counter.

"So no skydiving, parasailing, or climbing Mount Everest?" Luna asks.

"Not in this lifetime."

"You believe in reincarnation?"

"I believe in an afterlife," I say. "My grandmother always said that when a person dies, they buy the farm. I know that's just an expression for dying, but when I hear it, I think of a farm with people having picnics, and horses and cows grazing in the meadow."

"I've heard that expression," Luna says. "I can't stop thinking about your bucket list." She takes a deep breath. "Especially the one about dying of old age. Is that possible?"

"Anything's possible," I say.

"Hopefully we'll both grow old." Luna sets her Coke can on the counter. "How's the bucket list coming?"

"I have my driver's license."

"You should keep working on it."

"You have a bucket list?"

"In my head," she says.

"What's on it?" I ask.

"Skydiving, hang gliding, surfing, doing something illegal."

Wow. My bucket list was written by a simpleton. "I'll get a blanket and pillow for you," I say. "Unless you want to sleep in one of the guest rooms."

"No. I like to sleep with the TV on, if that's okay."

"I keep a light on," I say. "If I keep the TV on, the program becomes part of my dream. Once I starred in *Nightmare on Elm Street*."

Luna laughs until she cries.

✚ ✚ ✚

The first thing I do when I awaken is sit straight up in the bed, and I'm thinking about Luna asleep on the sofa. I make a beeline downstairs where I see the comforter I gave Luna last night neatly folded on the sofa. I hurry to the window. Her car's gone.

In the kitchen, I see a note on the table. *Thanks! I'm going to be really busy the next few days. I'll talk to you one day.*

I'm kind of glad we don't have to see each other and say awkward stuff in person like "I'll talk to you one day." It's like maybe she will and maybe she won't. Luna's not exactly predictable.

I follow my schedule and keep my cell phone where I won't miss a call or a message.

CHAPTER 21

I'm not feeling too well, but I know it's because I'm wondering what Luna is doing, and I can't sit around doing nothing. If she doesn't want to be around me, that will have to be okay.

I'm going to do something, and it's not going to kill me. When I'm showering, I remember Cameron sitting on his porch all day with his service dog. He came to Nana's funeral and sat near the back door with Scruffy. He came to my birthday party although I don't really know him, but what the heck? I hardly knew anybody there.

I still haven't sent those thank-you notes, but I write one to Cameron.

It's seventy-five degrees when I get up enough nerve to walk down the road to Cameron's house with the thank-you card. Sometimes I've seen a dog walker walking Scruffy. I figure Cameron needs somebody to help, and I guess I might give it a shot. I don't know yet.

I stop at Cameron's mailbox and take a deep breath. He's not much older than me, and I could become like him. Cameron's sitting in his wheelchair on his front porch, and Scruffy's lying next to him.

I admit, I feel bad for the dog now, but I never did until recently. I didn't pay much attention before.

I go up to the porch. "Hey, Cameron. Remember me? David?"

He smiles. "Of course I remember you."

I hand him the thank-you card. "I was going to mail it, but I decided bringing it to you would be quicker."

I had written on it, *Thank you for the donation to the Alzheimer's Foundation.*

I met him the day the town had a celebration for him, and he rode in a parade waving at everybody. I felt like crying. He always seems to be on the porch waiting for something to happen.

I don't want to become like him, but maybe I am in a way when I drive up and down the road.

The dog is barking at me, but his tail is wagging. "Quit," Cameron tells Scruffy, and he stops barking. "Should you be outside?" Cameron says.

I didn't know he knew about me. "It's okay for a couple of hours," I say. "Did you know my grandmother well?"

"I didn't know her at all," he says. "But she helped me get Scruffy." Cameron tells me Scruffy was a starving puppy in Afghanistan, and he took care of him until he was wounded. He had to leave the dog behind, but an organization helped bring Scruffy to him and train him as a service dog. Scruffy did not pass his final exam.

For once I feel like I know how to do something. "Maybe I could help him," I say. "I could exercise him."

Cameron looks me up and down. His eyes fix on my cane. "I'm sorry, David. To be honest, I don't think you can manage Scruffy."

At least Cameron didn't start laughing.

I stick out my hand and let Scruffy sniff it. "I really need a job," I say. "I am sure I can manage."

This would be the perfect job for me, and it's the only thing I can think of to do. A job standing or sitting all day wouldn't be safe for me. I'm prone to joint deterioration because I don't feel it if I'm standing, sitting, or sleeping the wrong way. I could end up with a joint infection and lose a limb. I know it sounds like I'm a hypochondriac, but I'm not. That's just the way I have to live so I don't end up in a wheelchair. A job outside or in a hot kitchen wouldn't be safe for me either.

"How come somebody like you needs a job?" Cameron says.

I shrug. I don't know if he means the genetically mutated me or the me with money. I smile at him. "Getting a job is on my bucket list."

"Wow," he says. "You make it hard to say no."

"I can take Scruffy to my house, and we can swim in the pool," I say. "He'd get a good workout, and he'd be happy."

"Scruffy has behavior problems," Cameron says.

"Because all he does is nothing," I say. That's how I was. I remember banging my head for attention when I was little.

A motorcycle goes by, and Scruffy sticks his tail between his legs. He's scared. Whenever I've seen Scruffy walking in front of my house, he's barking and lunging. I lean against the porch post and it moves, so I stand up straight. "He needs more exercise," I say. What he really needs is to gain confidence. Exercise would help.

"Do you know anything about dogs?" Cameron asks.

I shake my head. "I love dogs, and I know about exercise and swimming," I say. And I know about feeling insecure.

"I'm sorry," he says. "I wish I could hire you, but I can't."

"I'm doing it for free," I say.

"Why?"

I shrug. "I don't need money." It's lonely at my house. I need to have a purpose.

Cameron smiles again. "I don't need you to feel sorry for me," he says.

I shake my head. "I'm jealous," I say. "You've done a ton of things. I've never done hardly anything."

"Okay," he says. "I need a backup person I can depend upon. Just be careful and avoid trucks. Scruffy chases trucks."

Wow. Nobody has ever needed to depend upon me before.

"I'll bring him back in an hour," I say.

Cameron hands me the leash. "If you're sure," he says.

I am. You'd think I was desperate to do something.

✦ ✦ ✦

Scruffy drags me down the road, and it's hard for me to keep my balance and go any faster. My hands don't stop shaking until after we go through the back gate and stop at the pool. Then I untangle my hands from the leash. I check my shoulder to make sure it isn't dislocated and set Scruffy free. He only looks around. I find a stick and toss it into the water. He charges, jumps in, and starts paddling, but he's sinking.

Right away, I learn that not all dogs know how to swim. I pull off my shirt and shoes, jump in, and swim to Scruffy. I hold him up and take him to the shallow side of the pool where he climbs out and shakes water on me.

It was time for me to get into the water anyway. The sun's bright. I bet it's already gotten hot.

I'm like a vampire that needs to stay out of the sun. When I was a kid, I liked to look at blood. It fascinated me the way it would suddenly appear on my skin or mouth for reasons I couldn't figure out. Then Nana taught me it meant danger.

I have a vague memory of going to sleep in a car once, and when I woke, I was in the hospital.

I sit next to Scruffy on the pool steps where the water comes up to my waist, and I pet him. I tell him I want to help him and how my grandmother died, and how my parents don't care about me. I figure it's okay to whine in self-pity to a dog. He won't tell anybody how sad I am sometimes.

I made the right decision to help Scruffy. He's helping me back.

I tell him I don't know what I'm going to do, and I need his help. I massage Scruffy's ears, and he licks me. I think he likes me now. I tell him about Luna and how I miss her, how I'm just another person she used to know. Scruffy stays sitting with his tongue hanging out the side.

It's like I've made a connection. How come a dog understands me and people don't? Maybe I should get a dog.

I get the stick, sit on the pool steps, and toss it into the shallow part a couple of feet away. Scruffy jumps in and sinks again. I pull him to me and let him sit next to me for a minute before I toss the stick. I do the same thing over and over, figuring that one of these days he'll go farther out. I know how he feels. Sometimes I think I go after the prize and sink before I grab on to it. I'll have to get Scruffy a life jacket. And a ball. He eats sticks.

I dry Scruffy off, put him into the backseat of the Lexis, and drive to Cameron's. He's not on his front porch, and his van is gone. May as well do something else.

I drive to the pet store and take Scruffy inside with me. Scruffy's way too tired to pull and lunge. I buy him a life jacket, a bag of tennis balls, a tug toy, a box of good treats, and a hairbrush.

✦ ✦ ✦

Every morning for the next few days, I pick Scruffy up, go swimming, and take him home. Sometimes I hang out at Cameron's for a few minutes and change lightbulbs or do something he can't. Sometimes I don't want to go home. Veronica's there, and I like her, but it's not the same anymore. In the evenings, I watch TV.

"You have a dog in the pool wearing a life jacket," Joe says on Friday.

I swim to the side where Joe is and hang on. I hear Scruffy paddle after me. "I've been teaching him to swim, but I'm nervous about taking it off."

Joe rolls his eyes. "You're teaching a dog to swim?"

"Yes. It's my job. You wanted me to show you I can be independent."

"You aren't teaching him anything when he has to depend upon a life jacket."

"He's supposed to be Cameron's service dog, but he's a scaredy-cat," I say. "You remember Cameron? He was at Nana's funeral and my birthday party."

"Funeral" and "birthday party" should never be used together in a sentence.

Joe nods.

I stand on the pool steps, call Scruffy, and then remove his life jacket. I throw a tennis ball and watch him paddle to it. Scruffy scoops it into his mouth and swims with his nose held high, the yellow ball glowing in the sunlight.

"Did you see Luna on Monday?" Joe asks.

I turn around. "Yes." It's been five days. Five long days. "Why?"

"Her mother called me. She hasn't heard from Luna in two months."

Scruffy swims to the steps. I clip the leash on his collar and lead him out of the pool. "She's all right," I say. "She works at the Holly Building. She's been having roommate problems and car trouble. She doesn't want her parents to know."

Joe raises his eyebrows. "She should call them."

Scruffy jumps on me, and I turn away. "Luna's an adult."

"So was your dad."

"He's been gone for years."

"There's no difference," he says loudly.

"There is at least an eleven-year difference."

"Your grandmother was frantic when she hadn't heard from your dad in two months. You were frantic. You cried every night."

"I don't cry."

"Okay, so you howled. Don't you remember how it felt?"

My stomach clenches. I have a faint memory of my dad going away and not coming back. "Her cell phone's damaged," I say. "That's why she hasn't called."

"Tell her to call them. I leave for Belize tomorrow, and we need to come to an understanding. If you are irresponsible, you're not going to be able to live here without supervision. You can have friends over here as long as Veronica says it's okay, and you're not to go anywhere unless somebody is with you."

"I'm eighteen," I say. "I don't need to be treated like I'm a kid."

"Just because you're eighteen doesn't mean you're responsible. Actually it probably means I'm crazy for not taking you to Twin Falls for a week or hiring a full-time person."

I shrug. "I haven't done anything wrong."

"It's not about what you do wrong. It's about what you don't know. Did you know your arm is bleeding? Did you know you have scratches all over your arms?"

I look at both my arms and see blood from a scratch that runs from the middle of my arm to my wrist. "Scruffy gets excited when we play tug-of-war," I say.

CHAPTER 22

After taking Scruffy home, I unlock my front door and walk inside.

The house is quiet. Veronica's around somewhere, maybe watching a court program on TV. It's fine with me, but I think something else would be more interesting.

She's not in the living room so I stretch out on the sofa, feeling my cell phone in my pocket. I take it out and message Luna. I don't usually call or message anybody unless I have a reason.

Your parents called Joe looking for you.

I sit up and set the phone down on the arm of the couch. It's too early to take a nap, but I'm sleepy. I close my eyes. I hear Veronica come into the living room, and I open my eyes and watch her. She dusts the TV, the coffee tables, the end tables, and then me. She doesn't say a word, but I have a feeling she wants me to do something like get out of the way and write the thank-you cards.

I wonder what Spencer, Cameron, and Luna are doing today.

I'm almost asleep when I hear Veronica yell, "David! Answer your cell phone! Do I have to do everything around here?"

I sit and pick up my phone. "Hello."

"Hey, David," Luna says, sounding out of breath.

My heart speeds up. "You got my message?"

"Yeah," she says. "I called them."

Veronica turns on the TV. "Hold on," I say and go into the kitchen. "Are you in trouble?"

"They were worried about me. They're not now."

"Your car's fixed?" I ask.

"I dropped it off this morning. It won't be ready until tomorrow, but at least I have a cell phone now. Can you give me a ride home?"

There's no way I'll say no. "Yes," I say. I don't know what Joe will do if he finds out. I hope Veronica doesn't try to stop me.

Luna gives me directions.

I find Veronica in the study dusting and moving some of Joe's stuff around. "I wouldn't do that if I were you," I say.

She looks over at me. "Why?"

"Joe said to stay out of the study."

She shrugs. "He won't know. I've put the cards and letters on the desk where you can work on them without getting sidetracked."

"I will later, but Luna's stranded," I say. "I'm going to give her a ride."

Veronica nods. "You haven't been showing you're responsible," she says.

I hate looking at sympathy cards. It makes me feel like Nana died yesterday.

I go to the garage and climb into the car. I open the garage door and back out. Ten minutes later I arrive at the auto repair shop. Luna's waiting out front for me.

It's turning out to be a great day, and I want the afternoon to last forever.

We talk as I drive her home. Her mother cried and cried when Luna called. She thought something had happened to Luna. They were either going to call the police or come to Waterly. They showed up unexpectedly another time during the middle of the night after not hearing from Luna. They made airline reservations, took an evening flight, rented a car, and went to Luna's apartment. There were about four or five people passed out on the floor. There was garbage and dirty dishes all over the place. Her parents went to a motel and left the next day. Her mother called later on and said she'd never been so disappointed in her.

"Worse words ever," I say.

"I hate to call because I feel like they're disappointed that I work at low-paying jobs, I take courses online, and my car's a piece of junk. I'm not getting anywhere." She smiles. "They don't see how hard I'm trying."

My grandparents never expected me to get anywhere, but I had speech therapy because it was hard to understand me when I talked. I had the best doctors, the best clothes, the best tutors. They made me practice playing the piano as exercise for my fingers and to help my hand-eye coordination. They built me a nature trail.

Some of the houses on Luna's street have junk in the yard. Others have uncut lawns or are for sale. I park in front of a small apartment building with a concrete yard. I imagine hanging out with Luna for the rest of the day. Maybe we'll go to dinner or to a movie. I don't know what. "You live alone now?" I ask.

"My roommate moved before I had the chance," she says. "I'd invite you inside, but I don't have air-conditioning."

"That's fine," I say, not looking at her. "We could do something else."

"There's a party tonight."

"Sounds good," I say.

"Pick me up at nine?"

She probably only needs a ride, but I'm thinking maybe she'll discover she really likes me. I don't have anything to lose. Besides, I'm following my doctor's orders to get out more, even if Joe doesn't want me to do anything. Anyway, he hasn't left for Belize yet. His rules aren't in effect yet.

Thirty minutes later, I'm walking in the front door at my house. I hear the TV in the living room, and I go to check if Veronica's there.

She is. "What are you watching?" I ask.

"*Flip This House*."

I sit on the sofa. "What's it about?"

"Remodeling houses." She stares at the TV. "We need to remodel our house before we sell it."

"Sell it? Why?"

"We want to buy a condo."

"Where?"

"Closer to our kids."

That's not anywhere around here. Her kids are adults and live in other states.

"I want to be able to spend time with my grand-children," she says. "I barely know them." Veronica keeps talking. "I found your birth certificate on the floor in the study," she says. "It's on the desk. You should put it back in the safe."

"I will."

"Now," she says and looks at me with a frown. "And do the thank-you notes."

CHAPTER 23

I go to the study and sit in the chair at the desk. I have about a hundred thank-you notes to write, but the sympathy cards are mixed in with a bunch of junk mail. I'm thinking I'm a failure for not reading the cards sooner, but I couldn't stand to look at them. I'd write something special on each one, but I don't know what to say.

My birth certificate is on top of the sympathy cards. I pick it up. Underneath it is a legal envelope. I pull a letter out. It's from STP Investigations.

Joe told me about this. He didn't say he had an official letter.

It contains a list of dates and times and billing hours, but what's interesting is that two months ago the detective located a woman named Elizabeth Tharp, formerly known as Carlee Hart. Her address is given along with the time, place, and date of her upcoming wedding.

Joe forgot to mention that.

The detective has written, *Does not want to be bothered. Threatened to call police.*

Next to the info, Joe has scribbled, *TC to Stanley. Investigation closed.*

That was a few days before Nana died.

All these years I've wanted to believe my mom had good reasons for dumping me, and maybe she did, but she could've taken a few minutes to tell Nana thanks or tell her what she knows about my dad. Nana never asked for anything else except for me to have a good life.

I put the birth certificate in the safe and sort through the cards and letters, hoping to find out more. Maybe there is a stupid sympathy card here. Maybe my mom even wrote me a letter.

I wonder what else is in the other pile of papers on his desk. I know I shouldn't snoop. I have a conscience.

I'm wondering why Joe wouldn't tell me everything. Like he keeps me hanging about moving to Twin Falls. He holds it over my head like a threat.

Like that trip to Belize he had to take alone. Every year he goes on a trip alone to meet somebody.

I don't have anything else to do but write thank-you notes, so I search the study.

Thirty minutes later, I haven't found anything. I start writing thank-you notes and have a stack finished when Veronica knocks.

"I have to go," she says. She picks up the stack of cards. "You did great."

"You saw the letter. Why didn't you tell me?" I ask Veronica.

"It's none of my business," she says and puts down the cards. "But you needed to know. Joe made the decision not to tell you, but it's because he didn't want you hurt."

I think keeping secrets hurts.

"Luna invited me to a party tonight," I say.

"Go. Have fun but no drugs, alcohol, or sex. Be home before midnight."

"Gotcha," I say.

CHAPTER 24

A big sign in front of a ranch-style house two blocks from Luna's reads *Happy Birthday, Jasmine.*

Luna says Jasmine works in the lab and her boyfriend, Lucas, is giving her a birthday party. Jasmine was Luna's former roommate.

"And you still get along with her?" I ask.

"I don't hold grudges," Luna says. "But I have to warn you, this might turn out badly." Luna tells me Jasmine has been planning on breaking up with Lucas, but she couldn't do that when she found out he was giving her a party.

We're an hour late because I got caught up in writing and searching the study again for more secrets Joe's hiding. I didn't find anything else.

I open the front door for Luna and follow her inside.

Music plays, people dance, others talk and laugh. Most seem to be in their early twenties. Luna takes my hand and we walk across the room.

It's like a dream. Her hand feels good holding mine. I don't have anything to worry about. Not tonight. It's only us at a crowded party.

We stop to talk to four people standing in a circle.

"This is David," Luna says. She introduces Jasmine, Piper, Kirk, and Gerald.

"Holy shit," Piper says. "David Hart. I thought—I thought you didn't make it." She looks at the others. "He was really sick a few years ago and in the hospital. When I was a medical assistant, I used to sing to him, but then I went back to school to become an x-ray tech. Holy shit, David. You're okay now? They cured you?"

"I'm okay," I say and smile at her. "But I'm not cured."

"David has an extremely rare disease, and he doesn't feel pain," Piper says.

"So what's that like?" Gerald asks.

"What?" I ask.

"Not feeling pain?"

I glance at Luna. "It's normal for me," I say with a sigh. "I don't have anything to compare it with."

But it hurts not to feel.

Because I have messed up lives.

"It would be wonderful not to feel pain," Jasmine says.

"Oh no, it isn't," Piper says. "Pain tells you when there is something wrong. It's there for a reason."

"Have you ever been in trial drug studies?" Gerald asks.

I shake my head. "Not really. It's dangerous. Experimental drugs can kill you."

"How do you think discoveries are made?" Gerald says.

I know how discoveries are made. "What I'm saying is

that you really have to be careful with any experimental drug or treatment," I try to explain. "And nobody's interested in spending money researching a rare disease. I'd actually try an experimental drug if there was one."

"I think money for research should go to common diseases like cancer," Jasmine says. "Too many people die from cancer."

"Where's Lucas?" Luna asks Jasmine.

Jasmine rolls her eyes. "Who cares?"

I stare at Jasmine, thinking she should care since Lucas is giving her the party.

"When are you moving?" Gerald asks Luna.

"One week," she says.

"Just give me a call if you need help. You renting a U-Haul?"

I take a deep breath. I knew this was going to happen sooner or later. Pretty soon the population of Waterly will be down to one if everybody starts moving on to bigger and better things.

"I'm giving away what I can't carry with me," Luna says. "Come on by. I have some good junk." She smiles at him.

Piper touches my arm. "Do you remember me?"

"No, but I remember somebody singing to me."

Actually, I don't remember that, but I figure it was nice of her to sing to me.

"Really?" she says. "You were in a coma, but I felt like you could hear me. Just knowing you could hear me makes my day."

Luna says she's starved and is getting some food. She walks away.

"Nice to meet you," I tell Piper, Jasmine, and Gerald.

"Where are you going?" Piper asks.

"For food," I say with a smile.

At the kitchen table I get a small plate of sausage balls, cheese, crackers, and brownies. Luna's acting like I'm not in the room. I follow her outside and sit at a table by the pool.

"You can be with Piper if you want to," Luna says. "She likes you."

"Why would I want to be with Piper?" I ask.

"Having a girlfriend is on your bucket list," Luna says.

"She's a few years older than me," I say. "And I'd rather hang out with you unless you're waiting for Gerald. I think he likes you."

"He likes me for my sofa," Luna says.

I see a guy staggering around the pool. "He's going to fall in."

Luna turns her head. "Jasmine's boyfriend, Lucas," she says. "I predict before the night's over, Jasmine will dump him."

I kind of feel sorry for Lucas.

"She probably is with another guy right now," Luna says. "Or else they would be together." She looks over at Lucas. "He's not always like that."

Lucas pushes a girl into the pool.

"Did you grow up here?" Luna says.

"Sort of. When I was six, my dad dropped me off at my grandparents' and never came back. I haven't seen my dad since then. I don't remember my mom."

Luna flinches. "I remember that finding them is on your bucket list."

I shrug. "Yeah."

"When?"

"When what?" I say.

"Are you going to look for them?"

"Maybe I'll see my mother soon. I have to talk to a detective first." I look at the pool. Lucas is dragging another girl toward the water. She's laughing as he throws her in.

Luna looks me in the eyes. "What's going on?" she asks.

"I have her address." I look away, tapping the table. "She lives in North Carolina, but she doesn't want to see me."

"Maybe I shouldn't have asked. I should've waited for you to tell me if you wanted me to know."

"It's okay." I'm watching Lucas. "He's coming this way. I bet you're next to go into the water."

"I just have a big mouth," she says, not listening to me. "I didn't mean—"

Lucas grabs her by the arm and pulls her toward the pool. She starts yelling, "Get your hands off me!"

I stand and knock my chair over.

When they're at the edge, she somehow flips him into the water. He goes under, then surfaces and hangs on to the side. Luna comes back to the table.

Lucas climbs out of the pool and curses at Luna. He pulls his iPhone out of his pocket. "You have to pay for it," he says.

"Leave her alone," I say.

She turns around. "Moron." She throws a sausage ball at him. It hits his chest and bounces onto the concrete. He picks it up and squashes it with his hand. He stomps toward us, eyeing me.

Is Luna crazy to be calling him a name? I want to keep breathing.

She clutches my arm.

"We don't want any trouble," I say to Lucas.

Lucas gives me a look, and I take a step backward. I trip over the chair and fall. He grabs my neck and tries to stuff a sausage ball into my closed mouth. I smell grease and garlic, and I feel some grit. I never tried holding my breath this way before.

"Release him or I'll sausage your balls," Luna says. Of course she can talk and use non-verbs. I'm the one smothering.

A couple of guys pull his hands off my throat and drag him away. I stand up. Jasmine appears and starts cursing him. She tells him to pack his stuff or she's calling the police.

Lucas starts crying.

"I should've just let him throw me into the pool," Luna says and starts gasping. "He doesn't deserve to be thrown out tonight." She starts crying and places her hand on her chest. Gasping, she grabs on to me.

I help her to the chair and sit next to her.

"Try to take some deep breaths," I say. "I'll take care of you."

I hold her wrist and check her pulse. It's fast and faint. Her skin's damp. I'm afraid something's wrong with her heart. I know about heart attacks. When I was younger, I watched Grandpa have his last one.

Grandpa was slumped over in the kitchen floor and clutching his chest.

I called 911. A man answered. "What's your emergency?"

"My grandpa is having a heart attack," I said.

"Is he breathing?"

"He's gasping, and his skin is wet and bluish."

It took eight and a half minutes for help to arrive.

Luna's pulse isn't running away now, and it's strong, but I hold on to her wrist to keep checking it. "You'll be okay. Just stay still a few more minutes."

"It's nothing. I hurt my funny bone," she says. "When he grabbed my arm, it hurt. And then the pain made my heart beat fast, and I felt nauseous for a minute. I'm fine now."

I didn't see her bump her elbow.

"I can't take pain," Luna says. "It kills me when I get a paper cut."

I didn't know paper cuts hurt. I've seen Nana suck her finger when she's gotten one. I check my watch. I've been outside a half hour, and my body temperature's normal.

"You are so sweet," I hear. I turn my head and see Piper. "Protecting Luna like that."

"I didn't do anything," I say.

"Lucas is such a loser," Piper says.

I hate it when people are called names. "He was trying to fit in," I say.

Piper laughs and walks away.

"Are you saying I shouldn't have thrown him into the pool?" Luna says.

"No."

"He'll never fit in."

"He shouldn't have to try," I say. "Jasmine is supposedly his girlfriend, but she wants to break up with him. She decides to use him so she'll have a birthday party. That's not right. She should've told him in the first place." I shrug. "I didn't see her with him at all earlier. Instead she was hanging out with her friends from work."

We sit there for a while people-watching and talking about nothing in particular. Pretty soon, there are only a few couples left in the pool making out.

"I guess we'll be heading in different directions about the same time if you decide to go to meet your mother," she says.

"You're definitely moving?"

"I have to go. I've quit my jobs. My apartment's rented."

"I have a crazy idea. What if we go to North Carolina together? I can leave anytime. We could go to the beach or to the mountains. Whatever you want to do."

"I can't," she says.

"Okay," I say.

The overhead lights start going out.

"I think that's our hint it's time to go." Luna gazes at me. "Let's go to your house, okay? Watch TV or something? But don't get the wrong idea, okay? I don't feel like going home yet, and I like talking to you. In a few days, I'll be gone, and you'll probably be headed to North Carolina." She gives me a smile. "You should not miss an opportunity to meet your mother."

✦ ✦ ✦

Luna looks through the movies in the study and chooses two: *Garden State* and *Eternal Sunshine of the Spotless Mind*. She says I should make the final choice. "We can watch both," I say although I'd rather watch something like *Indiana Jones*. "Or we can find something new on cable."

We watch a new movie. I don't even know the name or who is in it. It's a romance kind of like *Romeo and Juliet*, and the lovers both die at the end. Luna weeps. I don't. I knew the ending at the beginning.

Then we decide to go outside to the pool.

I turn on the lights, and the wind's making the water ripple. Luna heads back inside to get a blanket. The water looks so great that I jump in, swim a lap, and then dry with a towel. My clothes are dipping wet, but I'm not in the mood to change. The water might help keep my body temperature from going up. It's fine right now. It's only ninety-seven.

I've sat out here lots of nights when the sky was starry. That reminds me of the meteor shower I heard about on the news, but it's not going to happen for a week. It has a name I don't remember. Having Luna come over and watch it with me would be pretty great, but she's going to be gone by then.

Watching meteors would be too sad to do alone. You'd think about them as falling stars, and of course you'd have to make a wish on every one of them, while knowing the whole wish-upon-a-star thing is a lie.

But I like to believe it's true, just like I want to believe Pinocchio became a real boy.

"Hey," Luna says. She has a blanket hanging over her arm, two drinks inside the blanket pressed against her chest, and a bowl of popcorn in her free hand. She sets the popcorn and drinks in the space between the lounge chairs, lies down, and covers up with the blanket.

It's like I'm floating. I'm feeling great, but maybe I've been sniffing too much oxygen or nice-smelling hair.

Then we eat popcorn and watch the sky. We don't talk. After a while I look over at Luna, and she's asleep holding the empty bowl of popcorn. I take it and set it down. I think about waking her, but I don't want her to go home.

I sit and wait for her to wake up.

But she doesn't. She's still sleeping. I touch her wrist with my hand.

"Don't check my pulse," she says.

CHAPTER 25

I'm dreaming and I missed all the good parts, or I've died and gone somewhere else. Water washes over me from my head to toes. I wipe my face and open my eyes. Luna's shaking and holding a bucket.

I'm not dreaming. I'm still in the lounge chair by the pool. "What's going on?" I ask.

"We fell asleep. You've been in the heat for hours, and you could be confused. It's hot out here. Get into the water."

But it's dawn, and the normal July temperature at night is seventy-five degrees. Maybe I am confused. I mean, I never know. If a person could know, they'd start acting not confused. I get up and jump into the pool. My brain's a little foggy, so I only hang on to the edge and go underwater a few times. Then I climb out and dry off.

I'm fine. "What time is it?" I ask.

"Six thirty."

I smile at her. "Thanks for waking me," I say.

"You're okay?"

"Yes."

"I overreacted."

"Not really," I say.

"That's just great," Luna says. She wheels around and picks up the empty drink cans, the empty popcorn bowl, and the blanket. She heads inside.

My grandmother would've been calling the paramedics, and Veronica would have been in the driveway waiting to wave them down. That's overreacting.

I go into the kitchen. Luna's not there, but I can hear water running. I go to my room, change into dry clothes, lie down, and fall asleep.

✦ ✦ ✦

My watch beeps me awake.

I do my routine, and on the way to the kitchen I hear Veronica and Luna laughing.

"Hey," I say, walking into the kitchen kind of wondering what Veronica thought when she arrived and Luna was here. I'm kind of embarrassed.

"I was telling Luna to always expect the unexpected around here." Veronica smiles at Luna. "One morning when I came to work, the air-conditioning unit had quit working, and his grandmother hadn't noticed. Temperature was over eighty," she says. "David was practically in a coma. That was when he was much younger, and back then his temperature would spike quicker."

"What did you do?" Luna asks.

"We threw David into the bathtub and called to have the air conditioner repaired." Veronica laughs.

Luna cracks a smile.

"There is always something happening around here," Veronica says.

Because Nana and Veronica would overreact, I think.

Veronica places her cup into the sink and turns toward me. "Let me know if your temperature gets above a hundred and two. I've got work to do."

I check my watch. "My temperature's only ninety-nine." Actually my temperature is a couple of degrees higher, but it isn't at the danger level. "I'm taking Luna to pick up her car. Is that fine with you?" I ask Veronica.

"If you're sure you're okay."

"I am."

A moment later, I hear the vacuum cleaner roar to life in another room.

Luna's writing in a notebook.

"What are you doing?" I ask.

"Making a list of what's dangerous for you."

I grin. "Ironing boards," I say.

"What?"

"Ironing boards. Have you ever read *This Hurts*?"

She shakes her head and keeps writing. I hope she's not writing "ironing boards."

"It's a play about a guy who doesn't feel pain. He keeps a list of what hurts. He's sitting in a laundry room when he gets hit with an ironing board, and he adds that to his list. Then he has trouble deciding if ironing boards are dangerous or if he should only be afraid of them." I shrug. "Anything can be dangerous to anybody."

"This is documenting number of hours outside, your

body temperature, and the outside temperature."

"More research," I say.

"You'll be able to see on paper if you're making progress. You need to keep track."

I shrug. "I don't want to. I rather not know," I say.

"Let's go pick up my car," she says, sounding annoyed.

I get the car keys from the spider plant. I don't know why I still keep them there.

On the way to the auto repair place, I'm trying to think of something we could do today. I wish we could go on a hike or rafting down the river.

We're told the car won't be ready for an hour. We sit shoulder to shoulder in plastic chairs in the auto-repair waiting room. I probably should've skipped a chair and sat in the next chair, but somebody was already in it. A country love song is playing on the radio. It's about this guy who loved this girl until he died, but she never loved him back. You'd think she'd have cared a little. Lately I've been thinking it would be wondrous to be loved.

Luna gets paper from her notebook, and we play Hangman for a while.

Then she takes out a calendar and looks at it. From the look on her face, you'd think she was reading the worst book ever.

I stretch out my legs. Waiting in an auto repair shop and inhaling oily smells is better than I ever imagined it could be. There's no place else I want to go, no other person I'd rather be with.

"What all are you having done to your car?" I ask.

She looks up from her notebook. "Just getting the

radiator fixed. It'll get me to where I'm going."

"To the Magic Kingdom."

"I haven't decided yet. Have you ever been?"

"No."

"It's hot and crowded."

"And magical."

"It was when my parents took me years ago," she says. "They acted like little kids."

"I'll have to visit you."

"Definitely, if I go there."

Then my cell phone rings. "What's taking you so long?" Veronica asks.

I sigh. "We have to wait for the car. It won't be much longer."

Sometimes it's like I'm on a long rope, and it's getting tighter around my neck.

"I've been worried to death," Veronica says. "All you need to do is call me when you're late and check in with me." She's out of breath.

This is how I know she cares. "Sorry," I say. "I'll be home soon."

When Luna's name is called, I go to the counter with her and offer to pay.

She shakes her head. "You are wonderful, but no thanks."

✦✦✦

It's getting dark outside, and I'm sitting looking out the front window. There's nothing moving around. I wish I could look out and see more.

Veronica left a few hours ago.

I asked Luna if she wanted to do something today, and

she said she had to deep clean her apartment, paint, and fix some holes so she'd get her deposit back.

I go to the top of the stairs and slide down the banister like I used to do when I was a kid. It's kinda fun. At the bottom I hear knocking. I tiptoe to the front door and look out the peephole, my heart pounding.

I see Cameron and open the door. He's smiling, and Scruffy's wagging his tail. "I have good news. Scruffy's a certified service dog now, and I have a job at the pet store. I can take him to work with me."

"That was quick," I say.

"I hired a trainer for service dogs, and then Scruffy passed the test right away with flying colors. I'm here to take you out to celebrate at Maxwell's Pub. It's a hole in the wall, but the food is good."

"That's terrific," I say.

"Spencer and Marcello are meeting us there," he says. "I tried to call, but you didn't answer."

I check my pocket. "Be right back," I say and head to the kitchen. My wallet and cell are on the counter where I left them.

I text Luna.

Going to Maxwell's Pub. Want to meet me there?

✚ ✚ ✚

At first, the hostess at the door says dogs aren't allowed, but Cameron takes Scruffy's certificate out of his pocket. The hostess reads it.

"I don't know," she says.

I explain about the Americans with Disabilities Act. Nana made me learn about it once. She figured I would need to know, even if I didn't end up in a wheelchair.

The hostess talks to a manager, and I see her nod. She shows us to a table in the back close to the bathrooms.

It's the first time I've been in a real bar. I've always wanted to go to a bar.

Cameron tells me to order him a beer. He's going to the bathroom. "What if they ask for an ID?" I ask.

"Then wait for me, but they usually don't," he says and wheels away with Scruffy at his side.

I turn my head. From where I am, I can see about a dozen booths filled with people.

"Can I get you something to drink?" the waitress asks without looking at me.

I look down. "Beer," I say.

"What kind?"

"What kind do you have?"

She lists about six kinds. I choose the first.

"You want the twenty-four ounce?"

"The regular size," I say. "I'd like water too."

Then Spencer and Marcello arrive and order Cokes. I turn and glance toward the door, hoping Luna's coming too. I don't see her. Cameron returns and orders a Bud before I can say I already ordered his.

I guess I'll drink the beer.

"Guess what?" Cameron says. "My little brother's coming to live with me."

"How old is he?" Spencer asks.

"Twelve. I figure he's better off with me than with my aunt now that I'm back on my feet." He taps the armrest of his wheelchair and grins.

"It may take him a while to get used to it," I say.

"He'll have his own room and stuff. At my aunt's he has to share a room with his two cousins."

It took me forever to adjust to living with my grandparents, but I kept expecting my dad to show up. Maybe I need to learn how not to worry, but planning and thinking ahead is part of what's kept me alive.

The waitress brings our drinks, and I order nachos. I wonder if I'd get a hangover and maybe a headache if I drank a lot of alcohol. As I take a sip, the beer reminds me of the time I had to drink a gallon of gross stuff before having x-rays. I gagged a lot.

Cameron reaches across the table and grabs my beer. "I'll take this," he says. "You're too young, and you are the designated driver."

Then I get a text message from Luna.

I can't meet you. Painting.

I write Come over later if you want to. I have to write thank-you notes.

The waitress brings our food. My nachos are a great change from the cereal I usually have. We talk, laugh, and joke around, but Marcello sits silently, the way he usually does.

After we eat, Spencer and Marcello play darts. I'd play too, but I'd probably miss the dart board and stab somebody.

Cameron and I talk about video games his brother would like, and I say I have a bunch he can borrow. Books and movies too. It seems like I have everything, but I lost what matters the most. My mom and dad, Nana, maybe Luna.

I'm beginning to think I'm only somebody Luna knows, somebody she's going to leave behind and forget about quickly. Why shouldn't she? She doesn't even call her parents much.

Cameron's still talking about his brother.

"I don't know him anymore," Cameron says. "He was a little kid when our parents died and I enlisted." He takes a long drink. "After I was injured, I thought my life was over. The pain totally consumed me, and my aunt said he needed to be in a stable environment. She was right at the time, but now I need to reconnect with my brother. He can go back to my aunt's house if he doesn't want to live with me."

I admit, if my mother and father showed up right now and asked me to go with them, I would, not knowing if I'd be jumping into a frying pan. I wouldn't have gone with either of them a month or two ago. Plus, Nana or Joe would've stopped me.

"Your brother's really lucky," I say. "Really lucky."

Cameron laughs, but for the first time I notice he has tears in his eyes. "My brother thinks I'm some sort of hero. I'm not. I was at the wrong place at the wrong time."

"Why did you enlist?"

He takes a drink. "It seemed like a good idea at the time. It was going to be my career. I wanted to save the world."

And now he's going to be working at a pet store, maybe for the rest of his life. I think it would be great to work at a pet store, but not the kind that sells puppies.

"How's Luna?" Cameron asks.

"I see her sometimes," I say. "And I asked her to come

tonight, but she's painting. She's moving to Florida or Texas soon."

"I saw her one day," he says. "I had to have some blood drawn, and she was in the lab waiting room. She only said she was waiting for a friend, but after I had my blood drawn, I heard her name called."

I shrug. "She's a private person," I say. "It took a while before she'd talk to me about anything but my body."

"Your body?"

"You know, stuff like 'How's your temperature?' She was my personal assistant then, so we really don't have a close relationship."

Cameron's shaking his head.

"I said that the wrong way," I say.

"You didn't, actually. It's just weird," Cameron says. "Don't worry. One of these days you'll meet somebody else and fall in love. My mother and father didn't meet and get married until they were in their thirties."

I nod and smile. He could've given me advice instead of telling me to meet someone else. I don't want to meet someone else. It's painful when you know it'll end.

CHAPTER 26

Sunday I go into the study and get back to writing the thank-you cards. That way I won't daydream about Luna. If I started a list of things that are dangerous, I'd put her name on it.

It takes me an hour to finish the thank-you cards, and I'm relieved.

I pick up the letter from the detective and read it again.

I have more questions than answers. What did Joe say to Stanley? Did he contact Carlee? Did Stanley meet with Carlee? Did she ask about me first? Did Carlee say anything about my dad? Why didn't Joe give me details? Why did she change her name? Why don't I just find out for myself?

I Google the address of the detective. His office is not far from the town square. I also Google Ruby's address.

The next morning I swim early, get dressed for the day, and head downstairs. I go into the study and get a pad of paper and a pen. I write a note.

"I'm going out," I tell Veronica.

"Did you finish the thank-you notes?"

She's sounding like Nana. "I have," I say and hold them up. "I'm taking then to the post office."

This is my good excuse to do some investigating.

"Good," she says. "You even have stamps on the cards."

I found them when I was snooping.

"You're learning," she says.

"Yes, ma'am," I say.

✦ ✦ ✦

Luckily, the post office is on Waterly Square, and STP Investigations is inside an old house less than a quarter mile from the square.

I drop the thank-you cards in an outside mailbox at the post office and head to STP. I pull into the driveway of the agency and park behind a black van. Getting out of the car, I hear dogs barking and then see three little mutts at the back fence.

A bell chimes when I walk in. Nobody's in the front room. I see a desk, a computer, a pot of coffee, and a bouquet of dead roses.

A man comes into the room. He's wearing shorts and a T-shirt. "Hello," he says, sticking out a hand for me to shake. I'm not big on handshakes, but I do it anyway.

"I'm Stanley Peacock," he says.

"Hi, I'm David Hart."

"I recognize you," he says. "I had a feeling you'd show up here one day."

"I wanted to ask a few questions about Carlee Hart."

"That information is confidential."

"I have the right to know," I say, not feeling like a helpless kid for once. "And I've been searching for her and my father for most of my life. Why should it matter what you tell me at this point? Joe's fired you, right?"

"He said he didn't need my services any longer."

"I might," I say. "Not today or tomorrow but one day. I'm not giving up on finding my parents."

"I told Joe all I could find out." Stanley opens a desk drawer. "I only know she's getting married from checking her trash." He hands me a wedding invitation, torn halfway down the middle. "She evidently threw this one away because of its condition. Somebody probably used a knife to open the box."

I start taking notes. "But you talked to her and said Joe was looking for her?"

"She said she didn't want any contact with Joe, Mrs. Hart, or you."

"Can I keep the wedding invitation?" I ask.

"Suppose so. Joe didn't want it."

"Have you ever found out anything about my father, James Hart?"

"No. Joe asked me to stop after Mrs. Hart died," Stanley says. "I think he had to have changed his name too, or he's deceased."

"After James Hart disappeared, a detective was hired to look for him," I say. "Was it you?"

"I'm not that old. My dad could've been hired, but some of his files are gone. When he died, my mother got rid of everything she thought was unimportant," he says. "But I do have a newspaper article from five years ago. I emailed Joe a copy." He opens the folder and pulls out a yellowed paper.

It's a newspaper article in the *Pine Branch Gazette* from five years ago.

"I've searched online," I say. "Never found anything."

"The newspaper folded," he says. "A neighbor had initially reported him missing. She called your grandmother a few years ago asking if she'd heard from him. Your grandmother gave Joe her number, and I followed up."

I read the article.

Police are asking for help in finding James Hart, a local man reported missing. Sam Tink, manager of Blue Water Apartments, remembers last seeing Hart around 8 a.m. a week ago. "He had his head down and was getting into his car, but that wasn't unusual. I rarely saw him unless he was paying his rent, and he always paid a couple of months in advance. He took frequent trips."

"There is no evidence of foul play," an investigator said. "We checked Hart's apartment, and it appears he had moved. He is an adult, and deciding to move or disappear is not a crime."

At the end of the article is a phone number for anyone with information to call. I scribble down *Pine Branch*, *Blue Water*, and *Sam Tink*.

If I disappeared, people would say, he went swimming as usual. He stayed out of the sun. He was related to Dracula. He was a dummy. There were no calls on his cell phone. He ate, played video games, and went to bed.

He wasn't depressed. He was awkward. He was happy. He was concerned. He didn't care about anything. He was a daredevil. He was always careful. He wouldn't hurt himself. He'd hurt himself without knowing it. He resented his grandmother for driving him crazy.

"I called the number," Stanley says. "The investigation was closed. I also called Sam Tink at the Blue Water Apartments. He didn't recall anything new. Nor did Evelyn Winters, the neighbor who reported James missing."

I run my finger down the wedding invitation. "Did you go see Sam Tink or Evelyn Winters?"

"No," he says. "Evelyn Winters asked not to be bothered anymore."

Looks like I'm going on a road trip this weekend. I add her name to my list. "Did you find out anything else?"

"I talked to a cousin of your grandmother's, but she said she didn't know anything."

That would be Ruby. I'm going there anyway, but I don't plan on talking to her.

✚ ✚ ✚

I crank the car. I bet Ruby would have some answers if I could get the courage up to talk to her, but I have a feeling she wouldn't tell me anything. She hates me. I'm not going to think about her. It takes too much energy, and my brain's running low on adrenaline.

I remember a joke I heard once.

How many golden retrievers does it take to change a lightbulb?

The sun is up, the sky is blue, and you're worrying about changing a lightbulb when there's grass to roll around in?

I don't want to do this. It's a great day, and I have plans to make.

✚ ✚ ✚

An hour later, I stop in front of a yellow house with a matching picket fence. The curtains are closed, and the driveway's empty. I'm scared to get out of the car so I wait for a few minutes. Then I grab the paper with the note I'd written earlier.

I take a deep breath and get out of the car. I stand facing the house, and I wonder if anybody's watching me.

I ring the doorbell. One time. Two times. Finally the door inches open, but I can't see much. A chain lock keeps the door from opening all the way.

"I don't want to talk to you," Ruby says.

I try to hand her the note. She starts to shut the door. At the same time, my fingers get stuck in the door frame. I push the door a little and move my hand.

Ruby slams the door shut.

"I'm going," I call out. "I won't bother you again." I stick the note into the door frame. I should've done that in the first place.

My finger looks okay. It's not bleeding. It kills me inside that she shut the door on my fingers on purpose.

When I look up, I see a police vehicle pulling up behind my car. Holy crap. I walk to the curb.

"You're not allowed to park on the street," he says.

I didn't know that. "Sorry," I say. "I didn't see a sign." My voice cracks.

He points to one that's leaning backward like somebody ran over it. He asks to see my license, registration, and proof of insurance.

I get the stuff out of the glove compartment and show him my license. I figure it must be really hot because he's sweating.

"Wait in the car," he says.

I clear my throat. "I have a condition," I say. "And because of it, I get heat stroke quickly. Can I turn on the air conditioner?"

"No."

I used to have a medical alert bracelet, but there was no reason to wear it when I didn't go anywhere.

He goes back to his car.

I look around and toward the house. Somebody's looking out the window. I'm pretty sure I made a big mistake, and Ruby called the police.

Joe was right about my bad judgment.

Three people are standing on the corner looking this way. I stare straight ahead and wish I could disappear. If Joe finds out about this, I'll have a strike against me. I'm not sure what I did that was so bad. It's not like I'm stalking her or anything. I bet nothing like this would ever happen to Spencer or Luna or Joe.

The officer returns.

"I'm not going to give you a ticket this time, but I better not catch you parking on the street again."

"Thank you," I say. Thank goodness I can't cry.

"Don't come back here."

Why would he say that if Ruby hadn't called the police?

"I won't." I don't need to come here again. I crank the motor and turn on the air. As I'm pulling away, the officer heads toward Ruby's front door. Now I'm glad I came. I think I have closure. I think about what I'd written to Ruby.

I'm sorry I hurt your grandson.

✚ ✚ ✚

When I get home, Veronica's mopping the kitchen. You'd think the floor would stay clean with hardly anybody walking on it. She stops what she's doing and tells me not to track up the wet floor.

For some reason I need to tell somebody what happened.

"I'm sorry," she says. "I understand, but Ruby's as hardheaded as a concrete block. Your grandmother tried to talk to her a couple of times a long time ago, but Ruby gave her a piece of her mind. She's unforgiving."

"What'd she say?"

"I wasn't there." Veronica squeezes dirty water from the mop into a bucket. "What happened to your finger?"

I tell her, and she makes a splint for my finger from a tongue blade and gauze. "You're up to something," she says at last. "You know you can tell me."

"And you know because I went to see Ruby?"

Veronica shakes her head. "You left the directions open on your laptop to the detective's office." She washes her hands. "I'll drop your suit off at the cleaners on the way home." She wipes her hands with a paper towel. "Just in case you need it."

CHAPTER 27

I'm sitting on the deck with Veronica, which is something I've never done. She tells me that they're still renovating her house, and it will go up for sale soon. She is loving how the house has shaped up. "I wish we could take the house with us," she says. "It's my dream home now."

"It wasn't before?"

"The rooms were pink, and the yard was dirt and weeds. I finally have sod in the front yard. I've always wanted sod, but we could never afford it."

"Don't move," I say. "There'll never be another you."

"You can visit us whenever you want to," she says. "We'll take you fishing."

"I've never been fishing," I say.

"I know."

"I'm taking a road trip," I say.

"If you have to go, I'm not stopping you," she says. "The number one thing you need is life experience, but I'd feel better if you had somebody to go with you."

"I can ask somebody," I say.

"Good."

"You'll be here when I get back?"

"Of course."

Joe sends me a text message.

How is everything?

Fine. I'm about to go swimming.

Who's there?

Veronica. Don't worry about me.

I shut off my phone. "Joe?" Veronica asks me.

"Yeah."

"You tell him?"

"No. He'd stop me. He's been threatening to send me away."

"He won't." She looks down. "I'll have to answer any question he asks me."

I nod. I won't tell her anything else. I'll leave in two days. I'll pack the car on Thursday night and sneak away on Friday. Veronica won't even know I'm gone if I do the usual. She'll think I'm playing video games when it's time for her to go home. She'll figure it out Saturday, and she'll have to call Joe. He may fire her.

"Go swimming," Veronica says. "Neither of us can be out here all day. I've got work to do."

I jump into the pool. It's a perfect day, and the water feels great. I swim lap after lap thinking I'm finally doing something, and I'm excited.

✚ ✚ ✚

"What's this?" I ask Veronica, picking up a package on the kitchen table. It has my name on it.

"It was on the porch this morning."

I open the package and take out a gold necklace in the shape of a sideways eight. The words *Best Friends* run through the eight.

"Who's it from?" Veronica asks.

"I don't know."

"That's an infinity necklace," she says. "If I had to guess, I'd say it is from Luna. She must've dropped it off when we were on the deck. You should thank her."

I spin around and hurry to my room.

Luna answers on the first ring. "Thank you," I say.

"You're welcome."

"I thought we could get together before you leave," I say. "I'll be leaving on Friday. I have information about my mom and dad."

"I'll come over tonight."

"I'll pick up a pizza."

"No onions," she says.

"See you later," I say.

"Around seven," she says.

Then I go into the bathroom and apply a dry bandage and new splint to my finger. It looks fine except the nail has fallen off.

I get busy with more important stuff. Dirty clothes are strewn all over the floor, and I can barely find a place to step without getting tangled up. I start picking up clothes and throwing them into a basket. I take the overfilled basket to the basement, throw the clothes into the washing machine, and add detergent. I twist the knob to start.

I'll be all set to pack later, and my room won't be dirty if Luna and I play video games or something.

Then I finish cleaning my room, dry my clothes and fold them, and play video games. I listen for the sound of Luna's car, although she's not coming for hours.

At five p.m., I drive to Nate's Pizza and get dinner for Luna and me. It's great not having to ask if I can go somewhere and do something. It's great doing stuff by myself. It's great when a girl you really like is coming to dinner. Maybe I should've gotten something better like steaks to grill. I've never grilled anything before, but I don't have any worries.

On the way back, I stop at Spencer's. Luna's not coming over until seven. I probably should've waited to get pizza.

Spencer's in the driveway, standing next to a pile of lumber. "Hey," he says. His face is red, and he's sweating. "How's it going?"

"I have a date with Luna tonight," I say. I love times when everything is going right. Not like when Ruby called the police. That was wrong.

"Where are you going?" he asks.

"I picked up a pizza, and we're going to have dinner and talk."

"About what?"

"I'm not sure," I say.

"Sounds like lots of fun," he says in a deadpan voice. "Never done that."

"Never done what?"

"Had pizza alone with a girl in my house. Talk."

Then I ask him if he wants to take a road trip this

weekend. "I found my mother," I say. "I'm going to meet her."

He can't. He has to help his dad. "How about next weekend?"

"Maybe," I say. But I can't go then. Joe will be back from Belize. "I have information about my dad I'm going to check out on the way back."

Spencer's dad comes out from the garage and says hello to me. He tells Spencer to get back to work.

"We're building a screened-in porch, and my dad wants this finished in a week for the open house my mom's planning. She's already made flyers advertising the business and inviting the public to stop by."

"Why?"

"She's expanding the business and hiring a couple of preschool teachers. Want to carry some stuff to the garage for me?"

I guess I can do that. It's only five minutes after six.

Spencer heaves a couple of pieces of lumber onto his shoulder. Carrying a gallon of yellow paint and a bag, I follow. At a blooming rosebush, he turns around. The wood smacks me on the side of the head. I fall into the rosebush.

Spencer drops the lumber and rushes over to me. "I'm sorry! I didn't realize you were right behind me." He sticks out his hand, and I grab on to it. He pulls me out of the rosebush.

I look away. "It's my fault. I wasn't paying attention." I touch the side of my head and don't feel blood. "I'm not hurt."

That's the story of my life. I'm not hurt.

Spencer touches the side of my head. "You don't have a

lump, and there's no bruising." He examines my arms. Both have scratches and are bleeding from the thorns. "Come inside and wash the scratches."

"I'll do it at home," I say. A few scratches are nothing. I take the paint into the garage and set it against the wall.

Six gallons later I'm done.

"Thank you," Spencer says, placing the last two-by-four against the wall.

"It's nothing," I say.

He looks at my hand. "What happened to your finger?"

"It got caught in a door when I wasn't paying attention or thinking."

Spencer's shaking his head. "What's there to think about?"

I shrug. "It could happen to anybody," I say. "Anybody. It doesn't have anything to do with being painless. Remember that time you got your hand stuck in a car door? All you did was scream like a baby. When I got my hand stuck in the door, I just pushed it open."

"You shut the door on my hand."

"That was when we were kids," I say. "And I was sorry as soon as you started screaming."

When I pull into the drive at my house, Luna's about to drive away. I turn off the motor and go over to her car. She opens her car door and gets out, the motor still running.

CHAPTER 28

"Sorry I'm late," I say. The thing is, I'm not late. She's a half hour early.

"I'm not staying," she says. "Do you remember Derek?"

I shake my head. "I never heard of him."

"He's my ex-boyfriend from Texas. He's in town. He wants to have dinner, and I think I should go."

"You still care?"

"I'll always care, but the thing is, I don't want to regret not seeing him. I might always wonder about what might have been."

"Okay," I say. "I get it."

"What do you get?"

I turn my head so I'm not looking her straight in the eyes. "I get to eat the whole pizza," I say. "And you'll probably be late if you don't go right away." I'm not going to look at her. No way. I can't cry, but my face would scream, *I care*.

There's no point in letting someone see you care when they don't.

"We can get together another night," she says. "What about Friday?"

"I'm leaving Friday," I say.

"Sorry. I forgot. What about tomorrow night?"

"I can't. I'm tired of being an afterthought."

"Okay," she says. "Be that way." She gets into her car, shuts the door, and drives away.

I get the pizza out of the car. It's probably cold anyway.

On the front door I find a note. I take it and go inside, slamming the door behind me. I sit on the floor for a moment holding the pizza in my lap and the note in my hand. I read it.

Sorry I'm leaving a note, but I can't stay. It wouldn't be right. Please understand and don't be mad.

Don't be mad. Why would I be mad about Luna not wanting to stay? *Hurt's* the right word. Hurt like a hand slammed in a car door and you scream from the pain.

But I get the part about it "wouldn't be right." We're different. She'll probably live to be old and gray with children and grandchildren. I won't.

I came close to almost having a girlfriend once. Spencer had fixed me up with a girl from his school, but then she backed out. I think somebody told her that I couldn't feel pain.

I tear the note into small pieces. Then I tear the small pieces into tiny ones and drop them onto the kitchen counter. I know how to protect my body, but this is the only way I know to protect my heart. I can't breathe too well. We had fun, I think.

I go into the bathroom, and my mouth falls open when a see a streak of blood running down the side of my head. If it wasn't for the blood, I'd look normal. I wash it away.

I pick up the pieces of the note and stick them into a drawer in my bedroom. Part of me, maybe all of me, cares, and I want to keep the note as a reminder of pain.

CHAPTER 29

My body temperature is a hundred when I wake up. I'm feeling lousy, but I can't find anything wrong with me on the outside. My smashed finger is swollen, but there's no sign of infection. Heck, the door didn't even break the skin. And my head just has a couple of scratches.

I head downstairs, and then Veronica calls. She'll be late. She has a doctor's appointment this morning.

At nine o'clock I go into the kitchen and eat a banana.

At nine thirty Joe calls, and I say I'm fine.

Yesterday he went scuba diving.

I'd like to go scuba diving. I get choked up. I have to calm down. Shutting my eyes, I imagine Luna's next to me, and we're on a beach in the Caribbean sitting at a table under a palm tree. Then we're scuba diving. I open my eyes. This isn't the time for dreaming. I have to make it through this conversation. I take a deep breath. "Sounds fun," I say.

Today he's going hiking.

I clear my throat. "Good thing I'm not there," I say. It kind of hurts to know he didn't want me to go with him. I would've said no, but he could've asked.

"What do you mean?"

I probably should hang up before I explode. "I'd have to stay behind, and I'd be bored. I've got a new game I'm going to play. It's called *Devastation*."

I'm a liar too. Maybe I am stupid. Maybe I am a loser, and I don't know it because I don't know what normal is.

"I don't want you to be upset," he says. "I've been talking to friends, and they run a boarding school in New York. They'd like for us to visit. It would be a great opportunity for you."

Opportunity for what? "No thanks. I finished high school already."

"Why don't you give anything a chance?"

"So you're saying I should give my mother a chance?"

"No. I don't know why you want to bring her up. She was a lousy mother and doesn't deserve you."

"I have to know more," I say.

"Listen, David, don't do anything until I get back."

"It's my life," I say and disconnect.

I'm going to have an awesome time playing video games and watching TV, and playing video games and watching TV...Maybe I'll check and see if Scruffy wants to go swimming. Ha-ha. My best friend these days is a dog that's not even my dog. I rest my head on the table.

I hate being alone.

At eleven o'clock, I lie on the couch and watch TV. After about a half hour, my neck feels sore. I sit up and move my head around. It's weird that I wouldn't feel my throat getting cut, but I can feel sore.

Veronica calls as the TV judge is making her decision, but it's not Veronica.

"Hi. This is Ed," the person who is not Veronica says. "Veronica's husband. She was having belly pain all night," he says. "We thought it was either gas or a virus." I hear him take a deep breath. "She has an aneurysm. She's having surgery."

Suddenly I'm reliving the moment when I woke up and found Nana dead. I start breathing fast. I can't say anything. I know what an aneurysm is. It occurs when a blood vessel is weak. If the blood vessel ruptures, it's a dire emergency.

Ed continues. "The doctor said she'll do well. He found the aneurysm in time. Afterward she'll be in the ICU for a couple of days. She said to tell you to have a great time in North Carolina and to take care of yourself. She'll be back to work before you know it."

I hate it when somebody tells me something because they might die.

"Can I see her after the surgery?" I ask.

"She won't be allowed visitors, and she needs to rest."

That's what I figured. "Tell her I'll be fine, and I'll see her soon."

Then I try to call Joe, but I can't get through. The only reason I'm calling is because I don't want to piss him off any more than he already will be.

I'm supposed to head to my mother's wedding tomorrow. It won't be long until I'm cruising down the highway, windows open, road-trip music playing. Or maybe not.

I don't know if I can do it.

I decide I'll go to the bookstore and buy a road-trip CD.

What I'll do on Friday is drive a few miles listening to the music. I can turn back anytime I want to.

✚ ✚ ✚

I walk out of the bookstore, and it's storming. Standing under the roof, I press my body up against the building along with a couple having an argument. She's yelling at him about text messages she found on his phone. I know that voice.

Cassandra.

The guy walks off.

Cassandra calls her mom and asks for a ride. Next she calls her dad. Apparently, they both have said no. She just stands leaning against the wall. So what if she has to walk home? Why should I care? I don't.

I hear her sniffing. She either has a cold or she's crying.

As an expert at getting left behind, ignored, and dumped, I feel sorry for her.

"Hey, Cassandra," I say. "You need a ride?"

She glances my way. "Sure," she says.

So I take enough money out of my wallet for cab fare, give it to her, walk into the pouring rain, and keep going.

✚ ✚ ✚

I read *The Alchemist* for a while. It's about a boy following his dream of seeing the world. He's afraid of suffering, but he's told that the fear of suffering is worse than the suffering.

I watch TV and get interested in a missing person and forensic program. You wouldn't believe what some people do for love or money. They lie, cheat, steal, and murder. And you wouldn't believe how many people disappear and are never found. I do. My dad is one of them.

I check Facebook and read the Waterly High School page. They talk about who died during high school, who got married, and who hung out at the Tasty Cone. I don't have any of those memories because I never went to high school or to the cone place.

I think about my bucket list, how I may never have another opportunity to meet my mother or search for my dad, and how time's running out. If I am extremely lucky, I have a few years left in me, but I can't count on that.

I'll drive to my mother's wedding. Joe will return from Belize, walk into the house, and figure out I'm gone. He'll call my cell, and for once, he'll be the one who doesn't get an answer because I won't want to talk to him when he's going to be mad at me. It'll make me sad because I've known him longer than I knew my parents.

My mother will be overcome with joy when she sees me. We'll celebrate, and I'll forget about everybody here.

She'll tell me about me, and she'll ask me to stay.

But I won't.

Then I'll go see Sam Tink in Pine Branch.

✚ ✚ ✚

Around dinnertime, Cameron and Scruffy arrive with tacos. "I was afraid you'd be stuck here without anybody checking on you," Cameron says.

"I don't need anybody checking on me, but it's great to see you," I say, sounding way too happy about him coming over. "I'll get plates and drinks." I head to the kitchen and Cameron follows.

He's right. I am stuck here, and I should stay in contact with people too. It's like I've disappeared into the walls of this house. I don't want this. Nana would tell me to put on my blue shoes and dance. Joe would tell me to walk away from my mother, but what does he know? He doesn't have anybody, and he doesn't care. Joe's got a good reason to keep me from meeting my mother. He controls the money.

Most of my life I've dreamed of making my mother and father sorry they got rid of me—not with revenge or anything like that. More like *I'll show you I never needed you.*

"I heard Luna stood you up," Cameron says when we go into the living room to eat. I turn on the TV.

"Spencer talks too much," I say.

Cameron unwraps a taco. "When I was in the hospital, my girlfriend sent me a Dear John letter. She said she felt guilty, but it still sucked."

"She deserved to feel guilty," I say. I give him the remote control. "You can pick something out."

He keeps his eyes focused on the TV, channel surfs, and finally stops at a movie. "Have you seen *The Dark Knight*?"

I nod. "It's a great movie."

"The Joker's the greatest villain ever," Cameron says.

"He blew me away. How did he get the scars?" I ask. "He told different stories."

"Nobody really knows." Cameron is only kind of watching the TV. "But maybe he did it to himself to show the world how much pain he could take."

I look down at my arms. I bet the Joker is really scarred on the inside.

CHAPTER 30

I jump out of bed, fling open my closet door, and start throwing clothes onto the bed. My suit, dress pants, a couple of shirts, shorts, my black shoes, and my guitar. I take anything I might need. By nine a.m., the car's loaded.

And I call Luna. I need to say good-bye.

Luna's voice is groggy when she answers her phone. "This is David," I say. "I'm leaving in a few minutes. I wanted to say good-bye."

"You're really going to meet your mother?"

"I'm going to her wedding, and then I'm following up on a lead from a detective about my dad."

"Have you lost your mind?" she says.

"Yeah," I say. "Remember? It's on my bucket list to find out about my parents."

"The bucket list," she says. "When and where is the wedding?"

"Tomorrow evening at six. It's about an eight-hour

drive. And then on Sunday I'll be headed to check out my dad."

"When are you coming back?"

"Sunday evening or Monday."

"I hope everything works out for you," she says.

"A detective gave me the invitation to my mother's wedding. He found it in her garbage."

Luna laughs. "I'd love to be a fly on the wall when she sees you."

"Come with me," I say. "We can go as friends. Nothing more. We'll have separate rooms. I won't even hold your hand."

"I'd go, but you have to believe me when I say I can't."

"You have free will," I say.

"Not with this," she says. "Good-bye, David. It was great most of the time."

I get into the car wondering what's going on with Luna.

She's marrying Derek.

She's pregnant.

She's saying no in the nicest way possible because she doesn't connect with me.

I take deep breaths. All those times I was in the hospital because of CIPA, I never gave up. I never even thought about giving up. Sure, I was not in pain, but I've learned there are other ways to suffer without it.

Okay, David, I tell myself. Pretend this is a game. You're in the woods and you don't know which way to go.

It's like that part of my video game where Davy and Tyler have to make it through the woods to a tower and rescue the princess to restore order in the village, only I don't have friends or a princess to rescue.

I feel like I'm going to stagnate and start growing mold if I don't do something.

I have to do this.

Besides, if my plan explodes I'll still be able to sit on the beach for a while. I'll play my guitar. It'll be almost like home where there's no one around to hear me.

✦ ✦ ✦

I stop at Spencer's house and walk to the garage. He's got paint on his face and arms. "What's going on?" he asks.

"I'm going to my mother's wedding. I wanted you to know where I'll be."

"What about Joe?"

I shake my head. "I didn't tell him. He'd talk me out of going."

"Why now, David? Why not wait a week? I can go with you in a week."

"Joe would stop me."

"I'll explain everything to Joe if you want me to. He only wants to make sure he's doing what's best for you, but he doesn't know what to do," Spencer says. "But I'm glad you're giving this your best shot. Good luck."

✦ ✦ ✦

I go to the bank, and I stop for gas. Then I go into the store and buy an energy drink and chips. As I'm waiting in line, I see a kid who used to be on my grandfather's soccer team. Once in a while I'd go to their pizza parties.

"Hey, Wyatt," I say.

He looks at me and says hello. He asks about my grandfather, and I say he passed away. "He used to say you were the best goalie he ever coached."

"He was a great coach." Wyatt sets a twelve-pack of beer on the counter.

"I didn't know you were twenty-one already," I say.

The clerk asks him for his ID.

He pulls one out and gives it to the clerk.

"I thought your name was Wyatt," the clerk says.

"I hope you die," Wyatt says to me.

That's all right. Just because I'm off to a bad start, it isn't an omen that this trip is going to suck. If luck's based on breathing, I'm doing pretty okay. The worst thing that ever happened to me is going to become the best thing, and this kid doesn't rank in the top thousand of bad things that have happened to me.

I slide behind the steering wheel and fasten my seat belt. My cell phone rings.

"Can you stop by here before you leave?" Luna asks. "I can't say good-bye in a telephone call."

When I get to Luna's duplex, I see her sitting on her porch with a backpack. Her car's gone. I get out of my car and meet her halfway.

She touches the necklace around my neck. "You're wearing the necklace," she says.

"Yeah." I've been wearing it since the day she gave it to me. "I never gave you anything." I wish I would've given her something to remember me by.

"You're kidding," she says. "You rescued me tons of times."

"Not tons," I say. "Maybe two. Where's your car?"

"I donated it."

"Why?"

"I don't need it," she says. "I won't be needing it."

"Flying's better," I say. "Where did you decide to go?"

"Texas."

"I'll miss you," I say.

She looks away. "You're staying in a hotel tonight?"

"Yes."

"Did you make reservations?"

"No."

"You should've. Drive carefully, okay?"

"Come with me. You don't have to leave today."

"I can't," Luna says.

"You're leaving because of Derek?"

"I don't have a choice," she says.

"A couple of days won't make a difference. It's not like an asteroid is going to destroy the earth right away."

A cab pulls up in front of her house. Luna gives me a kiss. It's the first time I've really kissed her. Then she walks to the cab and gets in. I climb into my car and rest my head on the steering wheel.

There's a knock on my window, and I look. I see Luna and roll down the window.

"I hate you," she says. "I hate you for making me want to go with you. I hate you for making this harder."

"You called me," I say.

"You should've kept going. Will you be back before Tuesday?" she asks. "Are you absolutely sure you'll be back?"

"Yes."

"Promise?"

"I promise."

"Then I'll come with you as long as you understand that after this weekend, I probably won't see you again."

I'll think about that on Monday.

PART THREE

CHAPTER 31

I back out onto the road. "Will you be in trouble for not showing up today?"

"I'll call my mom," Luna says and punches a number into her cell phone.

"Hey, Mom. I've changed my plans. I'm taking a road trip with David…Okay. That sounds great…I'll meet you Tuesday morning…I will…Love you too." Luna sighs.

"Is she mad?" I ask.

"No. She told me to have a good time."

"She thinks you still work for me?"

"No. Are you going to get into trouble?"

"Probably. I didn't tell Joe I was leaving." I don't ask her anything about Tuesday. The days before are more important.

"Is it worth getting sent away?" she asks.

"It is now," I say.

Luna shuts her eyes and yawns, and we're not even out of the city limits yet.

"Want to listen to a road-trip CD?" I ask.

"Okay."

"It's in the console." I tell her how I went to the bookstore, heard Cassandra and her boyfriend arguing, and how he left her on the sidewalk when it was storming.

"You took her home?" Luna asks.

"No. I gave her cab fare."

"That would be embarrassing to her, I think," Luna says.

"It was late. My license restricts me from driving after midnight."

"So you're going to this wedding to get back at your mother?"

"Well, I don't want her to remember me as a disease," I say. "I want to show her I'm better off without her, and I'm more than all right." It only took me eighteen years to get where I am.

"Just don't expect anything from your mom." Luna slips in the CD. "Born to be Wild" starts.

"I don't."

"We can have fun doing other stuff."

She starts singing. By the time I turn onto the interstate heading north, we're singing together, and the windows are down.

"Your eyes are different," Luna says when the song ends.

"Bloodshot?" I ask. I turn the mirror and glance at my eyes for two seconds.

"Bright like you're happy."

"I am."

"Me too, except for one thing. I didn't bring anything to wear to a wedding."

"We'll stop somewhere," I say.

"Goodwill," she says.

It's a good day for driving. The sun shines bright in the morning sky, and there isn't much traffic.

"I'll reserve a couple of rooms," Luna says. "After we get there, you may have a problem because of your age."

I get my wallet from my pocket. "Use my bank card," I say. "There are maps in the console with the route we're following. Try to find a five-star hotel. Get a penthouse if you want to."

Luna starts searching on her phone. After a while I ask if she's having trouble finding something. "I'm reading reviews," she says.

She spends the next hour reading. I keep driving north on the interstate. I drive the speed limit except when someone is merging onto the highway, and then I slow down. There isn't much traffic, and it's interstate all the way. Along the side all I see are signs, trees, and exits to places I've never heard of. A car museum, campgrounds, a lake. I drive over a suspension bridge about a mile long. Below are water and boats.

"I found one," Luna says. "It has a restaurant, pool, and Internet access."

"Okay," I say.

Pretty soon I see a sign to an outlet mall at the next exit in a few miles, and I ask Luna if we should stop there.

"Let me check," she says.

A few minutes later we're inside the mall and at a

shop with racks of prom and pageant dresses. I watch her as she searches through the rack of gently worn dresses. She carries several into a dressing room and returns a few minutes later with a short, black dress. The neckline is low cut. It's on sale for twenty-five dollars.

"Are you sure black is a good color for a wedding?" I ask.

"Nobody will know me," she says. "Will I embarrass you?"

"Never," I say. "You can wear whatever you want to wear."

"I want to do something I've never done before," Luna says, looking over at a rack of shoes. She picks out black three-inch-high heels and tries them on.

I look up her body from the heels and meet her eyes.

"They match the dress," is all I know to say. I can't say she reminds me of Miss March from an old *Playboy* magazine.

"Is it too much?" she asks.

"No," I say.

Outside I open the trunk. She gently places the dress across the bags and turns to me. "Want me to drive?"

"Why don't you look up information on the town?"

Back on the interstate, she tells me it's a barrier island. "Average high temperature in June is eighty degrees, and the average low is sixty-five." She looks at me. "It's perfect."

"Good."

"It's believed that Blackbeard hid his treasure there. The island is only twenty miles long, and it's a sea turtle sanctuary. Most of the island is privately owned. There is a forest preserve. The only access is by one bridge. Visitors are limited."

My stomach drops. "Not good."

"Don't worry," she says. "We have the wedding invitation, don't we?"

I nod. "Are you a good swimmer?" I ask with a grin.

She sets her phone on the console.

"Since this is theoretically the last time we'll ever do anything like this, why don't we play truth?" I ask.

"But only one question per category and only three questions total," she says. "And we can refuse to answer. No, I am not a good swimmer, and if you're thinking we'll swim to the island, you're crazy." She sighs. "What are the top three craziest things you've ever done?"

"Three? That's three questions."

She shrugs.

I tell her about the time I lay on the railroad tracks, the time Spencer dared me to jump off a bridge, and the time we tried to stop a robbery.

"I thought you were scared to do anything," she says.

"I was after I jumped off the bridge. I ended up with a collapsed lung and almost died," I say. "Now it's my turn. Have you ever had sex?"

"Yes."

"With who?"

"One question per category," she says. "What's the name of the person you were with the first time you had sex?"

I keep my eyes on the highway. "June," I say after a minute.

"How long did you date her?"

"A few times when I was younger," I say, even though her question falls into the sex category.

"She sounds old," Luna says.

"She was older than me," I say. "Okay, so what do you think you and I will do this weekend?"

"Eat, dance, laugh, swim in the ocean, maybe sleep on the beach." She clears her throat. "And say good-bye when it's over."

Luna didn't mention anything about me meeting my parents. I glance at her. She's looking out the window. I turn my head toward the road and think about how in two or three days we'll be headed in the other direction. Together but separate. We don't say anything for a while.

Finally she rests her head against the window. "I've always wanted to sleep outside where I could hear the ocean," she says.

"I think I'd like sleeping on the beach as long as we don't get arrested."

"When I was fourteen and fifteen, we'd rent a condo on the beach, and I'd sit on the balcony for hours at nighttime."

"No partying?" I ask.

"No. It was in Mexico, and I spent most of my time ·with my parents," she says. "I think I'll take a nap."

I keep driving down the highway, and Luna sleeps. After a while I pull into a service station and fill up the tank. After I move the car, I get out without waking Luna and walk around. It's eighty-five degrees, the air is heavy with humidity, and the sky's cloudy. I hope it's not going to stay this hot and cloudy. I'd like to take a walk on the beach in the sunlight while holding hands with Luna.

I go to the bathroom and then head back. Luna's getting out of the car.

"Are you hungry?" I ask.

"Not yet," she says. "I need to pee."

I nod, get into the car, and turn on the air. Looking at the road map, I figure we still have four more hours to go. We've been on the road for four hours, but we spent an hour at the outlet mall. Still, we have plenty of time before it gets dark. I'm kind of worried about finding the hotel after dark.

Luna returns and doesn't say anything. I get back on the interstate heading north. I've never driven this far or long before, and I'm doing all right. Of course, all I have to do is drive straight and watch out for the big rigs and cars passing us.

It's mid-afternoon when I pull into a truck stop and park in front of the restaurant. Luna gets out, yawns, and stretches.

"Hungry yet?" I ask from the other side of the car.

Luna looks over at me and smiles. "I am, actually," she says.

We go inside the restaurant and sit by a window. I smell grease and onions. Even though it's late for lunch, the place is half full. There's a counter with a half-dozen people sitting on stools. A chalkboard has "liver 'n onions" or "chiken 'n dumplins" listed as today's specials. I kind of grin. Somebody doesn't know how to spell. A kid is crying at one of the tables.

The waitress arrives and recites the specials. We order burgers and fries.

I'm wondering where all these people are headed when a guy at the counter stands and yells, "I hate crying kids!"

Everybody turns their heads to look. The woman with the crying kid picks her child up, calls the guy a moron, and goes outside.

"We should get a T-shirt while we're here," Luna says, nodding toward a rack of clothes near the entrance.

"Okay." I need one that says, "I drove five hours and ended up with a cheap T-shirt."

As we're eating, I watch out the smudged window and see a guy with a backpack tie a dog to a post. The dog is big and skinny with its ribs showing. The guy comes inside the restaurant and looks around. He has long, scraggly hair and rumpled clothes. He snatches leftover food from the table where the crying kid was sitting.

The waitress watches, but she doesn't say anything. He goes back outside, gives part of the food to the dog, and starts eating the rest. I get up, go outside, and hand him a few dollars.

"Thanks," he says. He has a sign with "Dosta" written on it.

"Where's Dosta?" I ask.

"A couple of hours northwest."

I go back inside.

"You gave him money?" Luna says.

I nod. "He needs a ride to Dosta," I say.

"You offered?"

"No. We're not going his way."

"Have you ever picked up a hitchhiker?" she asks, watching out the window.

I don't look. I don't like seeing sad stuff. "No. Have you?"

"No," she says.

"It's out of the way," I say. It's a dumb thing to do. I'd

probably give him a ride if Luna wasn't with me.

We buy T-shirts and pay the cashier. I leave the waitress a nice tip only because if I had her job, I'd like to get a nice tip as a surprise. Besides, it makes me happy.

I pull onto the road and avoid looking in the guy's direction. He could be a thief or a killer or just somebody with a dog. He can't take a bus when he has a dog, but I bet that dog has mange or something.

I pull onto the interstate. Luna's reading, and I'm thinking how miserable the skinny dog looked. Probably still starving. It's not his fault he's on the side of the road with a guy who's a loser. I'm not going to think about the guy and the dog.

Here's what's going to happen when I go to my mother's wedding.

I'll watch her go down the aisle. She'll be looking at people and smiling. She'll see me and smile the same as she does for everybody else.

Because she's not going to freakin' recognize me.

Then at the reception she'll say hello quickly. Maybe she'll give me a hug and get back to greeting. After all, she's the star, and I have to be prepared for this. I should not expect more, but I'm hoping I have a minute to ask her about my dad.

It's drizzling rain. The windshield wipers make a fast *whack, whack, whack*, and I turn the switch to the low speed. The whacking isn't as bad. I bet the dog and the guy are soaking wet by now.

I see the next exit, and I don't know what comes over me. I move into that lane, stop at the red light, and then turn left. I see the sign for the interstate heading south. I make the left turn, and pretty soon I'm headed in the other direction.

"Are we lost?" Luna asks, sitting up straight.

"We're going back," I say, and the speedometer climbs to seventy.

CHAPTER 32

"Why?" Luna asks.

"Because I have to."

"I'm tired," she says.

"I'm sorry."

I take the exit to the truck stop and slow as I near the corner. I don't see the guy and his skinny dog.

"I thought you meant we were going home," Luna says, leaning forward. "He's on the next corner."

"You're okay with this?" I ask.

"It's your random act of kindness," Luna says. "And it's what I love about you."

I laugh. I don't think she means it the way I want her to mean it.

"And I have mace if he turns out to be a psycho," she says.

I pull into the drive and stop near the gas pumps under the covering. I take a beach towel out of my backpack and cover the backseat with it.

"Hey," I call to the guy. "Hey!"

He turns, looks in my direction, and takes off running toward me. My heart speeds up.

He smiles wide. "Thanks. My name is Eric."

"Hello," I say with caution.

"Where you headed?"

I tell him.

"Great," he says. "Just stay on the interstate and you can drop me off at my exit. That way you won't be going out of the way." He climbs into the backseat with his dog.

I take a deep breath and head back to the highway.

"What's your dog's name?" Luna asks.

"She doesn't have a name. She's a stray," Eric says. "I found her on the side of the highway a couple of days ago. She has a tag on the collar, but the phone number on it had been disconnected."

I decide Eric's okay. "Somebody dumped her," I say.

"Probably. I had her scanned for a microchip, but she didn't have one."

"So what's in Dosta?" Luna asks.

"I grew up there. I haven't been home for five years," he says. "I've been hitchhiking for ten days, but hardly anybody'll pick up a hitchhiker these days."

"So one day you decided to go for a visit, packed a bag, and ended up standing on the side of a highway?" I ask, glancing at him through my rearview mirror.

"My mother had a stroke, and I was short on money, so I decided to hitchhike. I didn't want my parents to think I was a loser by asking for money." He leans forward and tries to return the money I gave him.

"Keep it," I say.

"Give me your address, and I'll pay you back and send gas money."

"Do they know you're coming?" I ask.

"I'm going to surprise them."

"My parents had a fit the first time they visited me after I moved out. They tried to force me to come home," Luna says.

I think her parents have finally won that argument.

"My guardian tried to force me to move into an apartment where I'd be supervised," I say, sounding lame.

"David has a rare disease hardly anybody has heard of," Luna says.

"He looks like he knows what he's doing. Are you two running away?"

"Yeah," Luna says. "For a few days. I have to be on a flight by Tuesday morning."

I don't want to think about then.

"Last weekend together?" Eric says.

"Yes," Luna says. "We'll probably go to the beach."

"I slept on the beach a few times," Eric says.

"You were homeless?" I ask.

"I was a Boy Scout."

"I was a Girl Scout," Luna says. "It was too much like school, and I was always hoping it would get better. Once we went to a cave in Tennessee. We had to crawl through an opening to a large area, but the leader got stuck. I didn't think we'd ever get her out. Then we slept in our sleeping bags all night. The next morning we went home. The most exciting thing that happened was when the leader got stuck."

"I like to be spontaneous," Eric says. "And not have to follow somebody else's schedule."

"This trip was a last-minute decision," Luna says.

Not really. I've been thinking about a trip for days, and I've been dreaming of meeting my parents for years.

"Glad you decided to go," Eric says. "Or I'd still be standing on the corner begging for a ride."

"We almost didn't stop," Luna says.

"My parents would thank you too," Eric says.

"You're going too fast," Luna says to me.

I glance at the speedometer. "I'm not speeding," I say.

Eric leans forward. "My exit's coming up soon," he says. "I can walk the rest of the way."

"No problem," I say.

We drive him all the way home. It's a small ranch-style house in an older neighborhood.

"Give me your address," he reminds me.

I tell him.

He climbs out of the car, the dog behind him. I roll down my window.

"Good luck," I say. I've always hating saying good-bye, even to someone I only knew for a couple of hours.

"Thanks again," he says and heads toward the house with the dog.

I watch for a minute, kind of hoping to see his mother's face when she sees him. The front door opens, somebody hugs him, and he turns and waves to us. He goes inside. I hope he and his dog will be okay.

✚ ✚ ✚

"I like watching people," I tell Luna. "And wondering

what their life is like. When I first saw him on the corner, I thought he was a drug addict or a bum."

"What changed your mind?"

"He had given his food to the dog, and I kept thinking about him."

"One time I was walking along the side of the road with a friend, and we saw a dog lying in a ditch. I remember how he lifted his head and looked at us. I planned to go back and check on him, but I forgot about him until the next day. I went back, but he was gone."

"Somebody else helped him," I say.

"Hopefully. He could've crawled away somewhere."

"And then somebody helped him."

"But I've felt guilty about that," she says. "Whenever I've seen a needy dog."

✦ ✦ ✦

"We're almost at the exit to the hotel," I tell Luna.

"I almost didn't call you," she says. "I almost didn't get out of the cab, but when I saw your head on the steering wheel, I had to."

"I almost decided not to take this trip," I say.

"I would've been at my parents' house by now. We'd be sitting on the sofa watching TV."

"I would've been at home, but I don't know what I'd be doing."

"Alone?" Luna says.

"Spencer and Cameron come over sometimes. It's always been kind of lonely at my house, especially after my grandmother became sicker."

I exit the interstate and then Luna gives me directions

to the hotel. A few minutes later I pull into the parking lot. It's hard for me to believe I've made it this far.

It's hard for me to believe Luna is with me. I keep thinking any minute now I'm going to wake up inside my empty house. In less than twenty-four hours I'll be seeing my mother, and maybe just once, life will be fair and I'll find my dad. I'm not asking for much. I'm not asking for instant love.

I turn off the motor.

Luna sits straight up in the seat. "What do you think?"

"It's nice."

Luna gets her dress from the trunk. I carry our bags.

We enter a huge lobby and step up to the desk. I'm worried we'll have problems because of my age, but we don't. Luna only has to show the confirmation info on her phone.

Our rooms are next to each other. I watch her unlock her door with the plastic card so I'll know how. I get this image of me standing behind a man, and he's unlocking a door. It's something I had forgotten until now. I try to remember more, but I can only see that one image in my head. I concentrate harder trying to figure out who the man was, but I only see the back of his head. His hair was black like my dad's.

I go inside with her and place her bag on a luggage table or whatever it's called. The bed has a bunch of pillows on it, and a big-screen TV welcomes us. A sliding door spans one wall. I open it and step onto the balcony. It overlooks an outdoor area, where people sit at tables eating and drinking. Lanterns hang from trees. It's almost what I imagine a Caribbean paradise would be like.

I check my watch. We've been riding for over eight hours, but the travel was worth it to make it here.

"This is heavenly," Luna says. "Want to have dinner in the courtyard?"

"That sounds good."

"You know what we should do? Dress up. I'll wear the black dress."

"I don't know," I say. The people in the courtyard are dressed casually.

"Nobody knows us here," she says. "Anyway, I want to wear the dress more than once."

"The thing is," I say. "I can wear a shirt and tie, but I probably shouldn't wear a jacket."

"Heatstroke?" she says.

"Yep."

Coma or death by jacket.

"Bring it with you and wear it for our pictures," she says.

✦ ✦ ✦

Luna comes out of her room. She's wearing the black dress. It fits snugly, and it's revealing. The top of her breasts are visible. The hem of the dress hits mid-thigh, and the heels make her legs look longer. I think I'm in heaven.

"You look terrific," I say. I'm wearing a lavender shirt, black tie, and black pants.

"You smell terrific," she says.

I'm wearing the cologne for guys with their heads in the stars and feet planted on the ground, but tonight it's like I'm walking on a cloud.

We ride the elevator down and find the sign for Dinner under the Moon. Then we follow a hostess, and I feel like everybody's watching us. It's kind of like we've sneaked into a place where we don't belong, and it feels like we aren't us anymore. We sit at a table with a white tablecloth and upside-down glasses. When the hostess gives us menus, Luna takes a quick look and asks for a dessert menu. She says that tonight she's only having desserts. I swear Luna's glowing in the candlelight. The moon and stars are shining, music's playing, and a breeze is blowing. I can smell the flowers on the bushes along the sides of the courtyard.

After we order desserts, Luna says, "We have to memorialize our road trip. Pull your chair next to mine."

She takes a picture of us sitting at the table. I take a picture of us standing in front of blooming gardenias, and then she takes a picture of me. I take one of her.

Then the waiter brings our desserts.

First I taste the chocolate layered cake and then the strawberries 'n cream. They're like nothing I've ever tasted.

"I need to tell you something," Luna says.

I wipe my mouth with a napkin. "Don't tell me you need to take my blood pressure," I say.

Looking down, she smiles. "It was terrible of me to dump you that night we were going to have pizza." She takes a bite of cake and swallows. "But after I saw Derrick, I came back to your house. The lights were off so I left."

"You should've called," I say.

"I didn't want to wake you."

My heart's in my throat.

"And then I wanted to go on the road trip with you and do something neither of us had done before."

"Why?"

"Why not? It sucks when you're facing your mortality." She rakes up cake crumbs with her fork. "I guess you've been doing that for most of your life, but when you think about it, everybody is."

I meet her eyes. I don't know what she's talking about.

"Did I ever tell you I missed my senior prom?" she asks.

"No."

"I'd bought a long dress and everything, but then I didn't feel like going. Now it feels like I missed a milestone. Milestones are important."

"I've never been to a prom, and I don't feel like I missed a milestone," I say. "Milestones to me are graduating from high school and college, falling in love, starting a career, and maybe buying a house." I shrug. "I don't need a house so that doesn't count."

"Moving into your first apartment will count. Starting your first job. Getting a driver's license." She takes another bite of the cake. "You've done both of those."

"Going on a road trip with you," I say.

"Sex for the first time. Surviving a fatal disease."

"Weird that you think of those at the same time."

"Saying good-bye." Luna taps her glass. "Losing somebody you care about."

I know. "Realizing you aren't the only one with problems," I say.

"Helping Eric make it home," Luna says.

I smile at her.

We spend the rest of the evening listing the milestones of a lifetime.

CHAPTER 33

I awaken at six a.m., coughing and tasting blood. I hurry into the bathroom and see blood on my mouth where I've bitten my tongue and lips. I'm pretty sure it's because during the night I dreamed about my mother over and over again. I was a little kid, and she was driving me somewhere. When she looked at me, she didn't have a face, and I jumped out of the car and ran away.

She'd probably have a face if I remembered what she looked like.

It's a good thing Luna wasn't here to wake up and see the blood on my face. She would have screamed.

I wash my face, brush my teeth, and turn on the TV. I pick up my cell phone and check for calls I could've missed, but there aren't any. Joe doesn't know I've left yet. He's going to cause trouble when I return if he finds out, especially if the trip turns out badly. That will only convince him to put me where somebody else can deal with my problems. I tell myself that nothing bad is going to happen. Nothing can go wrong. I will be careful like always.

I wonder if he knows I went to Ruby's house. She acts like I should never have been born. I probably wouldn't have been, if genetic testing had existed for CIPA. I don't know if it does now or not. Joe didn't want my grandparents to adopt me because I'd be too much trouble.

I feel like I have fruit flies flying around in my stomach.

I step outside the sliding glass door. It's cloudy, and I can see the courtyard below where the waiters are setting up the breakfast buffet. Then I go inside, call Luna, and tell her about the breakfast buffet.

"I have a headache," she says. "Probably from all the sugar last night. I'll catch up with you later."

I think she's tired of me. Last night after we finished talking, I walked her to her room and she yawned. She said good night. That's all that happened.

I shower and dress. Sitting at the desk, I look at the four maps with directions I printed as I was packing. I pick up the directions to my mother's home address on the wedding invitation. I printed them out just in case I'm invited for a visit.

But Luna has to be back before Tuesday, and I promised she would be, so I don't have time to go to my mom's.

Chances are, I won't be coming back here. Meeting my mom at the wedding or reception with hundreds of people around doesn't feel like a good idea anymore.

She'll probably say hello and suggest we get together one day.

But people don't mean it when they say, "I'll call you," or "We'll get together."

They forget.

I wonder if my dad said, "I'll see you soon," when he dumped me at Nana's house.

I don't think he forgot to come back.

I don't have anything else to do, nothing to lose, and I only want to see the house where she lives in case this is my last chance.

✦ ✦ ✦

On the way, I stop at a sporting-goods store and buy sleeping bags and a battery-powered lantern. Tonight's the night we're sleeping on the beach after the reception.

Thirty minutes later, I turn off the motor and sit in front of my mom's house. It's light yellow like a baby chicken. A *For Sale* sign stands in the yard.

I climb out of the car and take a deep breath. I love the smell of mowed grass and gardenias. It smells like life. On the way to the front door, I stop to watch a squirrel nibbling on a pinecone. It's a great day unless you're terrified about what might happen.

I knock on the door. Nobody answers. I walk back to the street, and a man jogging by stops and tells me the house has been empty for a couple of weeks. It's going to be a hard sale because the inside is a dump and needs total renovation. "I'm just warning you," he says. He explains it was a foreclosure and will be up for auction.

I guess my mom couldn't pay the mortgage.

Back at the hotel, I go to my room and step onto the balcony. The courtyard is deserted, and all I hear is a bird singing its heart out. I call Luna. She still has a headache.

"I'll be right over," I say. I grab some Tylenol from the first aid kit in my backpack and a washcloth from the bathroom. I get the ice bucket and fill it at the machine next to the elevator. Then I head to her room.

When she opens the door, her hair's messed up, and she's wearing the big T-shirt she bought at the truck stop.

"I brought Tylenol and an ice pack," I say.

She nods, and I step inside.

She sits on the bed.

In the bathroom I fix her a cup of water and an ice pack.

Then I give her everything.

"You don't have to go to the wedding," I say. "I can go alone."

She lies down and places the ice pack on her forehead. "No, you won't. The pain isn't bad. I think I'm more afraid of it worsening. I want to go, and we'll be at the ocean. I really want to at least walk on the beach. I think the headache is from stress. I've had a stressful week. Why don't we skip the wedding and go to the reception? We can leave anytime."

"You really want to go?"

"Finding your mother and father is on the bucket list. You don't want to have regrets, right?" She takes a deep breath. "I know I don't."

✦ ✦ ✦

Luna pulls up to the security gate and stops. Ahead is the long bridge leading to the island. "We're here for the wedding and reception," she says and shows the guard the invitation. He opens the gate, and she drives through.

Minutes later she pulls onto the long driveway to the country club where the reception will be held.

We checked out of the hotel and packed the car before we left. Luna said we don't have much time and need to squeeze everything we can into the weekend. We don't want to come back here.

"Do I look okay?" she asks.

Luna's wearing her black dress. "You are beautiful," I say.

"You look really great," she says. "Your mother should be happy you're her son."

"Probably not. I take a road trip to see somebody who never wanted me around. Eleven years have gone by. Eleven Christmases. Eleven birthdays. I never heard from her." I glance around. The parking lot is practically empty. "Joe told me that one time she was supposed to come visit me and didn't show up."

"Maybe there is a reason for this." Luna parks at the side of the country club. "My mother says there is a reason for everything. Do you mind if I give you suggestions?" She doesn't wait for an answer. "At the reception, you need to have fun and not focus on whatever's happening with your mother."

"I will." I look out the window. There's a couple heading inside. The girl's wearing a long dress. The guy's wearing a tux.

I get out of the car and slip on my jacket. It's sixty-six degrees, so I'll be okay.

We enter through double doors and a man asks my name. I tell him, and he looks at a computer printout. "Sorry," he says, "your name isn't on the list."

"She's my mother," I say. I show him my driver's license, which in no way proves I'm the son of the bride.

"Okay," he says. "You can go in. Sometimes when there is an open bar, all sorts of freeloaders show up to eat and drink."

We enter a large banquet room. It looks as if we're attending a prom or something. I feel like an intruder, but Luna's acting as if she does this all the time. She's saying hello to people and smiling.

"Do you see your mother?" Luna asks, glancing around.

"No. I don't know what she looks like."

"Usually there is a receiving line, but we're running late."

That's fine with me. I don't want to have to get into a line to meet my mother.

We go over to a long table filled with appetizers, and next to it is a table piled high with gifts. There's an ice sculpture in the middle. "Is that a duck?" I get a cracker and look up and down at the six-foot creature.

"It's a swan," Luna says.

It looks like a duck to me. "I didn't get them a gift," I say.

"You made it here, didn't you?" Luna says. "Which is an almost miracle."

"Because of you," I say, looking at a painting on the wall of a naked man eating an apple. I take a deep breath and smell alcohol and smoke. I wring my hands and look around for my mother. I'll tell her...I don't know what I'll say.

We weave through the crowd holding hands. I hear talk about Chicago, LA, and New York. I see a gigantic sliding door and a deck.

"Let's go outside," I say.

"Why?"

"I think the ocean's out there."

We step onto the deck. A half-dozen people are standing around talking. The ocean roars, and the wind's blowing. We go to the railing. The view steals my breath. I can hear the waves and smell the salty air and the smoke from the smokers. The ocean stretches forever, and the crests of the waves are foamy white. This is like something I'd see on the National Geographic Channel.

"I've never seen waves so enormous," Luna says.

"There is a hurricane in the Atlantic," a guy standing a few feet away says. He's probably in his early thirties, and he's tanned. "It's great weather for surfing. If you're around tomorrow, you can join us."

"I can't," I say, looking at the ocean. "I probably need to be able to keep my two feet on the ground first." I grin.

Out of the corner of my eye, I see him looking at my cane. "What about you?" he asks Luna. "It's heaven on earth."

"I already have plans." Luna smiles at me. Heaven on earth is her smile.

I turn my head and see a woman on the deck wearing a wedding dress. At least I think it's a wedding dress. It's long, white, and lacy. She's talking to a man in a tux.

My heart picks up speed. There's nowhere to go. Nowhere to hide.

"I like her dress," Luna says.

My mother's looking in my direction.

"Go speak to her."

"I'll wait for her to speak to me."

I see Luna shake her head slightly. "She may not recognize you," she says.

I lift my hand to wave, but I stop. The look on my mother's face is like she's on a plane that's about to crash. Her heels click on the deck as she walks away. I see her glance over her shoulder as the man in the tux ushers her into the ballroom. I bet he's her new husband. My stepfather.

"Even if she didn't recognize me, it's weird she'd run from a wedding guest."

"Maybe she figures you're a freeloader?"

"And in a few minutes, we'll be thrown out?" I say.

We look at each other and laugh. It probably won't be funny if it happens.

A big woman comes onto the deck and tells everybody to go inside and find their seats for dinner. I tell Luna we won't have a place because we aren't on the guest list.

"There are probably extra."

"I really don't want to get thrown out," I say.

"You belong here." She hooks her arm around mine. "You are not leaving here with regrets."

The tables are only half filled. Luna and I find a couple of places in the back of the room. A waiter pours wine.

On the other side of the table, two ladies are comparing their watches. One watch was handmade and cost $20,000.

I take a sip of the wine. "I hope it's waterproof," I say, and everybody laughs, but Luna kicks me.

The watch lady sizes me up the way she might a piece of meat at the butcher's, and her nose wiggles like she has a big hair in it.

I lean over to Luna. "I sounded stupid?"

Luna gives me a look. "You sounded dead serious." She leans over to me. "What's your temperature?"

"You're not allowed to ask me that," I say. I check my watch. Ninety-nine.

My mother's table is across the room on a stage. An older man stands and welcomes everybody to the celebration of Barney and Elizabeth's wedding, even though storms are on the way. I wonder if he knows her real name is Carlee, and she dumped her kid years ago.

We start eating the salad. It has little flowers in it, but I don't eat them. I finish my wine just in time for the waiter to refill my glass.

Then the best man gives a toast. His speech is slurred. I think he's drunk. He starts talking about an urban legend where the bride had been unfaithful to the groom the night before their wedding, but the groom found out and placed pictures as evidence under the chairs. "Now, I would like you to check under your place mats," he says.

I hear gasps and then the rustle of place mats.

"Caught you looking," the best man says.

There's weak laughter.

Then he goes on and on about what a great couple Elizabeth and Barney are. They're meant for each other.

I eat prime rib, little potatoes, and asparagus. Butter drips onto my shirt.

The maid of honor gives a toast. In a shaky voice, she talks about how it sometimes takes an eternity to find your soul mate, and she's happy Elizabeth finally found hers.

I'm eating cheesecake when I see Luna looking at the wedding invitation.

"What?" I whisper.

"I don't know. It kind of felt like we were not at the right wedding."

I look at her. She looks at me. She starts laughing. "We could've been the ultimate wedding crashers," she says. "But I don't think we are. Are we?"

"We're crashers since we weren't invited," I say.

"But are we crashing the wrong wedding?"

"Maybe."

"Life event," she says and laughs.

Then Elizabeth and Barney dance.

After a minute, other people start dancing. Luna's busy talking to the people at the table about wallpaper, but I don't think she makes any friends when she says wallpaper makes a room look dated. Light, airy colors are timeless. Then she asks no one in particular, "Have you known Elizabeth long?"

My watch beeps so I get up and walk to the bathroom. It's a nice bathroom with an attendant and flowery wallpaper. I wouldn't mind hanging out in here for a while.

I use the bathroom and wash my hands. I'm feeling pretty good from the wine, but I won't have any more. I don't need to look any stupider than I feel.

The attendant, an old guy wearing a tux and a bow tie, gives me a towel.

I ask him if he likes his job. He says yes. He used to be an engineer and made a lot of money, but he lost his job and spent time in prison.

"I've seen a lot of crazy stuff," Fred says. He hates it when the drunks don't have good aim or they vomit all over everything. Most of the men have been drying their hands on their pants or not washing so they can avoid tipping him. "But I am so much better off."

I tip him and say I hope he has a good night. He says thanks and doesn't even bother looking at the money. He says he enjoyed talking with me, and it's one of the small things he'll remember. He says I should always remember the small things.

I step out of the bathroom. The band's playing "It Feels Like Rain." Luna's dancing close with a guy. I see the maid of honor talking to two bridesmaids by the ice sculpture, and I hear them talking about Elizabeth. I go over and get a grape. One bridesmaid says she's happy Elizabeth found somebody like Barney. She's had a very tragic life.

There's another slow song playing, so I take a deep breath and ask her to dance. I'd like to find out why Elizabeth's life was so tragic and see if anything sounds familiar.

The bridesmaid's name is Em, and she's probably ten years older than me. "I don't really know anybody here," I say as we're dancing. "Are you Barney's daughter?"

"I'm his younger sister," she says, smiling at me. "Neither Barney or Elizabeth have any children yet."

Okay. So Elizabeth doesn't have any children. I need to tell Joe to get his money back from that detective.

The song ends. "Do you want a drink?" Em asks. I shrug and follow her to the bar. She gets a martini, so I do too. I take a drink.

"Have you known Elizabeth long?" Em asks me.

I look around the room for Luna. "No." I finish the drink.

"Is the girl you're with your girlfriend?" Em asks.

"No. She's a friend."

Em smiles at me.

Em's friends come over and start talking. I listen and learn things I'm not trying to learn. Where to get the best massage (or tummy tuck), how it is insane to fly coach to Europe, and if you go to a doctor who sees mostly low-class people, you'll get treated well.

I scan the room and see Elizabeth by the ice sculpture talking to Barney. What if I just go over there and say hello? It's not like it'll kill me to find out whatever I can. I have to say something now or I may lose my chance, plus I've had two or three drinks, and I'm feeling brave. I set my glass on the bar, grip my cane, and walk over to her.

"Congratulations," I say to Elizabeth and Barney.

Elizabeth looks at me as if she's seeing an alien from outer space. She clears her throat. "Hello," she says. "I don't believe we've met."

So she's not my mother, and I'll probably get thrown out by security.

"I'm David," I say. "David Hart."

She stands looking at me for a few seconds. "Jan's grandson?" she asks.

"Yes," I say. "Jan was my grandmother." I think she has to be my mother unless there's another Jan with a grandson named David who was invited to her wedding. I swallow hard.

She introduces me to Barney.

"Nice to meet you," Barney says and shakes my hand.

"I'm sorry for your loss," she says.

Elizabeth has to be my mother. I look at her and see if there's any resemblance to me. I don't see any. I'll have to ask her. Maybe she had amnesia and forgot she had a son. "Would you like to dance?" I look toward Barney, and he nods.

I stick out my hand and lead her to the dance floor. The song is "You Raise Me Up."

"Who taught you to dance?" she asks as we whirl slowly past the ice sculpture, me ignoring my limp.

"My grandmother."

We move past the cake standing tall on a table. "What are you doing here?"

"So you are my mother?"

She takes a breath. "I'm not ready for this. I don't know if I'll ever be ready."

It's like I've been stabbed in the heart. "Is that a yes?"

"I gave birth to you."

"Do you know where my dad is?"

"I left the past behind me," she says. "I am sorry. I feel awful."

I have a feeling it's because I showed up at her wedding reception. Rejection wasn't part of my dreams, but it was my nightmare.

But I knew she didn't want to meet me. I had a crazy idea that if she saw me, she'd feel differently.

"We had no reason to keep in touch," she says.

No reason.

"He doesn't want to be found," she says.

When the song ends, I say, "I have had a good life." I

bow. "Thank you for giving me away, and thank you for the dance. I hope you and Barney have many years of happiness together. Congratulations."

"Go home. Forget about me. Take care, David." She's choked up.

I turn and walk away. *I've done great without you, and I have no reason to see you again.*

I don't want to talk to anybody right now. I go outside, stand on the deck, and watch distant lights from the fishing boats. The wind's blowing hard now, and I feel the size of a grain of sand when I hear the roar of the ocean waves and see the billions of stars. I can't move. It's hard to breathe.

"David."

I turn. "Hey, Luna," I say, fixing a friendly smile on my recently stepped-on face.

She hugs me. It's the best hug ever. She makes my heart race. It's also the worst hug ever because she sees my sadness.

"I almost cried watching you dance with Elizabeth. I knew she had to be your mother."

We keep looking at each other. "I'm fine. It's beautiful out here."

"Yes, it is. What did Elizabeth say?"

"She didn't want to meet me. She moved on long ago. We can go home tomorrow if you want."

"What about seeing Sam Tink? What about finding your father?"

"What if he says the same thing Elizabeth said?"

"You'll have closure," Luna says.

"There's a hurricane coming."

"We have plenty of time, and I love storms," she says.

"You're great, Luna. I am glad you're here."

"I am too," she says. "Ready?"

I fold my hands and watch the water. "Yeah."

Then we go down the steps and stand on the beach. Floodlights from the country club light up the sand.

I take off my shoes.

"Oh no, you're not," she says.

"Oh yes, I am."

I take off my jacket and walk out about fifty feet. The water's not deep until a wave comes along, and I bodysurf toward the lights on the shore.

CHAPTER 34

"This is the perfect place to spend the night," Luna says as I get out of the water. "Look at the stars."

They're so bright they look as if they're breathing with life when they twinkle.

After we get clothes, the lantern, and the sleeping bags from the car, we find a place out of sight under the deck where we can hear the ocean waves and the music from the wedding. I change into dry shorts and the T-shirt I bought at the truck stop. Luna puts on her T-shirt and shorts.

We have matching shirts with sea turtles on them.

We sit in the sand and watch the waves. "If we get arrested, will you bail me out?" she asks.

"Will I be able to bail myself out?"

"I don't know. I have never done anything illegal before."

"I've driven without a license before," I say. "I had an accident. Luckily I only got into trouble with Joe."

Then Luna opens a tote bag and pulls out a plastic pail shaped like a castle and a shovel. My mouth drops open.

"I bought them at the gift shop of the hotel," she says. "We need to be prepared, and I figured you'd never built castles before."

We build a castle in the sand and talk and laugh. "Time of Your Life" is playing inside the country club, and when it ends, the floodlights go out. Suddenly it's dark, but the castle is six stories high by now. I turn on the lantern, and we crawl into our sleeping bags.

When we awaken, we watch the sunrise.

"God shouldn't allow a person to die until they've seen the sunrise over the ocean," Luna says. "And at least a hundred other miracles." She looks at me. "I have a long bucket list."

✚ ✚ ✚

Luna is driving slowly as we exit the interstate and head south. It's early Sunday morning, and rain's now coming down in sheets. Traffic lights are swinging back and forth on wires. It's amazing how the clear sky suddenly changed to black.

"Pine Branch is about an hour from here," I tell Luna as I look at the map. "But in this weather, it'll take longer." I fold up the map. "Maybe we're wasting our time."

"You never know unless you do it," Luna says. "And we have a purpose."

It feels good that she thinks so. Still, I have doubts if I'll ever find out what happened to my dad. But we built our castle, and we saw the sunrise over the ocean.

My cell rings. It's Joe.

"Do you want to know how mad I am?" he says.

"No, thanks."

"Your mother called," he says.

"So you've known all the time where she was."

"Sporadically," he says. "She did not want to meet you, and your grandmother did not want you hurt. I didn't either."

"Meeting my mother is on my bucket list," I say.

"David," he says.

I shrug. "My life expectancy is on the short side."

"For god's sake, why didn't you tell me what you wanted to do? I'm your guardian."

"Because you'd stop me," I say.

"I told you how she felt," he says.

"I had to find out for myself."

"I'm sorry," he says. "You were a challenging kid. You needed constant care. She just couldn't handle it all. I can't handle it."

"Nana did it," I say. "And my grandfather did it."

"They were special people. Where are you?"

"Ten hours from home. Luna is with me."

"There is a hurricane watch along the East Coast," Joe says.

"I know. We've hit some rain," I say.

"Please go home," he says. He's at the Belize airport, but his flight has been delayed.

"I'm going to Pine Branch first."

Luna glances at me and wrinkles her forehead.

"No, David. The weather will only get—" Joe's saying when the call is dropped.

I set my phone on the console. I'm too close to turn back now. "He's no better than my father or mother."

"You can't get mad at him for doing what he is supposed to do," Luna says.

✦ ✦ ✦

We pass houses, a school, and a church. More houses. More churches. "It's coming up," I say. "Turn at the next right."

Luna pulls into the parking lot. The apartments look like a run-down motel. Cars are parked in front of doors. I don't know why my dad would've lived in a place like this when he could've been living with Nana and me.

Luna parks in front of the office. "You can wait for me," I say. "I'll only be a minute." I figure that's how long it'll take for me to walk in, the manager to say he doesn't remember anything, and me to walk back out.

"I'll come with you," Luna says.

A skinny man with a beard sits at the desk in the middle of the room.

I stick out my hand. "My name is David Hart. This is Luna."

He stands. "Sam Tink," he says and shakes my hand. "Are you looking for a one-bedroom or two-bedroom?"

"We aren't looking for an apartment. I'm looking for information on James Hart. He lived here years ago before he disappeared." My voice shakes. "May I ask you a few questions? I'm his son, and I've been searching for him for years."

"I've told the police all I know. I can't remember much about him, but I'll answer what I can."

Suddenly, I don't know what to ask.

"What do you remember?" Luna asks.

"He lived here for a year, but I rarely saw him. He'd pay his rent in cash two months ahead each time. He never caused any problems, but he took off without giving a thirty-day notice. I called the emergency contact number—turns out the person was his ex-wife. She said he had a history of disappearing for weeks at a time, but who knows what an ex-wife might say," Tink says, eyeing me. "The police weren't worried either."

"What happened to his stuff?" I ask.

"I put it into storage for thirty days, and then the unit was sold at auction. Evelyn Winters kept a few of his personal belongings, believing he'd be back. You should talk to her. She lives in apartment one thirteen."

"Will she talk to me?"

"She will talk to James's son," he says.

"Where did he work?" Luna asks.

"He was working for a video-game company for a short while, but then he was laid off. I don't think he found another job after that," the manager says. He walks around the desk toward the door. "You're lucky you caught me. I'm closing the office before the weather gets bad."

"Would you let us know if you hear anything?" Luna takes out a piece of paper and scribbles my name and number on it.

"Sure, but it's been years, and I haven't heard anything new since the day he went missing. I'll give Evelyn a call and say you're on the way over. Otherwise, she'd probably slam the door in your face."

"Why?"

"For a while she was a suspect. People thought she'd killed him." Tink walks us to the door. "You know, sometimes a man gets to be a certain age, and he just gets fed up and takes off. I'd do it if I had the nerve."

"Do you think you'd be some kind of hero for running off?" Luna says.

"No, but I might be happier," he says.

I'm barely aware of walking across the parking lot to Evelyn's apartment while Luna moves the car. A light rain is falling, and the sun is behind black clouds. I need a few minutes to think. I figure my dad took me to Nana's because of more child-abuse charges. They had already decided to leave me there. Was that best for me? Yes. I know it was. Then they divorced. Six years ago, Dad rented an apartment for a year, and then he disappeared.

Luna is waiting at Evelyn's door. "Make this quick. The weather is getting worse," she says and knocks on the door. I hear talking from inside and then silence. Somebody's probably looking at us through the peephole.

"I'm looking for Evelyn Winters," I say when the door opens. "My name is David Hart. I'm James Hart's son."

"I don't know anything," a middle-aged woman says. She gives me directions to the police station.

The rain's coming down pretty hard. "Thanks," I say. "Thanks." I turn toward the parking lot.

"You can't do that to him," somebody else says. "Come back, David."

I turn around and see a girl.

"You'd want somebody to help me if you disappeared," she says to the woman.

"Come in," the woman says in a trembling voice. "I'm Evelyn. This is my daughter, Rachel."

Luna introduces herself.

Evelyn doesn't smile, but I can tell by the way things are going, today's not a smiling day. I'm about to find the pot of crap at the end of the rainbow.

Their apartment is small. I sit on the sofa with Luna. Our legs touch. It's like we were meant to meet and end up here. It feels right.

"You don't remember me, do you?" Rachel asks.

"No," I say.

"We once lived in the same neighborhood," Evelyn says.

I tilt my head. "You knew my family?"

Evelyn nods. "You resemble your father."

"I had nightmares about you after you left," Rachel says.

"I was pretty scary back then," I say.

"Not really. Tyler and you were my best friends. I thought you had died."

I look at her and smile. "But Tyler wasn't real," I say.

"Wasn't real? He lived next door to you."

My jaw drops. Oh god. How could I have been that mixed up? How come nobody told me the truth?

"Tyler died a couple of years ago in an accident," Rachel says.

I wish I would've known.

"Do you want something to drink?" Evelyn asks.

"Sounds good," Luna says.

"We used to play cards together," Rachel says. "You'd wear those goggles, and Tyler thought that was what gave you secret powers."

"I sort of remember playing cards," I say.

Suddenly I'm a little kid again. Tyler, Rachel, and I are dressed up. She's a fairy princess. Tyler is a bunny rabbit. I'm Superman.

Evelyn comes into the room carrying glasses of iced tea. She hands me one.

My finger traces a line through the frost on the glass. Frost feels the same as steam or morning dew. Wet. To me, ice tastes like wet rocks.

Evelyn starts talking.

James moved here temporarily while he was building his lake house. He was a kind man who loved animals and nature. He didn't like being around people. He was working as an accountant.

"I thought he worked for a game design company," I say.

"He was the accountant. Someone called his employer and said he was stealing money. James was asked to resign. The accusation hit him hard."

"When did you last see him?" Luna says.

"Around seven a.m. the day he disappeared. He was heading to his lake house. He was only living here because it was closer to his job. He said he'd be back in two days."

My heart's beating fast. "Do you know what my dad did the day before he disappeared?" I ask.

"No. After he didn't return on time, I went to his lake house. He wasn't there. I went to the police, but I wasn't allowed to fill out the form. I'm not a relative. James was forty-five, the detective said. He could do as he pleased.

"James had left his cell phone. I went through his numbers and called everybody he knew. Carlee said he'd run off somewhere and not to worry because he had a history of running away to avoid sending her money. She accused me of being another one of his girlfriends." Evelyn smiles in a tired kind of way. "I don't believe James is dead. I think he changed his name and went somewhere to start over."

"I don't really understand," I say.

Evelyn shrugs. "He lost everything. Then he was accused of stealing money. He wouldn't do that. There was never any proof."

He didn't lose me. All he had to do was come back for me. I waited. Nana waited.

Evelyn keeps talking. "One day, I took Rachel over to play with you. Nobody was there except Carlee, and she had a fire going in the backyard. She was burning everything James owned, pictures, and toys. Then we moved, and years later James called me."

"Was my dad happy?" I ask.

"Sometimes," Evelyn says.

"He was sad most of the time," Rachel says.

"He loved you," Evelyn says. "You were the sweetest, most caring little boy I've ever met."

"Once I cut my finger, and you kissed it and cried," Rachel says.

I smile at her.

"The apartment manager said you have a few of his things," Luna says.

"Yes, I do. There isn't much." Evelyn goes into a back room and returns with a manila envelope. I open it and find a wedding band and a watch.

"I've always believed he'd be back one day," Evelyn says.

Written on the ring is "For Time and all Eternity." I'm feeling sick. The watch is engraved with "Let us be one until there is none."

To calm down, I take deep breaths. The room is loud with silence. I miss Spencer and Cameron and Nana and how my life changed from great to everybody's got a friggin' secret.

"David," Luna says, looking at the inscriptions. "We need to go now."

"Can you give us directions to the lake house?" I ask and glance at Luna. "I promise we'll be back home before Tuesday."

"What happens Tuesday?" Rachel asks.

"The end of the world," Luna says like she's kidding.

Evelyn pulls out a state map from a drawer at the bottom of the coffee table. She draws a route. From what I can tell, we'll be heading toward the storm, but the house isn't close to the coast. "James's place is about an hour from here, and the area is deserted. Most people started calling it Zombieville after the developer went bankrupt." Evelyn gives me the map.

"Do the police know about this?" Luna asks.

"Yes. The local police checked the house. It's been abandoned."

I give Evelyn my phone number.

Then I pick up a picture of Evelyn and a man. They're dressed up like they're going to Cinderella's ball. "That's James." Rachel hooks her arm around mine. "He was happy when he was with my mother."

I think of Luna and how we danced the night of the Spring Festival back when I was a kid and how we built a castle and watched the sunrise—and how things can change in a heartbeat.

CHAPTER 35

We're heading down a two-lane road. Luna's driving and trying to find a radio station to get a weather update. She turns off the radio. "You okay?"

"I'm tired," I say. My hands are trembling. I'm scared for both of us. We're heading to someplace known as Zombieville to look for somebody who probably isn't there.

There's a good chance we won't make it back before Tuesday.

The sky is dark, and the wind and rain are unforgiving.

"You don't have to come with me," I say. "We'll find a bus station."

"No," she says. "We're together, remember?"

I think the worst thing in the world would be dying without having answers.

"I don't know if it means anything to you or not, but none of what your mother or father did is your fault," Luna says.

I flinch. "I completely blocked Rachel and Tyler from my mind. I created an imaginary friend and a video-game character to replace Tyler."

"I think you were so sick a lot of times that you didn't know what was going on."

I'm speechless. My head is churning.

I had everything I wanted, and I believed what I was told—like I believed there was a Santa, an Easter Bunny, a tooth fairy, and a man in the moon, but don't most kids believe?

I lean my head against the window. Rain pounds the windshield. Puddles of water drown the highway. Pine trees trapped in moss bend back and forth. I put my hand on my chest and feel how hard my heart's hammering. I make a hurt animal noise.

"David?" Luna says. "What's wrong?"

I glance at my watch. It's 5:15 p.m. "I'm afraid we won't make it back by Tuesday."

"I think we will, but if we don't, there's always Wednesday," Luna says. "Or Thursday or Friday. It's not going to make a difference."

✦ ✦ ✦

Luna turns onto another two-lane road. "Why did your grandparents keep you inside most of the time?"

"There was a lady who used to come to the house, and she'd talk to me. Then she'd talk to my grandparents. She'd tell them I needed to be kept inside for safety reasons. I think my grandparents thought I'd hurt myself or somebody else. There really isn't much information about lifestyles and adapting when you have CIPA, so my grandparents developed a plan."

"It worked," Luna says. "It kept you alive."

"It did."

"It wasn't meant to be a life plan," she says. "And it wasn't as if you were a sociopath. You had to learn that others could feel pain. Evelyn said nice things about you, and Rachel was really happy to see you. Your doctor didn't seem to think you were dangerous."

"He said I was an introvert."

"I think he's right."

I think I was avoiding getting laughed at. But I had a couple of friends.

Luna turns on the radio and finds a station. Music's playing. "Things happen that we can't control."

Like the weather.

The landscape is flat, and the rain has almost stopped for now. From the looks of the dark sky, there's more to come. We pass nothing but tall brown grass and empty fields. Thick patches of trees bend with the wind on the horizon. I look over at the temperature reading by the radio. It's seventy-two degrees.

Luna glances at me and smiles. "No matter what happens, everything will be okay."

She's a pretty special person. "At least there's no traffic," I say.

The car hits a pothole. I wouldn't want to have a flat tire or break down out here.

A sign on the roadside reads, "Welcome to Flake. Population three hundred fifty."

In town there are five stores at the traffic light. All are boarded up and have closed signs except for a convenience store. "This place is dead," I say.

"It's the quiet before the storm," Luna says. "We should fill up while we can." She pulls into the convenience store.

I feel better. I feel like I have a part of me back. My dad probably died and I lived, and I can't change what was, but I can change what will be.

I pump gas, and Luna hurries into the store. When I'm done, I slide into the driver's seat.

Luna returns, quickly puts several bags in the backseat, and gets into the car. "I bought a bunch of supplies. Do you know why there's no traffic? The area's been evacuated. There's major action headed this way. Roads are flooding. The clerk said we should get to a shelter immediately. He was closing the store so he could get out in time."

CHAPTER 36

"We're almost there," I say.

Luna's shaking her head. "The house is by the lake," she says. "Have you ever been in a flood?"

"I've seen a couple on TV," I say.

Luna shrugs. "We need to be prepared. The clerk said the hurricane will make landfall later tonight, and it's likely to spawn tornadoes across the state."

"How far are we from the coast?"

"About an hour."

I thought we'd be far enough inland to miss most of the hurricane. I didn't figure on tornadoes and flooding.

"We don't know the condition of the cabin," she says. "It definitely won't have electricity. I bought batteries, flashlights, candles, and potato chips."

"I love potato chips," I say. I can deal with anything. "But we can eat them at a shelter."

Luna shakes her head. "I am a shelter expert, and we're

not going to one. Too many children crying and people farting," she says and reaches into the backseat. She pulls out two flashlights and a package of batteries.

"Why'd you stay in a shelter?"

"High school social studies project," she says, placing batteries in a flashlight.

"That was a shelter for homeless people. They're different."

"How would you know? Have you ever been homeless? Many are the same as us but with no address."

I understand. People think I'm different. I'm the same but without the nerve endings.

For the next fifteen minutes we don't see a single car on the road. The wind has picked up, and I can hear the moan and snap of trees. Black clouds roll across the sky.

At a pasture, I make a right onto a one-lane dirt road with foot-high grass in the middle, drive about two miles, and go through an open gate with a rotted picket fence. The words on a dangling sign hitting a post are faded. From what I can make out, the sign used to read Friendly Hill. There's nothing friendly looking. There's nothing but cut-down trees or houses under construction enveloped in weeds and vines. Limbs are blowing across the road.

At the end of the dirt road, a cabin sits in a thickly wooded area. "Too bad I forgot the weed whacker," I say.

Luna snorts. "And the boat."

I kill the motor, climb out, and get a lug wrench from the trunk. "We don't have a key," I tell Luna.

She hands me one of the flashlights.

We push through weeds and vines, and step onto a porch. We don't need a key or lug wrench. Luna pushes on the door, and it opens. She flips a light switch and nothing happens. "Just checking," she says.

"Hello!" I call. "Hello...hello?" I yell in the living room. From the corner of my eye I see movement. I turn and jump, my heart going fast. I shine the flashlight on the wall and realize it's only a mirror. I scared myself.

"It is abandoned," Luna says.

The master bedroom isn't anything special. The bed's neatly made, cobwebs hang in the corners, and a man's dusty clothes and shoes halfway fill the closet. Socks and underwear are in the dresser drawers. Somebody left a lot of clothes behind.

But if I was going to disappear, I'd take only what I could carry. I'd change my name.

I sit on the bed and gaze at the room. Then I lean over, open the bedside table, and see a bunch of pictures of my dad, my mom, and me. I get a lump in my throat. He didn't forget me. He kept pictures.

I'll take them with me when we go.

For right now I only want to sit here. It's lucky I rarely have tears for anyone to see, but it's funny how you could poke a finger in my eye, and it would feel like you were just touching me.

After a while, I stand and go into the two other bedrooms. They're empty.

The water from the bathroom sink is rusty and smells like rotten eggs.

The empty refrigerator smells like a sewage treatment plant. A mountain of freeze-dried food sits in a cabinet.

I open the back door and step into the yard.

Trees surround me. The wind's wailing. About fifty yards away and another fifty downhill, lake water sloshes on the bank. It's beautiful here. Looking at the view makes me feel both free and like I'm part of the universe. Like I'm a small part of something becoming big and wonderful.

I love storms. Whenever there were hurricane alerts on TV, I'd watch the reporters standing on the beach and see how the wind and rain would knock them around. I'd wish I was there. Once I asked Nana if we could go see a hurricane. She said no.

I hear Luna calling my name and head back.

"What are you doing? Waiting for a tree to fall on you?"

That reminds me of Seth and the tree that hit his car.

We go inside to the kitchen. The room is dark now, and I can barely see Luna.

"You know, I sort of wish we'd met up with the surfers. It's too late now, and by tomorrow the beach may no longer exist. But going swimming last night was great."

"You're not sorry you came?"

"No. I know my dad lived here for a while, and he went somewhere. I found pictures."

"I'm glad we're here now," Luna says. "It's soothing."

"The storm's soothing?"

"You are," she says. "I can see why your father liked it here. It's a good place to think. Let's unload the car. I bought drinks and sandwiches too."

We walk outside and get the sleeping bags, backpacks, my guitar, the lantern, and the supplies Luna bought.

Inside, Luna lights candles on the kitchen table. Then she puts sandwiches wrapped in plastic onto the table. "Egg salad, ham and cheese, and two hamburgers," she says. "The store didn't have many choices."

I take one of the hamburgers.

"It's cold," Luna says.

"I can't tell the difference."

"I forget sometimes." Luna unwraps the egg salad. "Are you all right?"

I nod. "I am. You know, I never asked my grandmother much, but I don't think she knew everything or she would've told me. It was a miracle Nana wanted me. I wouldn't have survived anywhere else." I tell her about having somebody watching me every second of the day, including when I was sleeping, until I turned fourteen. I talk about the tutors, the teams of doctors, the never giving up.

"Your grandmother was an amazing lady," she says.

"She learned to manage me and took it to the next level." I take a drink of Coke. "Managing was like a business to her. She used spreadsheets, graphs, and charts to keep up with everything. She'd say even if I ended up in a wheelchair, I'd be capable of doing whatever I wanted to do, but she mainly wanted me to try hard and be a good person."

"Your dad has to have felt guilty."

"Probably felt like a failure," I say. "Did you hear about that ferry that sank and lots of kids died? The captain made it out, but then he killed himself."

"I always felt like my older brother got all the attention. He made good grades and won every award possible in school. I never measured up to him. You know, the teachers called me 'Jonathan's sister.' They hardly ever called me Luna."

She gets a small radio from one of the bags, puts in batteries, and turns it on. I hear loud static. "I picked this up at the convenience store."

After a moment a voice comes on the radio, and we smile at each other.

"...be with you all night, soothing your soul with music and updating you with the latest weather conditions. Folks, get off the roads. Find shelter. This is an enormous storm."

CHAPTER 37

I pile wood shelves from the bookcase into the fireplace. I use old newspapers to start a fire. This way we will have some light throughout the night. Then I go into the bathroom and splash water on myself. I'll have to do this every couple of hours while the fire's going. Luna says it's in the high eighties inside, and the DJ says it's seventy-three degrees outside.

The outside temperature has dropped because of the storm. My temperature is a hundred and one point two, but Luna needs me to help, so I can't take a chance of my temperature getting too high. The first bad thing that happens before the last thing is the confusion. Seizures are next, followed by coma and death.

I text Joe.

We've stopped and found shelter. Bad wind and rain.

Good. How close?

Radio says enormous storm.

Okay. I can track you through your cell phone. I'll be here. Keep me informed.

I will. We're fine. Maybe call Luna's parents if you don't hear from me.

Okay.

Up until the past few days, I only had me to worry about. Nana was always there for me. Joe too.

"I sent Joe a message," I tell Luna. "Maybe you should send your parents one too." I take a deep breath. "So they know you're okay."

Luna nods and takes out her cell phone.

I can hear rain pounding the roof and the howls of wind as it comes and goes. "I'm going to sit on the porch for a while," I say to Luna. "Temperature regulation, you know." That's always been my biggest physical struggle.

"I want to listen to the weather for a few minutes," Luna says with concern. She has tears rolling down her face. "This is going to be worse than I imagined."

"You okay?"

"Yeah," she says and sticks her cell phone in her pocket.

"We'll be all right," I say. I've never been in a hurricane before, but years ago after a hurricane ripped its way across the south, it became a tropical storm and hit our house and blew trees onto our roof. Up until now, that was the worst storm I've been in. I sit leaning against the porch wall, the roof keeping some of the rain off me. In a way, I don't ever want to leave here. The thought makes me smile. I can see why James liked it here. I think how he really hasn't been my dad for years. My grandparents were my mother and father and everything to me.

"It's a Category five," Luna says, coming out the door. "But the winds are expected to slow to around a hundred and fifty when the hurricane makes landfall." She sits next to me, and our shoulders and legs touch. She shivers. "Four hours from now."

I'm wondering what the rest of the world is doing tonight when a sudden gust of wind blows the screen door away.

Luna and I hurry back inside. She lights a candle, and I grab the flashlight. I can hear snapping from outside. I go into the kitchen, struggle to open that door against the wind, and shine the light outside. Trees are on the ground, but I can't see much more. I shut the door. Hearing and seeing the destruction makes me feel the horror. It's like being on a railroad track with a train heading toward you, but your foot's stuck under the track.

I meet Luna in the living room. She's still shivering. I go over and put more wood on the fire. The DJ on the radio says winds are around sixty miles per hour. We have a way to go until the wind gets to a hundred and fifty, and already trees are falling.

Luna curls up on the sofa. The room smells like smoke. The sounds from the wind and rain haven't let up.

"I guess I should go sleep in another room," I say.

"Sleep? You're going to sleep?"

"I thought you'd want to sleep."

"We stay together, okay?"

The radio's still on, and the disc jockey is taking requests. We can either call in or send a text message.

I call the number and request "We'll Sing in the Sunshine."

"That's an oldie. Any special reason why you chose that song?" the DJ asks.

"Because it's raining," I say.

When I was a kid, my grandfather would play the guitar and sing the song with Nana.

"How is the weather there?" the DJ says.

"My friend and I are staying in a cabin at Friendly Hill. It's storming pretty bad. Trees are falling." I give him the address. When tomorrow comes, I want somebody to remember that we were here.

The DJ thanks me for calling and asks me to call tomorrow and tell him how we're doing.

Luna's scrunched up on the sofa like she knows why I was talking so much to somebody I don't know. "We're safe here," I tell her, and I hear a crash.

I get up and tell Luna to stay where she is, but she stands and reminds me that we stay together no matter what.

We walk through the house. She's holding on to the flashlight with one hand and my arm with the other. I don't mind, but I should be braver. I'm no hero. I'm too scared.

Luna shines the light into the bedroom and moans.

A tree went through the roof and landed in the bedroom, the limbs stretched out across the bed, rain dripping from the hole in the roof. I could've been lying under that tree. This is where I was headed a few minutes ago.

Luna folds her arms across her chest. "We're not going to make it back before Tuesday," she murmurs.

It's Sunday night. "I'll do everything possible to make sure you're back. Okay?"

"I know you will," she says in a shaky voice.

She's trembling. I follow her into the living room. She lies on the sofa, and I cover her with a blanket. Before I can turn around, Luna lunges off the sofa and hurries to the bathroom. I hear heaving, and then I hear flushing.

I sit on the sofa and lean forward crossing my arms. I won't bother Luna. When I'm sick, I want to be alone. My brain's jumping around with thoughts. What if she has something serious like appendicitis? The hurricane's only hours away. People die from appendicitis. Maybe she's having a panic attack. I'm terrified.

I text Joe.

Screen door blew away. Tree on house. Luna sick.

Okay. I'm here. Will be here all night.

I get up, walk to the bathroom, and knock on the door. "I can drive you to the hospital," I say. "Before the weather worsens." I hear the toilet flush again.

"I'm feeling better," she says, opening the door a couple of inches. "Go away, okay?"

I go back to the couch. "We'll Sing in the Sunshine" comes on the radio. It's about a couple who will sing and laugh in the sunshine, but the girl plans to leave after a year because the cost of love is too high.

I think maybe my dad felt like the cost of love was too high.

I start singing. It's kind of a happy and sad song. I know I'm weird. I know I'm a freak. It doesn't matter anymore. When it's life or death, you do whatever you can to make the bad go away. Singing works.

I hear footsteps and look up. Luna's walking into the room. "Don't stop," she says and plops on the sofa.

We sing together.

Next a woman asks the disc jockey if I'm dating anyone, and the DJ laughs. He says for me to call him back. The woman dedicates "Smile" to me.

The song comes on, and we sing to it. I don't feel self-conscious. I feel like I do when I'm playing my guitar or the piano, or when I'm singing in the shower or in my room. I forget about the world.

"Folks," the DJ says, "the hurricane will impact communication. We can't take any more calls. I've been informed that the cell phone system could become overloaded with calls and interfere with emergency calls. Because of the high winds, there is also a good possibility that the towers will sustain damage. If you have an emergency, you can use a landline or a pay phone, if you know where one is."

I kind of laugh. "Ever see a pay phone?" I ask her.

"I have a few times. I've never used one."

"I've never seen one," I say. "My grandmother kept our landline, but I don't know anybody else who has one." I don't know why I'm talking about phones. "We're going to ride out the hurricane, and then everything will be fine. This house is actually pretty nice, and I wouldn't mind staying here a while."

"You don't understand, David. I have to go as soon as we can."

I turn my head toward her. "You don't have to do anything."

"You're a dreamer," she says. "I am a realist."

"Realists don't crash a wedding reception or sleep on a beach."

"That was my alter ego," she says.

I force a smile. "I am a dreamer. You're meant for bigger things. You need to keep going to college and graduate. You'll do something great one day." I look down. Probably I'd die of loneliness if I stayed here. Probably by tomorrow everything that's happened will seem like a dream. Probably Joe will invite me to dine with him on Thanksgiving and Christmas. He'll probably give me a sweater or tie. I'll wait for Spencer to come home on break from college. I'll probably keep my dreams.

"There's something I should've told you right away," Luna says.

I stare at the fire, the wooden shelves becoming ashes. "I have bad breath?"

"I have regrets."

I look over at her. "So, you're afraid of the storm, and you're afraid you'll die having regrets?"

"It's more than that."

People who say I don't understand pain are wrong. It's written all over Luna's face, the way she grimaces and shudders, the way she squeezes her eyes shut.

No. No. No.

"Tuesday morning I'm supposed to board a plane bound for Houston. When I arrive, I'll be meeting my parents. They'll drive me to the hospital. I'll be admitted, and then I'll start chemo."

I think I have pain written across my heart. I think it's stopped beating. "You have cancer?"

"I was in remission from leukemia. I'm not anymore. I suspected it the night the guy at the party grabbed my arm and left it bruised." She pulls up her sleeve.

I see a black and blue lump the size of a walnut I hadn't noticed before. "I'll get you back in time." I look down. "You shouldn't have waited."

"I wanted to dress up and pretend I was a princess. I wanted to do something illegal and sleep under the stars. I wanted to come with you."

"I'll go with you to Houston," I say.

"I'll go alone," she says.

✦ ✦ ✦

A few hours later I awaken, still sitting on the sofa. Rain hammers the roof, and the wind shrieks. The room's dark, but I can see Luna at the end of the sofa holding the flashlight as she pulls things out of her backpack.

"Luna?" I say. "Did you lose something?"

"I need something for pain," she says. "But I forgot the pills."

"I may have something. You relax."

"Relax?" she says. "Relax? How can I relax?"

"Try to calm down. It'll help ease the pain."

"What the hell do you know about pain?"

"Nothing. I don't know anything about pain."

I think God was teaching me a lesson when he made me painless.

"I'll be back in a few minutes." I head for the kitchen.

I get my backpack and shine the light inside.

I have a first aid kit. It contains Band-Aids, antibiotic ointment, Tylenol in case my temperature starts going up, and some Robitussin with codeine I got months ago when I had a bad cough and my throat itched so bad I couldn't stop scratching. I had gone to the doctor. He did an x-ray, and I had a broken rib I didn't even know about. He said it could have broken when I was coughing.

I hold the bottle of Robitussin up to the candlelight. It's expired. The Tylenol is okay, but I don't think it will help severe pain.

Then I pull out the bottle of Nana's pain pills.

I don't know what made me grab them when I was packing. I put them in my backpack to make sure Ruby didn't dispute the officer's claim and say Veronica lied and could've placed any pills in a bottle.

Ruby truly believes I should be punished over and over again.

I take the flashlight into the bathroom to see what else I can find. The bathroom stinks, and my shoes stick to floor. I could step on a nail and not know it, but I can feel sticky and itchy. I fan the air with my hand and then sling open the door to the medicine cabinet. I should have taken her to the hospital before it was too late. She should've told me she was sick. I hate freakin' secrets.

There's nothing there. At home I have dozens of bottles of pills for just about anything.

I guess if it's needed, expired Robitussin with codeine is better than Tylenol, and the next choice would be Nana's pain pills, but I won't give her one unless I don't have a choice.

I return to the kitchen and get a cup of water.

Back in the living room, Luna moans a couple of times. She's shivering. I don't think it's cold in here. She's probably got a fever. I kneel next to her and open the Tylenol. "Here," I say.

She takes the Tylenol with a sip of water.

"Can you drink it all?" I say. "It will help lower your fever, and if your fever goes down, you'll be more comfortable."

She drinks the water.

"If that doesn't help in about a half hour, you should take a tepid bath."

I show her the Robitussin with codeine and tell her it's expired. "I'm not sure if it should be taken with the Tylenol," I say.

"It's fine. Thank you," she says.

Then I sit on the sofa and massage her feet.

CHAPTER 38

The next morning I go outside to crank the car and recharge my cell phone. The car has been smashed into a metal pancake by an oak tree. We won't be driving anywhere. I look up. The sky's cloudy, but there's not much wind or rain.

I didn't sleep at all. It's my fault Luna's here when she could've been safe in the hospital getting treatment.

Around four a.m. I gave Luna Nana's medicine because she said she was dying from pain. She was mad at me for waiting, and she said you should never wait too long to give pain medicine because it's harder to make the pain go away. I was relieved when she finally fell asleep.

I go inside and check my phone. It doesn't have a signal. Neither does Luna's. I don't think any amount of charging would help.

Nana taught me to always think about what I do before I do it. That mostly applied to chopping vegetables or touching something that could be hot. Now I'm thinking I better start walking and forget I'm lame and that the heat can do me in quickly. I may be able to get to where I have enough of a signal to send a text message. If not, I'll have to find a landline or a pay phone.

I wake Luna. She opens her eyes.

"I'm going down the road to send a text," I say. "The car has a tree on it."

"I'll go with you."

"Sorry. You'll slow me down." That's something I've never said in my whole life. I place her cell phone in her hand. "Sooner or later there should be a signal. Go ahead and call for help if you finally get one." I pull the blanket over her shoulders.

Luna pushes it off. "We stay together," she says.

I pack my backpack, and I make a backup plan just in case I don't find a cell signal. I'm thinking it's about thirty miles to town because it took around a half hour to get here. How long would it take me to walk thirty miles to town? It takes an hour for me to walk a mile, but that's when I'm being careful.

Thirty hours to walk to town would be too late. If I were the hero in a video game, I'd set out to find help. I could take a knife in case I meet a bear, but then I doubt he'd run away if I showed it to him.

A walk to the main highway where we could catch a ride or a find a house would take me two hours. That alone could be fatal, but I have to take a chance. I can't let my condition stop me this time.

I go into the bedroom, get the pictures, and stick them in my backpack. Then I pull out a pencil and paper, and I write.

Dear Dad,

Nana is buried at the Garden Cemetery in Waterly.
    I believe you did the best you could. I think you
had to have been brave and strong. I hope I will be
one day. I haven't forgotten you. I never will.
    Thank you for taking me to Nana.

David

I go back to the living room.

"David," Luna says, "write your name on the wall."

I write my name next to her name.

If things had been different, I probably wouldn't have ever left Nana's house or done anything. I would've been too scared. I'm still scared, but I'm getting over the fear because I don't have a choice. "Ready?" I ask Luna.

"Yes."

Luna and I step out the front door and make our way through the storm debris.

CHAPTER 39

A blind person uses their other senses to get by. So does a deaf person.

I figure I'm the same. I don't feel pain, but my eyes and ears can feel the world. Sometimes I can taste it. All that stuff travels to my brain and to my heart. I feel pain that way.

I need to find help before the rain quits and the sun gets hot. We start walking, and it isn't long before the rain stops and the sun comes out. We keep going. It's a quiet day without any wind or animal noises. Downed trees line the road.

For some reason, I think about nursery rhymes so I don't think about how long the road ahead is, and after a few minutes I can't get "Humpty Dumpty" out of my head. I hate it when a tune won't go away.

Humpty Dumpty sat on a wall,
Humpty Dumpty had a great fall.
All the King's horses

And all the King's men

Couldn't put Humpty together again.

I know what Humpty's problem was. The king was an idiot. He asked the wrong people to put Humpty together again.

Then the wind blows hard, and we hold on to each other to keep standing. The rain starts pouring. Luna says she's freezing. I say I'd probably be freezing if I could feel. We keep going, and soon the road is muddy and we're drenched. This is good for me. The rain will keep my body temperature from going up, but it could get the best of Luna.

Hail hits me. I lean down and pick up a piece. It's big enough to knock Humpty off his wall.

After about a quarter of a mile and a thousand Humptys, I check my cell and have one bar. I tell Luna and make a quick decision. I text the radio station figuring everybody's calling 911. I can't afford to be placed on hold.

Send help.

I give the address. The DJ will remember us if he's around. I bet he hasn't gone anywhere.

Then I text Joe.

Walking to find help. Tree on car.

No! Go back!

Straight ahead in the distance a lightning bolt stabs the ground, and then I hear thunder. "Joe says to go back. He'll send help."

We turn around. I can make it one step at a time. I'm not cold or hot or in pain, but Luna is moaning. To me, the hail is only one big raindrop or a concussion waiting to happen. We take more steps and more steps, and pretty soon it's just us and the wind and the rain.

The sky gets darker and darker until it's a black hole. Then there's a roaring in the distance like a freight train. I turn around and see a funnel cloud far away.

"Oh my god," Luna says.

Then it touches the ground. It's hypnotizing. I don't move for a minute.

Wow. I've never seen this kind of destruction in my life. I don't ever want to see it again.

"We are seeing something horribly spectacular," Luna says, gasping.

I still have one bar on my cell phone. I text Joe and the radio station again.

Tornado on the ground.

Maybe the radio station can alert people.

"Run!" Luna cries.

The tornado is tearing up the road. We run for our lives.

But I can't run so fast. "Go!" I yell to Luna. "I'll catch up with you!"

She looks at me.

"I stay with you." She touches my face.

We make it to the house, wind whipping us forward, debris flying through the air. We get down on all fours and crawl into the crawl space. I can't move my arm. I turn my head. It's spurting blood. When I look at my arm, I see bone. "Are you okay?" I ask Luna, and she says yes. Then I tell her I need a tourniquet. She's crying as she pulls off her T-shirt and ties it around my forearm.

"I lied," she said. "I never took a first aid course." She rests her head on my chest, and the lights in my head go out.

CHAPTER 40

I blink my eyes several times. I'm hallucinating or else there really is a wicked witch on a broom in the sky.

I'm sorry, Luna. I'm sorry I can't get you home in time.

I'll pretend I'm somewhere else. After all, it's my hallucination. I can do whatever I want to do. There's a carnival. The lights are brighter than anything in the sky. I'm going to ride the roller coaster. I stuff my hands into my jeans pockets. I pass food counters, bumper cars, and a merry-go-round. The ground's littered with dropped hot dogs, spilled drinks, and cigarette butts. I hold in the smell of popcorn and cotton candy.

I get on the roller coaster, and it comes to life. It begins rolling and clanking and speeding up. It slings me from side to side as it rounds the curves. *Hang on, hang on,* I scream inside. The car ascends the steep incline. My heart thuds in my ears.

This is great. I'm not going to waste a second of this ride.

The car stops at the top. I see stars like fireworks exploding. If I could be here in a billion years and look up, I'd see nothing but black. The universe is speeding up; life is moving faster. One day there'll be a flicker and the universe will be gone. Everything goes to nothing. That's all there is. The car plunges. Taking a deep breath, I stretch my arms high into the air and feel the beautiful horror of the fall. I can feel.

Then in a flicker, the ride skids to a stop.

I cry raindrops. My heart's beating harder and harder inside my throat.

I get off. The roller coaster starts again and people pass, laughing and talking. The Ferris wheel moves gracefully toward the sky, and music from the merry-go-round plays on. I turn and watch the roller coaster ascend without me.

Nana was wrong, I think. When you die, you don't buy the farm. You go to a carnival and ride a roller coaster.

✦ ✦ ✦

I can hear my heart slowing. Then I can hear it not beating. My brain's as alive as ever, at least for three to seven minutes after my heart quits.

"We're losing him," somebody says.

Emergency, emergency, my brain screams. Where's the adrenaline that's supposed to kick in?

I'm drifting down a river with Spencer and Cassandra singing "Somethin' Stupid." Rachel, Tyler, and I are playing hide-and-seek and laughing. Grandpa's reading Goodnight Moon. *Nana is teaching me to swim. After I finish playing a song on the piano, Nana, Grandpa, and Joe applaud. Dressed in a Spider-Man costume Nana handmade, I win the contest for cutest, and Nana and Grandpa cry. Spencer and I are celebrating jumping off the bridge. I'm teaching a dog how to swim, but he's drowning. I'm dancing with Luna, and it's beautiful the way we move together. Spencer and Cassandra stop singing.*

I hear a snap, and I think it's the sound of my heart breaking.

"Yes! We've got him back," somebody says. "He has a pulse."

✚ ✚ ✚

Flat in a hospital bed, I hear voices and find out I'm hypothermic and have broken ribs, a collapsed lung, and a compound fracture of my left arm.

Luna, where are you?

I have a tube in my mouth that goes to the breathing machine. The tube's like an umbilical cord to a mother, the breathing machine. The nurse says to stop fighting the machine. I have to cooperate. She's giving me drugs to sedate and paralyze me. That way the breathing machine can help me live.

Luna?

✚ ✚ ✚

The door to my hospital room opens, and I hear footsteps coming toward my bed. The breathing machine pushes air into me, and the heart monitor instantly beeps faster than ever.

I'm unable to open my eyes, but I can hear the rattle of the curtain as it's pulled from around my bed. The person's standing next to my bed now, and I can feel eyes glaring down at me. To anybody who didn't know, I would appear unconscious.

Somebody touches my skin. "You're so cold," my mother says, pulling the covers over my shoulders.

I stare back with clouds in my eyes. I can't talk. I can't move. There are noises.

Beep.

Click.

I love to hear noise. It means I'm alive.

"Can you hear me?"

I can't move or anything.

I hear her sigh. "I have made mistakes. I have regretted much of my life. Just know, your dad and I tried. We believed your grandparents were the only ones who could give you the best life possible. I have always felt guilty and ashamed," she says. "I'm sorry." She kisses my forehead and goes. I don't think I'll ever see her again.

I think suffering has been a good teacher.

CHAPTER 41

I'm back from the dead. I don't know when it happened.

"Can you hear me, David? It's Joe. You're going to make it, and you're safe now."

It can't be Joe. He wouldn't ever cry.

"*Luna*," I mouth around the tube.

"She made it." He's holding my hand. "I've made sure she's getting the best of care."

I trust him. I know he will, and Luna will live.

I remember remembering. Parts of my life didn't pass before my eyes because I was dying. It was because I was fighting to live.

✚✚✚

My breathing tube's out. I don't remember when it was removed. I look around for the nurse call light, but it's hooked on the wall behind the bed. Usually the call lights are on the bed. I sit up, try to get out of bed, and accidentally pull out the IV.

My arm's bleeding. I press on my skin with the sheet. My head swims. I lie back down. I don't want to pass out and go back to la-la land.

I have to go find Luna.

I'm better now. I climb over the bed rail safely, but hit the floor hard. It's all right. I didn't even break the cast on my arm. All I have to do is crawl a few feet. I become aware of the alarm of an emergency buzzer. Nurses rush into the room.

Then three nurses lift me and throw me into the bed. I could've done it by myself. I'm probably not wearing underwear.

"I have to go," I say.

"You're confused. You pulled out your IV."

"I'm not confused."

Somebody puts a tourniquet on my arm and sticks an IV into the vein. "See if he has anything ordered to relax him, and get the restraints."

"You don't need to tie me down. I'm relaxed. You don't understand. I have to see Luna."

"You're all right, sweetie."

"I am not a sweetie."

"Check his oh-two sat. He's probably hypoxic."

"I am not hypoxic. I'm breathing fine. See?" I breathe. "Look at my face. Is it blue or pale? I'm getting plenty of oxygen."

Then I'm given something to relax me.

✚ ✚ ✚

I have an IV in one arm and a cast on the other.

The nurse hangs another bag of IV fluid and then

looks at the TV. The news is on. There have already been stories about stolen food stamps, security at the airport, a murder, and a traffic accident.

Now an update on the tornadoes that swept through Flake after a category three hurricane struck the coast.

The day started hot and cloudy with thunderstorms in the forecast. Most of the residents of this small community were going about the business of the cleanup.

Then WKRY received a text message from David Hart, a survivor. It read, "Tornado on the ground."

Some thought it was the end of the world when alarms went off, but residents had a few minutes to seek shelter.

By the end of the day, one unidentified person was confirmed dead. Five others were injured, and two remain in critical condition, but it could have been worse if David Hart had not sent the message. Our best wishes go out to him for a quick recovery.

"Hey," I say to the nurse. It sounds like my throat is full of gravel. "Can you tell me about Luna Smith? Was she admitted here?"

She turns around. "So you're awake. I heard that she was transported to another hospital."

"Was she in critical condition?"

"I'm sorry, honey. I don't know any details. You were brought here by helicopter without any identification. We were not sure who you were until the police found your backpack."

Oh no. "How long have I been here?"

"Seven days. We've kept you sedated."

"Then I can be discharged soon. I feel fine."

She laughs. "You're still under the influence of medication," she says.

"Can you change the channel to music?" I ask.

In my dreams, I feel pain. Earlier I dreamed I was running toward the house, the tornado behind me, and I was falling. I want to dream some more and reset what happened.

"Hello," I hear.

I turn my head and see a young Tyler dressed for battle. I blink a bunch of times. It's all right. I've done this part of the game and lost.

"I heard about you on the news. You're a hero."

I blink again. "Okay," I say like I'm drunk. It's the drugs affecting my brain.

Tyler smiles. "You looked like a baby Darth Vader."

"I'm glad to see you even if you're a hallucination," I tell Tyler.

"Me too," he says and grins. He melts into the hospital curtains.

✦ ✦ ✦

The next morning, my brain's a little fuzzy, but you wouldn't believe how glad I am to be alive. I turn my head and blink. A vampire's sticking a needle into my hand because the IV is in my forearm. I've had so much blood drawn in my lifetime that I could fill the Gulf of Mexico, and I've had so many x-rays I probably glow in the dark.

Joe's looking up at the ceiling. He never could stand the sight of blood. He's dressed like he's living on some sort of tropical island. His shirt looks like a morning sunrise.

I try to smile at the girl drawing the blood. I try to smile at most girls. She grabs an end of the rubber tourniquet, pulls on it, and pops it free of my arm. She places a bandage where the needle was and covers it with a pink elastic thing to hold it in place. She picks up her tray of tubes and needles. "Maybe I'll see you around."

I kind of smile. I hope not.

"Will you untie me now?" I ask, alert and ready to get out of here.

"I'll ask," she says and leaves.

"What would you do, David?" Joe says. "Climb out of bed again? Keep getting into trouble?"

"I don't have anything to do with acts of God," I say. I have a watermelon-sized lump in my throat. I'd go see Luna. She's surviving. I know she is. I feel her. "I want to see Luna."

"You cannot. She's at MD Anderson Cancer Center. It's the best," he says. "And she's doing okay, but if you settle down and cooperate, I'll call and get an update."

"I will," I say.

He unties my wrist. My arm in the cast isn't tied down.

All of this feels like a movie where you're scared the bad ending's coming, but you keep hoping for a miracle. Kind of like the first time I watched *The Wizard of Oz* and I was scared of the witch and those flying monkeys. The thing is, all Dorothy ever had to do was click her heels, and she'd be home. The answer was right in front of her if she had looked down.

"What about the update?" I ask.

Joe leaves the room and returns a few minutes later.

He says Luna will be in the hospital a while. She's scheduled for a bone marrow transplant.

"What?"

"She's going to have a bone marrow transplant. Luna and your story of survival went viral. You did good."

I didn't actually do anything except call a radio station and then send the text messages. "When can I see her?"

"You're in no condition to go anywhere, and she can't see anybody for a while," he says. He tells me she's in a special unit where visitors aren't allowed. Her immune system is weak. Her parents are with her. The transplant will be in three weeks. She's getting chemo, and then on the day of the transplant, she'll have full-body radiation. He explains that the day of the transplant is called Day 0. The next hundred days after the transplant will be a marathon for Luna and her parents.

I think Day 0 should be called the first day of the rest of your life.

Joe says I have my own marathon to run and not let anything get in my way.

"My mother came to see me."

His eyebrows rise.

"She said she was sorry."

Joe sighs. "Sorry, buddy. You were heavily drugged then, and you were confused."

I think about this. I'm good with it. I have a new family now. I take a deep breath. "What about my grandparents? Didn't they know?"

Joe shakes his head. "Your grandfather and dad had an argument. I think it was when you were a baby, and Carlee refused to let them see you. I don't know the details, but your dad didn't return home until the day he brought you to live with them."

I figure I should forgive my mother and my father. I figure I don't want to be mad forever at the way they are.

The next day, Spencer and Cameron show up. They've driven for hours to see me. I have a family. A good family.

I think I'll still feel bad for what might have been.

I'm going to keep looking for my dad. I have questions only my dad can answer. I'll find him one day. Finding my dad is all that's left to do for Nana. I loved her, and she loved me, so it matters.

I talk to Joe about where I'll go when I get out of the hospital. "Just listen," I say to him. "Let me believe I have a choice."

He nods. "Talk," he says.

"I could get my own place. I could go to Nana's house. I could go to the cabin. You know about it?"

"Yes," he says. He went to check on the car and had it towed to be sold as scrap metal. The house lost the roof and the porch, but it can be rebuilt. If we'd been inside, we probably wouldn't have survived.

"What do you want to do?" Joe says.

"I want to go home."

I want to start over. My dad could find me there. People lose track of people when they move around too much.

✦✦✦

Joe goes to get the car to pull to the front of the hospital, and then the nurse pushes a wheelchair into my room. "Ready to go?" she asks.

"Yes." I get my backpack and put it into the wheelchair. I have been in the hospital way too long. I have to get back to living. It's addicting. "I'm walking," I tell the nurse. I don't ever be want to be wheeled out of the hospital unless my heart's quit beating.

In the car, I ask Joe where we're going.

"Home," he says. "But don't get too excited. I'll be living there. You'll need me."

"I know," I say. "I understand. I'll always need somebody. You've seen Scruffy, right? He's a service dog. If I had a service dog, I can be more independent, and you can have your freedom too." I take a deep breath. "Unless you want to go to college with me."

Joe nods and smiles. We've come a long way, Joe and me.

"It will take months for a service dog to be trained," I say.

"We'll find an expert. You should list what exactly you want the dog to be able to do."

"I will." I look out the window and think about Luna. "What day is it?" I ask.

"Minus five," he says, knowing why I've asked.

This means there are five days until the transplant.

We arrive at a small airport and board a private plane. After I'm seated, I decide I hate small planes. It's like if you make the wrong move, you'll fall out the side.

✛ ✛ ✛

I open the door to the house, and I feel like I'm six years old again, and my dad's bringing me here for the summer, but I ended up starting my life over.

This time, Veronica's waiting for me. She's recovered, but she needs to follow a diet and exercise plan. "I'll be staying a while," she says. I say she can start swimming with me.

When I think about it, each day I open my eyes, I'm starting over. I get another chance. And I wake up smarter.

A few minutes later, I head upstairs. I left Joe downstairs. He's already looking at shelter dogs. He says we should find a homeless dog to train as a service dog.

I drop my bag onto the bed, sit on the floor and play my video game. It's kind of hard with one arm in a cast, but it's not impossible.

It's crazy, but I'm happy to see Davy, Tyler, and the girl character. I finally give her a name. Rachel. I imagine my brain like one giant house with separate rooms for people I have loved.

Spencer shows up for dinner. He'll be leaving for college soon, but he'll be back for fall break.

It's good to be home.

✚ ✚ ✚

I go through the stuff Joe got out of my crushed car. I find my bucket list and update it.

1. ~~Graduate from high school.~~ *Graduate from college.*
2. ~~Meet a girl I really like.~~
3. ~~Live in my own apartment where somebody's not watching me all the time.~~ *Live here with Joe. Make a list of what I need in a service dog, find the right dog for me, and hire a trainer.*
4. ~~Find a job.~~ *Get another job.*
5. ~~Get my driver's license.~~
6. ~~Go to the beach and swim in the ocean at least one more time.~~ *Do it ten more times.*
7. *Perform random acts of kindness.*

8. ~~Find my parents and laugh in their faces.~~ *Find my
   dad.*
9. *Don't break any more bones.*
10. ~~Fix my temperature problem.~~ *Check the thermostat
    frequently.*
11. ~~Feel pain.~~ *Understand pain.*
12. ~~Make tears.~~
13. ~~Stay alive and die of old age.~~ *Live well.*
14. ~~Ask Luna out.~~ *Go see Luna.*
15. ~~See~~ *Do something spectacular.*
16. *Find enlightenment.*

✦ ✦ ✦

It's evening, and Joe and I are sitting at the kitchen table. He's showing me pictures on his laptop of his trip to Belize. He's standing on the beach between an elderly couple. He tells me they're Grace's parents, the girl he was going to marry. "It was their fiftieth wedding anniversary." He says he visits them every year. Grace died the same year I came to live with my grandparents.

"I'm sorry you didn't find your father," Joe says. "We'll keep trying."

I nod. "Thank you," I say. I'll always remember my dad and my mom. A part of me will always yearn to know them.

CHAPTER 42

It's very early morning, and I can barely get out of bed. My temperature's a little over a hundred and three, but it's been a lot higher. I only know I have to get up. Luna's calling me this morning.

I sit at my desk and stare at my laptop. Then I look out my window, and the sun's getting ready to rise. It's still nighttime in Houston.

I hear a *bing* and answer. Luna's wearing a hat and a hospital gown. She has oxygen tubing in her nose, and she's holding a little stuffed elephant I sent her.

"Today's my big day," she says. "I'm scared. It's like my last chance, you know?"

"It's another chance," I say.

"A priest is going to bless the bone marrow when it's time."

"I'll be thinking of you every single minute," I say, choking on the words. "I'm sorry I can't be there."

"How are you?" she asks.

"Fine," I force myself to say. I don't want her to worry about me.

"I'll always remember our road trip. It was spectacular."

"I'm happy for the times I spent with you." I smile, and then I sing. "Happy transplant to you. Happy transplant to you. Happy transplant, dear Luna. Happy transplant to you."

"Thank you," she says with a giggle.

"You'll do great."

I wave my hand, and she waves back. We look at each other for a few seconds, and then the screen goes blank.

I close my eyes and rest my head on my desk. I need a few more minutes before I ask Joe to take me to the hospital for a checkup. I'm not sure I'll be coming back, but this isn't the first time I've felt that way.

Surviving is what I do best.

ACKNOWLEDGMENTS

Thanks to Catherine Adkins,
Debra Garfinkle, Verla Kay,
and Steven Chudney.